A CENTURY
OF STORIES
NEW HANOVER COUNTY PUBLIC LIBRARY
1906-2006

Winner Takes All

Winner Takes All

Diane Amos

Five Star • Waterville, Maine

First Edition
First Printing: July 2005

Published in 2005 in conjunction with Tekno Books and
Ed Gorman.

Set in 11 pt. Plantin by Liana M. Walker.

Printed in the United States on permanent paper.

Library of Congress Cataloging-in-Publication Data

Amos, Diane.
    Winner takes all / by Diane Amos.—1st ed.
      p. cm.
    ISBN 1-59414-366-8 (hc : alk. paper)
    1. Raffles—Fiction. 2. Motor homes—Fiction.
  3. Recreational vehicle industry—Fiction. I. Title.
PS3601.M67W56 2005
  813'.6—dc22   2005009373

Dedication

To my four children
With Love

Michael D. Amos
Jeffrey D. Amos
Gregory D. Amos
Kathleen D. Amos

Acknowledgements

To my dear friends and fans who buy my books,
I appreciate your support!
Special thanks to:
Monique Couturier, Anita Stone, Doreen Jordan,
Jessie Jordan, Jessica Haynes, Claudette Simms,
Diana Tozier, Suzanne Parent,
Lorraine Dandeneau, Georgia Richardson (Jawjaw),
Carol Voss, and Karen Boml (Kiki)

Pat Rose, Greene Library
Priscilla Payne, Gray Library
Thanks for ordering my books

Laurie and Dan St.Pierre, owners of The Book Burrow.
You're the greatest!

The best critique partners a writer could have.
Marie Morey and Joyce Lamb.

Chapter One

"And the winner of the brand new, thirty-nine foot deeee-luxe, fully equipped, finest Winnebago in the industry is . . ." The plump turkey holding the microphone, moved away from the barrel filled with entries, anchored a lit cigar in the corner of his beak, and pointed a winged arm at the motor home parked in the showroom.

The crowd drew a collective breath.

Thomas O'Leary ran an impatient hand through his hair and said to his brother, "Joe, let's get out of here before I'm arrested for hunting out of season."

"We can't leave until we hear who's won. I bought us each a chance," Joe said, raising his left hand and holding up two tickets. "I penciled your initials on one."

Gobbling roared from nearby speakers. "And remember you saw it at Floyd's RVs, where price is no problem because . . ."

"We talk turkey!" the crowd shouted in unison.

"I figure if you win, it'll help even the score," Joe said, his youthful face lit with excitement.

"Floyd's a scam artist. Mark my word the winner won't be anyone from around here. This is nothing more than a publicity stunt." Thomas inspected the tickets clamped tightly between his brother's fingers. "Just as I thought, it says in tiny print only one number will be drawn and that person has to be present to win. How much do you want to bet the winning ticket holder will be conveniently absent?"

Joe threw him a cocky grin. "I got twenty bucks says this contest is legit."

"It wouldn't surprise me if you still believed in Santa and the tooth fairy."

"There's nothing wrong with dreaming once in a while," Joe pointed out.

Thomas stopped believing in dreams the night his parents' car skidded out of control on an icy road, instantly killing both of them. Since then, he'd cared for his brothers and his sister, paid the bills, and helped with their college tuitions. He didn't bother to wish for the impossible, and he certainly didn't want to waste time on Floyd's crazy shenanigans. But for Joe's sake, he reined in his patience and clamped his mouth shut.

A hush fell over the room as the five-foot tall turkey strutted across the floor, dug his wing into a large drum, and pulled out a ticket. "Before I read the winning numbers, let me point out this Winnebago has two sliders, one in the living area, the other in the bedroom. Quality, that's what you get at Floyd's. And to sweeten the deal, I've thrown in a Volkswagen Beetle for day trips. All the owner of the winning ticket has to do to claim this prize is cruise around New England for a month and drum up a little business for Floyd's RVs."

"Get ready," Joe said, elbowing Thomas.

"Gobble, gobble, twelve, seven, six, eight, four, fifteen."

No one stepped forward.

Floyd repeated the numbers. "Twelve, seven, six, eight, four, fifteen."

"Holy shit." Joe slapped a palm between Thomas'

shoulder blades. "You've won!"

Hoping she wasn't too late, Karen Ann Brown grabbed her purse from the front seat of her Toyota and dashed across the parking lot. Out of breath, she pushed the door open to Floyd's RVs in time to hear a loud cheer. Balloons floated down from an overhead net fastened to the ceiling. A tall red-haired man waved a ticket above his head. "We've done it," he said, pulling an even taller stunned looking man towards the front of the room.

While cameras from the local television stations recorded the moment for the evening news, Karen's heart plummeted. Granted she'd known her chances of winning were slim, yet she'd purchased the ticket and had chided herself for throwing away one hundred and twenty-five dollars. She gave herself another sharp mental kick. Buying the chance had been her last ditch effort to impress her parents. She'd intended to give them the motor home for their thirtieth anniversary. Now she'd never see the admiration on their faces.

The man in a turkey costume grabbed the ticket from the red-haired man and eyed the numbers for a long time before aiming the microphone at his face. "What's your name, son?"

"Joe O'Leary. This ticket belongs to my brother, Thomas." Joe pumped his arms in the air like a winning prize-fighter.

Looking disgruntled, Thomas shook his head as if to clear his mind. "What's the catch?"

The turkey stared into the closest camera lens. "Floyd's RVs, located on upper Lisbon Street in Lewiston, Maine, is a business you can trust. Smile for the cameras, son." Floyd pulled off his headpiece and grinned. "Remember this, at Floyd's we're always ready to talk turkey."

Instead of jumping for joy, Thomas O'Leary raised a cyn-

11

ical brow. Karen figured no man in his right mind would act this calmly after winning such a valuable prize. Floyd grabbed a black marker and jotted the winning numbers on a large poster board in the front of the room:

12, 7, 6, 8, 4, 15

Newspaper photographers snapped pictures. The flashing lights temporarily blinded Karen. Once she stopped seeing spots, she studied the man standing beside Floyd: about thirty years old, over six feet tall, broad shoulders, thick auburn hair that skimmed the collar of his knit shirt, and a deep scowl. His rugged build and tanned complexion suggested he might be an outdoorsman. He shifted his weight from foot to foot and tucked the tip of his fingers into the back pockets of his Levi's, indicating he was uncomfortable in the limelight. Not a mild mannered man, she surmised by the deep frown etched on his face.

Just for the heck of it, she reached in her jacket pocket for her ticket and read the numbers. Her breath caught in her throat. She double and triple checked the ticket, stared at it until tears sprang into her eyes. Surely, she was mistaken. She blinked and read the numbers again—12, 7, 6, 8, 4, 15.

The winning ticket!

She didn't bother to question her find. Instead, she flung her purse in the air, threw her arms above her head, and screamed.

From the corner of his eye, Thomas spotted a projectile flying toward the front of the room. A hysterical woman several feet away distracted him. For a moment he lost his train of thought. A leather object slapped his left cheek; its contents rained over him, landing at his feet. His cheek stung, but he pretended not to feel the blow.

He looked down and saw a partially emptied handbag with enough paraphernalia to fill a small trunk. Before he could bend to pick up a comb and several lipsticks, the woman from the back of the room elbowed her way to where Floyd stood. Tears streamed down her face as she jumped up and down, wrapped her arms around Floyd's neck, and planted a kiss on his forehead. Garbled sounds fell from her lips. Thomas didn't pay much attention until she inhaled a shaky breath, speared him with a loathsome look, and while frantically waving her arms, she yelled, "Throw that man in jail! He's a forger."

For a few seconds her comments threw Thomas off guard, but when she flashed her ticket within inches of his nose, he understood all too well. He stepped closer to let her know she didn't intimidate him. "I've been expecting something like this. How much did Floyd pay you to stage this?"

Floyd wiped his forehead with the back of his feathered hand and tried to figure what had gone wrong. There wasn't supposed to be one winner, much less two. His idea had backfired, big time. He flashed his best salesman's grin at the battling couple and pushed his arms between them, forcing each to step back a few inches.

News reporters rushed forward, bombarding him with questions.

"What do you intend to do?"

"Will you give them both an RV?"

"Will you have to substitute a less expensive model?"

"What's going to happen to the person who tampered with his ticket?"

"Will you press charges?"

"Will the forger do jail time?"

Floyd's heart threatened to explode, disproving the rumors he was a heartless bastard. As if ready to take flight, he raised his winged arms. "Whoa, let's not jump to conclusions. I'm sure neither of these fine folks would tamper with their ticket. I'm certain there's a perfectly reasonable explanation."

It was simple all right. Both were damn crooks. Floyd would see to it that Thomas and the woman spent time behind bars. He stepped out of his costume and grabbed both so-called winners by their elbows. "Why don't the three of us discuss this privately in my office?"

Once the door slammed shut behind them, Floyd's smile vanished. "Cut the crap. Which one of you is trying to rob me blind?" He set the two tickets next to each other and studied them for a considerable time. "They both look forged to me." He lifted his eyes to gage their reaction.

"What's your name?" he asked the woman dabbing her eyes with a tissue.

"Karen Ann Brown," she said, pulling back her shoulders, drawing his attention to a nice set of boobs.

Floyd struggled to stay on task. He slid his gaze upward, past the gold chain hugging her neck, past her luscious mouth, until they made eye contact.

"I won't seek legal action if you come clean now. Otherwise, you'll wish you'd never set foot in my place of business. I'm a reasonable man. Before I go to the expense of hiring a professional to figure whether one or both of you doctored your ticket, I'm willing to make a deal. I'll give you each two hundred bucks to quit the bullshit this second, no questions asked. We'll have ourselves a good laugh, and you can have a meal on me."

The woman yanked her ticket off his desk. "That's outrageous. You can't be serious."

Thomas fisted his hands by his side before snatching his ticket away too. "I won fair and square. If you think I'm going to fall for this, you're both out of your minds. Tell your girlfriend to back off, or you'll hear from my attorney."

Karen turned toward Thomas. "I never set eyes on this man until a few minutes ago."

"Lady, save your far-fetched tales for somebody else," Thomas said, planting his nose inches from hers.

She folded her arms below her breasts.

Floyd admired the goods. Round, pert, ripe for the picking. His mouth watering, he cleared his throat.

"I'll sue you," she said to Floyd, instantly redirecting his thoughts back to business.

"Look, sweetheart, I was ready to declare bankruptcy when I got the idea for the motor home giveaway. If you drag me through the courts, neither of you will win. Anyway, I'm certain, you're both thieves. When I prove it, you'll be going to jail."

A knock interrupted the discussion. Barney, Floyd's loyal, underpaid, and not so bright salesman, poked his head into the room. "I think we've finally figured out what went wrong. The computer virus we caught last month screwed up the programs on our hard drive. It seems we printed some duplicate entries. Isn't that a riot?" Barney slapped his hands together and laughed as if he'd told a whopper. "As I see it, Boss, you're one lucky son of a gun."

Heat flooding his face, Floyd pounded his fist against his desk. "How the hell did you jump to that asinine conclusion?"

"When we checked the other tickets, we discovered the computer had made some triplicate and quadruple entries.

Giving away two motor homes is a lot cheaper than giving away four!"

They'd agreed to give Floyd the night to come up with a solution to their problem. The next morning Thomas arrived at Floyd's RVs and paced in front of the establishment, waiting for the business to open. Karen turned up a few minutes later and stood several yards away. Her calm demeanor didn't fool Thomas for a second. He'd seen her in action— swinging arms, tears, completely unglued. He liked his women more stable and more in control of their emotions. He liked his women sane.

She was pretty in an immature way. He particularly liked her deep brown eyes and the color of her dark mahogany hair. The short haircut didn't do much for him, but then, he wasn't surprised. They were opposites, and given the chance they'd drive each other crazy. Fortunately, after today, there'd be no reason to see each other again. She caught him looking at her; her cool gaze proved she shared his views.

When the doors to the RV center swung open and Barney smiled at them, an uneasy feeling tightened Thomas' stomach.

"The boss should be here any minute. If you'd like, you can wait in his office."

Barney led the way and left once they were seated. Karen chose a chair to the right of Floyd's desk; Thomas sat on the small couch across the room and waited impatiently for the owner to arrive. He occasionally stole a glance at Karen and tried to decide whether she was an innocent bystander. If she was one of Floyd's flunkies, the man had gotten his money's worth.

Thomas had watched the circus act on the evening news. Not only had the cameraman zeroed in on his red cheek right after the moment of impact, the television station ended the news clip after Karen accused him of forging his entry. Clearly, not good publicity for his construction business.

Ten minutes later Floyd sauntered into his office as if he didn't have a care in the world, easing Thomas' concerns. Given the choice, Thomas preferred cash, but he wasn't against accepting a smaller motor home. Floyd lowered his bulky frame into the leather chair behind his desk and tented his sausage-like fingers. "I was up half the night, trying to figure ways to do right by you two. Now if I were a rich man, I'd give you each a Winnebago like the one parked in my showroom, but with my overhead, and lately, money's been tight . . ." He frowned convincingly and continued, "Anyway, you folks don't want to hear about my financial problems so I'll quit the small talk and get down to the nitty gritty."

Thomas exhaled an impatient breath and watched Floyd light a cigar and fill his lungs with smoke.

"So after lots of thought, I found the only equitable solution that would be fair to you both." With the cigar angled in the corner of his mouth, Floyd leaned back in his chair and grinned.

Thomas wanted to ring the weasel's neck for dragging this out. Across the room, Karen chewed her lower lip, looking as uncomfortable as he felt. He wondered again whether Floyd had hired her. Floyd blew out smoke rings. "That little beauty in my showroom lists for $225,000. The only equable solution would be for one of you to buy the other one out by paying half the list price."

"There's no way I can come up with that sum," Karen said jumping up.

Thomas shot to his feet and leaned over Floyd's desk. "You slimy son of a bitch, you sure as hell had better come up with a better solution than that."

Floyd dropped his cigar in the ashtray and waved his hands. "Calm down, I have another idea. I didn't mention it right off because it'll make only one of you happy."

At the end of his rope, Thomas bit back a curse. "Let's get this over with."

Floyd rolled his chair out of arm's reach. "There's no need to shout. I'm not responsible for this mess. I'm holding my business together by a thread and trying to do right by you two. Blame the cussed computer for screwing up the contest entries. If you'll both sit down, I'll tell you about my other idea."

Thomas stepped away from the desk and found himself sitting close to Karen. She smelled good, a combination of roses and spices. Her makeup was done just so, and her long red nails were polished to a high gloss. She had four piercings in her ears adorned with gold loops. Thomas preferred low maintenance women with a more natural look. He and Karen were worlds apart, which suited him just fine.

Floyd cleared his throat nervously. "I want you to let me finish before you object to what I have to say. When I hatched the idea of giving away the best Winnebago in the industry, I did it to save my neck. Floyd's RVs was going down the toilet, and I wasn't ready to flush it away. So here's the deal. Why don't both of you each take a month and tour the New England states? The person who gets me the most publicity wins."

Karen twisted her hands together. "That'll work only if I go first. I'm between jobs. Otherwise, I won't be able to take four weeks off to tour the countryside."

Thomas studied her face and still couldn't decide whether she was for real or one of Floyd's cohorts. "That's not possible. My brother just graduated from college. He'll be taking over my business until he finds a position in a civil engineering firm so I can't postpone a publicity trip."

Floyd smacked his hands on his desktop. "Perfect! I don't know why I didn't think of this before now. The Winnebago is big enough to share. It sleeps six easily. Why don't you both go together?"

Thomas and Karen jumped to their feet. "That's impossible!"

"There's no way I'd spend a month with this man cooped up in that trailer," Karen said.

"Motor home," Floyd corrected.

Thomas didn't like the conviction in her tone. "You don't have to make it sound as though I'm an axe murderer."

"You're not Mr. Personality either."

"Consider this a challenge," Floyd said with a foxy grin. "If one of you can't tough it out for thirty days, that person loses by default."

That idea appealed to Thomas. Miss Waterworks would crack under pressure. He figured a few days, a week at the most, and the Winnebago would be his. "What happens if Karen isn't willing to give this a try, and I am?"

"Then she loses."

Karen pushed past Thomas. "Not so fast. Don't count me out so quickly. I'm going!"

"Don't expect me to baby you," Thomas said, feeling sure of himself.

Her umber eyes narrowed to slits. "I'm in this for the duration. Now put that where the sun don't shine."

Thomas knew how to press her buttons. With little effort, she'd throw a tantrum and quit. Floyd leaned back in his chair. "Just think, one of you will have your prize within a month, and I could get a lot of press coverage. If all goes well, this could play out like one of those reality shows you see on television."

"Does the loser get anything?" Karen asked.

Thomas sent her a cocky grin. "I can see why you'd ask that question."

She arched her penciled brows. Bad vibes radiated toward him.

"There's no second prize." Floyd picked up a pen and jotted down a few words on a notepad. "Winner takes all."

Chapter Two

While balancing a bag containing cat food, treats, bowls, toys, and a favorite pillow along with an animal crate, Karen managed to press the doorbell with her elbow.

From inside the cage, her high-strung sealpoint Siamese emitted intermittent hisses and high-pitched meows. Karen's cat, Luce, didn't travel well and had already thrown up its breakfast. Through the metal bars, the animal's sharp claws snagged Karen's stockings and scratched her knee. A few drops of blood trickled down her leg.

Looking haggard, Abby, her best friend opened the door. "Come in, come in." From inside the house came a loud clang, followed by cries. Abby turned and rushed back inside.

"We're baking cookies for you to take on your trip," she shouted over her shoulder.

Karen closed the door, set the bag down in the hall, and after tucking Luce into the crook of her arm, she headed toward the commotion. She looked forward to the day when she'd have children of her own. Preferably four little darlings, two girls and two boys. But her children would be well-behaved, unlike . . . The faces of three little boys sprang to mind. She entered the kitchen to find Abby and her three sons picking up broken cookies off the floor and filling a brown paper bag.

"We made these for you," Peter, the seven-year-old, said

proudly with a lisp, air escaping through the gap of his missing front teeth.

"It's Peter's fault," Charlie, the five-year-old said.

"Is not."

"Is too."

"Is not."

"Peter told Byron to stick his foot on the cookie," Charlie pointed out, his upturned cherubic face lit with excitement.

"Tattletale."

"Am not."

"Are too."

Abby pressed two fingers to the bridge of her nose. "You guys promised you'd behave while Karen was here."

Charlie ran a toy dump truck over cookie crumbs on the floor. "Peter stuck his wee wee in the dough when mama wasn't looking."

Peter shoved Charlie. "Did not."

"Did too."

"Did not."

Abby caught Charlie's arm in a tight grip. "I swear I don't know where you get your ideas. Peter did no such thing. You tell Karen the truth this instant."

Charlie scraped his right foot back and forth and giggled. "I was joking."

"You're a butt head," Peter whispered under his breath.

"If you say that again, I'm gonna tell mama you stuck your nose in the dough."

Abby rolled her eyes.

Karen's stomach lurched.

"Poop head," Byron, the three-year-old, added with a grin before sticking his fingers in his mouth.

Heaving a loud sigh, Abby dropped her hands to her sides. Three pairs of eyes looked up.

"Boys what have I told you about name calling?"

Charlie and Peter pointed toward the baby. "It's Byron's fault. He shouldn't a stuck his foot on the cookies." Plump tears crested the toddler's eyelids. Abby set the bag of cookies on the table and scooped Byron into her arms.

"Sweetie, don't cry, it was an accident. You didn't mean to knock the cookie sheet on the floor. A little dirt won't stop Karen from sampling the best peanut butter, chocolate chip cookies in the world." Byron turned tear-filled eyes toward Karen and jutted out a wobbly lower lip. An ear-piecing shriek reverberated from his mouth, from which hung long threads of drool. Luce leaped from Karen's arms and dashed into another room.

The boys' clothing was stained and their faces smeared with chocolate. Never, ever would her children look as messy as these. Her children would not only be well behaved, but they would also be well groomed. Many times Karen had suggested that Abby incorporate positive reinforcement in her parenting. Again she compared the behavior of the children she'd have someday to Abby's unruly brood.

With an apologetic smile, Abby shoved a cookie into Karen's hand. "Go ahead, take a bite. The kids worked hard to make these for you."

Karen inspected the cookie: indents of small fingers, burnt edges, and chocolate chips arranged into a smiley face. She looked down at the three small boys, waiting for her reaction. She couldn't hurt their feelings. Praying only fingers had touched this particular cookie, she bit down and swallowed one small nibble. Expectant gazes met hers.

The words wee wee sprang to mind. Surely, they hadn't! The crumbs lodged in her throat like granite. "These are absolutely, positively, the best darn cookies I've ever tasted."

Looking pleased, the boys scattered into the other rooms.

"Can you hear that?" Abby asked, cupping her hand over her ear. "I love that sound."

Confused, Karen replied, "I don't hear anything."

"Precisely."

Abby poured two cups of coffee and put a plate of home-made cookies on the table. "You'll have to excuse the boys. They're at that age."

"What age is that?" Karen asked unable to control her tongue. "You're too easy on them."

"I know, but since their father left, I've been trying to make up for his absence. Anyway, they're just spirited."

Karen clamped her lips together and managed to keep her opinion to herself.

"Charlie is at that age where he enjoys saying dirty words. His favorite word this week is wee wee. And of course, Byron likes to mimic his older brothers. He calls everybody a poop head. I've scolded him until my voice is hoarse, but I can't get him to stop. I guess I'll have to wait until he outgrows this phrase."

Karen could no longer remain quiet. "Why not make a chart and log down the good and the bad words he says? Give a reward whenever he substitutes an appropriate word for a forbidden word."

Abby's mouth tightened. "Charts might work for you with the employees at the bank, but these are children."

Karen reached across the table and covered her friend's hand. "People are people, regardless of their age. The techniques I incorporate at the bank would work just as well with your boys. I'm sure of it. I've worked hard to develop my people skills. I know what I'm talking about."

Abby looked at her doubtfully. "Just wait until you have children of your own. Then you'll understand that childrearing is not as easy as it sounds in your psychology books."

Her children would not have the problems exhibited by Abby's boys because Karen planned to start teaching them from birth. "You need to set parameters and see to it your sons know what you expect of them."

Abby exhaled a weary sigh. "I see what you mean."

Was that sarcasm in her tone? Did Karen detect a slight rolling of her friend's pupils?

"When do you start your new job?"

"Next month I'll be the branch manager at People's Savings," Karen replied, excited about her position at another bank. "The severance package I got from Mechanic's Savings will allow me to concentrate on winning the Winnebago."

"Speaking of the Winnebago . . ." Abby's mouth curved into a teasing smile. "What's he like?"

"Who?" Karen washed the taste of the cookie and only God knew what else from her mouth with the strong coffee.

"The hunk you're going to shack up with the next four weeks?"

Karen choked. "Would you care to rephrase that?"

Her friend laughed. "Nope. Tell me about him?"

"Thomas, the hot-headed brute, accused me of working for Floyd's RVs. He probably still believes I do. The man doesn't know how to smile. He's the type who bottles up his true feelings inside."

"Is he handsome?"

Karen gave the question some thought. Thomas was the outdoorsy kind of man. His wide shoulders held some appeal, but handsome? *Incredibly good looking.*

"I've seen better." Hoping to change the subject, Karen added, "Be sure to feed Luce only a small amount of his food six times a day. Otherwise, he'll be sick."

"I've got it covered."

"Every night he crawls under the covers and stretches out

25

by my feet. I slip on a pair of socks, otherwise, he licks my toes."

"I'm sure I'll manage."

"The last time I went away for a weekend, I put him at the Pet Motel. He didn't eat a bite the entire time he was there. I couldn't rest if I thought he was starving himself. I can't thank you enough for taking him."

Abby waved her hand dismissively. "It's nothing. The boys love your cat. Besides, I'm certain if I ever needed you to care for my sons, I could count on you."

A shiver raced down Karen's spine. She'd babysat the boys several times, but only for a few hours. She suspected it would only take a few days for her to whip Abby's hellions into shape. There was nothing wrong with the boys a little psychology and positive reinforcement couldn't fix. Karen smiled. She and Abby had been close friends since grammar school and there wasn't anything they wouldn't do for each other.

Abby offered her a cookie. Under the circumstances, she thought it prudent to decline. "I'm on a diet."

Her friend took a large bite. "Four weeks is a long time to be cooped up in small quarters with a stranger. You might find yourself attracted to him."

"Not a chance," Karen said with certainty, checking her watch. "I'd better be taking off. I still have lots of packing to do."

She stood and started down the hall. Planning to say goodbye to Luce, she entered the boys' bedroom where she saw Byron jumping on the bed, Peter throwing Velcro darts at a bulls eye, and Charlie running around the room with his arms out by his side, shouting, "Vroom, vroom!"

Wearing a bow around his neck, Luce sat in the back of an approaching toy dump truck, the cat's blue eyes wide with fright as it leaped up and sent the truck catapulting across the room. Karen jumped out of the way.

Abby wasn't so lucky. She stepped onto the rolling toy; her arms swung, her feet flew out from under her. Helplessly, Karen watched her friend land on the floor with a loud thud.

For what seemed like the hundredth time, Thomas glanced at his watch.

"Maybe she won't show," Joe said, reaching down and scratching Thomas' black lab, Bear, between the ears.

"I wish."

"If you win, what will you do with the prize?"

"When I win, I'll sell the motor home and pay off some of the tuition bills."

"We don't want that. We want you to spend the money on yourself." Joe elbowed Thomas. "Floyd's on his way over here with a bunch of reporters. Maybe Karen called to cancel the trip."

As he approached, Floyd rubbed his hands together, his face aglow with a phony grin. "I got some good news for you, son. The pretty lady is on her way."

A cameraman snapped Thomas' picture. "Do you have a strategy?"

"Yes, I do." He'd drive Karen crazy and win by default when she refused to live in the motor home with him. A dozen microphones landed near his chin. "Care to divulge a few details?"

"That's top secret." Thomas curbed his annoyance. Floyd had made it clear he expected personable replies to the press. He could put up with this phony bologna for a few weeks.

"What's with the dog?"

"Bear goes everywhere I go. Besides, this motor home was built for family living," Thomas said, laying it on thick. "Most families have pets."

Floyd spoke into a mike. "Yes, sirree, the average American family has at least a couple of pets, and this Winnebago is large enough to handle them all. Besides, Mr. O'Leary has assured me he'll pay for any damages caused by the animal."

"Since I'm going to win the motor home, I won't have to spend a dime," Thomas said with certainty.

A woman reporter for the local paper jotted notes on a tablet. "Have you spoken to Ms. Brown since Floyd set up this competition?"

"No, I haven't."

"Don't you think you should have consulted her about your dog?"

"As I see it, as long as it's all right with Floyd, Ms. Brown should have no say."

"Who's going to cook?"

Thomas flashed an arrogant smile. "I make a mean peanut butter and jelly sandwich. But if Ms. Brown insists on cooking, well, that's fine with me."

Pop, a reporter for a tabloid magazine known for its outrageous stories, piped up: "Have you stocked up on condoms?"

Usually Thomas wouldn't have given the guy the time of day. But he wanted to push Karen over the edge. He winked at the reporters and cameramen.

"I packed a gross in my suitcase."

He heard several snickers, cheers, and a deafening cry. When he looked around, he spotted Karen running toward them, carrying a suitcase in one arm and a bawling toddler in the other. Behind her were two boys dragging a box and shopping bags of paraphernalia.

Joe whispered in his ear. "Looks like the send off committee has arrived."

Thomas inhaled a ragged breath. "This is going to be the

longest four weeks of my life."

"I think she's kind of cute," Joe said, appreciatively.

"It's too bad you aren't the one going instead of me."

Karen's well-groomed exterior had taken a beating. She had runs in her hose, dried blood on her leg, and guck in her hair, deposited, Thomas suspected, by the toddler's fingers. He wondered where the children's parents were and decided they were probably parking the car and had sent the young culprits ahead to gain sympathy from the masses.

Well they'd succeeded. For the blink of an eye, Thomas' heart went out for his harried looking competitor. He knew all too well the work involved in caring for children. He'd raised his siblings, and though he looked forward to settling down with a woman, he never intended to have children.

A few women in the crowd oohed and aahed at the boys. Beneath their cute faces, Thomas saw childhood illnesses, sleepless nights, and heartaches. He saw sullen faces and heard words spoken in anger. He remembered the teenage years and all the hurt that went along with them.

"Sorry I'm late," Karen said, her face flushed. "I've left the rest of my things in my car."

Thomas had packed one bag, only one. He stared down at the suitcase, the large box, and the overflowing plastic bags. "The first thing I intend to do when we get inside," he said with a nod toward the motor home, "is run a piece of tape right down the middle. I'll have my half and you'll have yours."

"Fine by me," she said, pushing her bangs off her forehead.

"Who gets the master bedroom?" a reporter asked.

"Since I drew the first winning ticket, it's only fair I get the bed," Thomas said with what he hoped was a cocky smile. "That is unless Ms. Brown has other ideas." Karen's cheeks glowed a delicate pink. He was sure of himself. Any minute, she'd turn tail and run. The motor home would be all his.

Looking flustered, she stole a glance at him. He threw her a lecherous grin. "Of course, I'm more than willing to share." He congratulated himself for rendering her speechless. Glancing at his watch, he calculated she wouldn't last another ten minutes.

The female reporter who had questioned him earlier approached Karen. "Do you have a battle plan for surviving the weeks ahead with this chauvinistic Neanderthal?"

Exchanging sympathetic looks with the woman, Karen replied, "I've brought my troops along to help me win the fight."

It took less than a fraction of a second for her words to sink into Thomas' skull. "Your troops? These are your kids?"

"No."

Relieved, he released a slow breath.

"But their mother is in the hospital, and she has no one else to look after them."

"Are you saying you offered to take them?"

"I had no choice. Luce was responsible for her fall. I couldn't turn my back on her."

A few low chuckles circulated through the crowd. Thomas saw nothing funny about the situation. "Don't you think you should have consulted me?"

The woman reporter butted in. "As I see it, as long as it's all right with Floyd, you should have no say."

Recognizing his own words, Thomas turned toward Floyd who looked as though he'd hit the jackpot in the Tri-State Lottery.

"Are you going to allow her to take the children along?"

Floyd puffed on his cigar. "Son, there's thirty-nine feet of luxurious living space in the Winnebago. Of course, there's still time for you to back out and allow Ms. Brown to go by herself with the children."

The female reporter aimed her mike at Thomas' face. "Weren't you the one who pointed out the motor home was built for a family?"

Thomas frowned.

"What are your names?" the woman reporter asked the boys.

"Peter," the oldest said before pointing toward the toddler in Karen's arms. "That's my baby brother, Byron."

"I'm Charlie," the last boy said while digging a cookie out of a brown paper bag.

Floyd blew out a series of smoke rings. "Course, if you can't take it, Son, you lose by default."

Thomas gritted his back teeth. Karen stared into the camera with wide-eyed innocence.

"Then Karen and the kiddies will tour the New England states by themselves. Did I point out the two sliders, one in the living space, the other in the bedroom? There's a shower, lots of cupboards, and plenty of storage." Floyd paused and looked at Karen, then at Thomas. "There's plenty of room for you both, along with the boys and the dog. Hell, even if you decide to take along a couple of the children's friends, you'll still find the motor home very spacious."

Thomas allowed Karen a point for deception. He'd thought himself clever when he'd brought along Bear, but she'd bested him. Karen was a conniving, lowdown . . .

Before he'd finished his thought, he felt a hand on his knee.

"Can I pet your dog, Mr.?" Clutching a toy dump truck to his chest, Charlie handed him a cookie. Knowing the cameras were rolling, Thomas took the child's offering and swallowed it in two bites. "Sure, go ahead, Bear loves to be petted."

31

A small hand reached out and touched one of the dog's ears. "Mr., did ya like the cookie?"

It was a little burned, a bit too hard. He remembered baking with his mother. The memory warmed his heart. Thomas smiled at the kid. "Sure, did you help to make it?"

A mischievous grin surfaced. "My brother, Peter, poked his wee wee in the dough."

Chapter Three

Cameras rolled. People cheered. The high school marching band played a catchy tune. Karen and the boys were all smiles as they boarded the motor home and waved like brave soldiers going to war. Floyd instructed Barney to help with their bags. After the last of their belongings were tucked inside, Thomas climbed into the motor home with Bear.

The noise outside the Winnebago paled compared to the sounds inside. The child who'd offered him the cookie was running around with outstretched arms, shouting, "Vroom, vroom." The toddler was using the couch as his trampoline. Peter sat in the driver's seat, playing with the knobs and the steering wheel.

"Take the bedroom," Thomas said, hoping to preserve some semblance of peace.

"Are you sure?" Karen asked over the din.

"I insist." Thomas stepped over his dog, elbowed his way past the boxes, the bags, and the children, removed his suitcase from the bed, and walked to the front of the bus where he set down his luggage and removed the offending child from the driver's seat. He angled his stiff neck against the headrest and closed his eyes. One month. Thirty long days and nights! For a moment he doubted his stamina.

His survival instincts kicked in. To put his brother and his sister through school, he'd mortgaged his business and his house to the hilt. He'd fight to the bitter end, and he'd win. As he sat there behind the wheel, he felt sticky fingers on his hand. He opened his eyes to find the toddler grinning at him. Thomas had underestimated Karen. She was a shrewd opponent. Somehow, she'd discovered his Achilles' heel. It wasn't that he hated children. He loved them—when they belonged to someone else, and when they lived far away from him. He yearned for adult conversation without interruptions. He yearned for a woman who'd love him without getting all teary eyed each time she saw an infant. Figuring he'd make the most of a bad situation, he patted the boy's shoulder and offered him a lollipop he'd taken from Floyd's showroom. He was a cute kid, round cheeks, sky blue eyes, and wet pink lips. Thomas ruffled his hair. "We men should stick together."

The youngster grabbed the candy and smiled. "You're a poop head."

Karen's suitcases were still full after she'd tucked the boys' clothing into the drawers in the master bedroom. It amazed her how much space three little boys needed. The bed was strewn with games and toys. At her feet lay three tightly bound sleeping bags, her makeup kit, lots of positive reinforcement material, and Luce's crate with the cat curled into a ball.

"Now boys, you have to be very, very good and very, very quiet."

"Why?" Charlie asked.

"So the mean man in the other room doesn't get mad at us, that's why," Peter said with a smirk that indicated he thought his brother a moron.

Byron bounded onto the bed and jumped. "Poop head."

"Bad, bad, word," Karen scolded, waving her finger at the

toddler. "If you promise not to say that *bad* word again, I'll give you a stick of gum."

He giggled. "Poop head."

"Do you want some gum?" The child nodded.

"Do you promise not to say that *bad* word again?" An enthusiastic nod. She dug in her purse and handed the boy a stick of sugarless gum. His smile reassured her she was on the right path. Giving herself a congratulatory pat on her back, she lifted Byron off the bed. "From now on, you aren't to jump on the beds or the furniture."

Another enthusiastic nod. "Gum."

"Do you promise to stop jumping on the furniture?" He nodded eagerly. Karen gave the toddler one more piece.

Byron laughed and extended his hand. "Poop head."

Taken aback, she stared down at the child.

"Gum."

"No," she said sternly, waving her finger, but tears welled in his eyes. Maybe she'd spoken too harshly. "This is the last piece of gum I give you," she said, patting his head. His face broke into a watery grin.

"Poop head, poop head, poop head!" Peter and Charlie sang, loud and clear.

She splayed her fingers over her hips. "What's going on here?"

"We want gum, too."

She doled out gum to the older boys, opened the door, and peeked into the front of the motor home. She was pleased to see Thomas at the wheel with his eyes closed. Before they could get on their way, Floyd wanted the reporters to come inside and see for themselves how easily a family of five fit into the spacious Winnebago.

She'd already used up all the storage in the bedroom, and she needed to hide some of the boys' toys and her luggage before they entered. Quietly, she slid open the shower door and stacked some of their belongings along with the crate housing Luce. She draped a spare blanket she found in the closet over the glass enclosure and hoped no one asked questions.

As she and the boys tucked the sleeping bags next to the bed and smoothed out the bedspread, Karen caught a glimpse of herself in the mirror. A stiff strand of hair stuck up like a horn. Her blouse was wrinkled, her skirt torn, her leg bloody, and her nylons ruined.

After Abby had fallen, Karen called an ambulance. She herded the boys into her car, went to the hospital, and waited for news from the doctor who later informed her Abby would need surgery on her broken lower leg. They were lucky, he said, that she hadn't injured her back. Abby would need complete bed rest. Four weeks tops, but if she recuperated quickly, then the boys could go home in two weeks.

The enormity of Karen's situation hit, and she had burst into tears. Her crying had upset the boys so she'd gathered her wits and smiled, though there was absolutely nothing to smile about. Because her options were nil, she called Floyd's RVs and pleaded her case. She feared he'd disqualify her. Instead, he seemed pleased with the idea of a family living in the Winnebago.

Before she had a chance to ponder the enormity of living with a stranger and three unruly children in confined quarters, she rushed to the boys' house and allowed them to pack their belongings. Once they'd crammed their toys and clothing into her car, there was little room left for passengers.

She stared at her reflection in the mirror. Her pride would not allow the cameramen to take more pictures of her in this disheveled condition. And the boys looked worse than she did.

"You need to change into clean shirts," she instructed them.

"Why?" Charlie asked.

"Because the ones you have on are soiled."

"Looks clean enough to me." Peter glanced down at his stained jersey. "Mama says a little dirt never hurt anyone."

"I'm sure she's right, but we want to look our best."

"Why?" Charlie asked.

"Because our pictures will be in the newspapers." Karen quickly removed Byron's shirt and put on a clean one. She noticed Charlie hadn't budged. Thinking he might need some help, she reached down and grabbed hold of the material. Charlie clutched handfuls of his shirt with both hands.

"What's wrong," she asked him.

"It's his favorite shirt," Peter said. "He don't go nowhere without it."

"I'm sure you have lots of favorite shirts," Karen said, remembering her psychology lessons.

"Nope, this one's my bestest."

"I'll wash it, and you can wear it tomorrow."

He paused for a moment, and she expected him to relent.

"Will ya give me gum?"

She heaved an exasperated sigh. "Yes."

Charlie removed his shirt. Her positive reinforcement plan still needed a few small tweaks. For now, she'd allow the boys to blackmail her with their demands for gum. It was a small price to pay for well-groomed children. She handed Charlie the gum and slipped a clean T-shirt over his head. He insisted on tucking one sleeve of his favorite shirt into the waistband of his jeans, allowing the rest of it to hang by his side. It wasn't the well-groomed appearance Karen had in mind, but she kept her opinion to herself. If she didn't choose her battles wisely, they'd spend the entire four weeks in the parking lot of Floyd's RVs.

Peter tore off his shirt and heaved it across the bedroom. "I'm too big to have a favorite shirt. But I'm not too big for gum."

She insisted they allow her to run a comb through their hair. She doled out gum to everyone and applied a little hairspray.

"Boys, I need you to sit on the couch in the living room and wait for me. Can you be really, really quiet?"

The baby stuck out his hand. "Gum."

She handed the boys another stick of gum and watched them tiptoe to the couch. Feeling proud of her progress, she closed the door and hurried to get dressed.

Thomas was aware of whispers behind him. He turned and saw the boys removing cans of soda from the refrigerator. "Do you need any help opening those?"

Peter stared at him as if he'd sprouted a second head. Charlie shook the can and popped the lid before Thomas could object. A dark fine mist sprayed over the three boys. Byron laughed and licked his fingers. "More, more."

Charlie removed his white T-shirt, wiped his face and neck, and then slipped on another shirt he had tucked at his waist. He plopped down on the couch and took a large swig of drink. "Want a cookie?" he asked Thomas with an impish grin.

"Thanks, but I'll pass." Thomas' first inclination was to get a towel and clean up the boys, but that would have defeated his purpose. They belonged to the enemy camp.

He swung around in the thickly padded driver's seat and reached down to rub behind Bear's ear. The dog rewarded him with a deep sigh. Dogs were easier to care for than children. They were happy with little, and they never talked back.

Dogs came when called and obeyed commands without question. Most animals were like that, Thomas thought, with the exception of cats. He never understood how people got so attached to the aloof, worthless creatures.

"Isn't that right, Bear?" he asked, as though the animal could read his thoughts.

Thomas knew the instant the bedroom door opened because Karen uttered a sound that was a combination of a scream and a moan. Music to his ears! He heard footsteps running toward the front of the motor home. "What happened? You guys were so clean just a minute ago."

He kept his gaze straight ahead. The enemy might have its teeth in his Achilles' heel, but they wouldn't stick around long enough to cause much harm. Floyd pressed his face against the glass panel in the door. "Can we come in?"

Thomas stood and swung open the door to the Winnebago. "You might as well. We're as ready as we're ever going to be."

Heart drumming up a storm, Karen leaned against the kitchen counter and tried not to think of her parents' disapproval when they spotted the pictures of the trip in the newspapers. If only she hadn't called them. If only . . .

But it was too late. They knew. They'd watch the local news. They'd remember. Her stomach convulsed. Now they'd see how inept she was caring for children. *How inept she was at being their daughter.* She needed to win. When she handed them the keys to the Winnebago, they'd wrap their arms around her and beam proud smiles for a job well done.

"Folks, this way, please. Allow me to demonstrate how easy it is to open the sliders," Floyd said, cigar dangling from the corner of his mouth. "It's so simple, even a child can do it."

The lady reporter eyed him skeptically. "If that's true, let one of the boys demonstrate."

"Great idea." He nodded to Peter. "Young man, show us your muscles."

Proudly, Peter jumped up from the couch and flexed his arm.

"Me too, me too." Charlie and Byron followed suit.

Hoping to quiet them, Karen hurried forward and handed the boys a stick of gum.

Floyd hefted Peter in the air. The child pressed the button on the wall and the room widened thirty inches.

"This is like having a home on wheels. Right kids?"

The three children nodded and continued chewing. The lady reporter jotted notes on a tablet. "If it were up to you boys, where would you want to go first?"

Peter's eyes widened. "Old Orchard Beach, I'd go swimming in the ocean. I'd eat lots of cotton candy and French fries, and I'd go on lots of rides."

"Me too, me too," Charlie added.

"Me too," the baby said, looking pleased.

"That's up to your folks," Floyd said, sounding as though he were dealing with a real family.

"Can we please?"

"Please?"

"Can we?"

"Me too."

The reporter looked from Karen to Thomas. Until now Karen had assumed they'd have a planned itinerary. She glanced toward Thomas, who shrugged and said, "It doesn't matter to me. You're the surrogate parent."

"Do we have to follow a particular route?" she asked Floyd.

"No sirree, it don't make no never mind to me where you

40

go as long as you drum up business for Floyd's RVs." He wiggled the cigar in the corner of his mouth and faced a camera. "That's Floyd's RVs located on upper Lisbon Street, Lewiston, Maine. No deal too big, no deal too small. Because at Floyd's, we talk turkey. So unless you folks have other plans, I suggest you take the kiddies to Old Orchard Beach."

He handed the boys each a ten-dollar bill. "Here's a little something for refreshments."

All smiles, the children tucked the money into their pockets. Floyd swung his arm to indicate the interior. "This Winnebago has plenty of room for a family and a large dog."

"Cat too," Charlie said.

Karen's heart skipped a beat.

"Yes, there's room for dogs, cats, gerbils, hamsters, and what have you. Did I mention this motor home comes complete with a washer and dryer? As you can see there's a fully functional kitchen with a stove, an oven, and a microwave. There are two televisions, one in here, the other in the bedroom, and a VCR, DVD, and a small satellite dish. Everything the average family needs for trips and lots more."

As photographers snapped pictures, Floyd made his way toward the master bedroom. "Let's have a look at the sleeping quarters." He shoved open the door with great flare. "And here we have another slider. Where's that young lad? I'd like him to demonstrate again."

Charlie made a mad dash toward Floyd. "Let me, let me."

"No, he wants me," Peter pushed his brother aside.

"I got an idea, why don't you both press the button at the same time?" Karen suggested, proud of her diplomacy.

Floyd positioned a chair for both boys to climb onto and started a count down. "Three, two . . ."

Charlie punched the button.

"That's not fair," Peter shouted, knocking Charlie off the chair.

Karen wrapped both arms around the falling child. He knocked her off balance, and she landed against the shower door. On the other side of the glass partition came a frightened shrill meow.

"What in the dickens was that?" Floyd asked, raising a skeptical brow.

"That's Luce," Charlie said. Before Karen could object, he yanked off the blanket she'd hung to hide their belongings and whipped open the door. Boxes, bags, toys, books, poster boards and markers fell to the floor. The animal crate toppled into the center of the room.

Growling, Bear ran circles around everyone. Charlie released the clasp on the cage, freeing the cat who dashed to the front of the motor home, climbed up Thomas' pant leg and planted itself on his shoulder. Thomas jumped to his feet and tried to free himself from the tenacious animal's sharp claws. "This is absolutely the last straw!" But Thomas' words were lost amidst the clamor of startled adults, screaming children, barking, and incessant meowing.

Some time later Floyd lowered his considerable bulk onto the leather chair in his office and smiled at Barney. "Those two will kill each other before they cross the New Hampshire border."

"There's no love lost between them, that's for sure, Boss."

"The tension inside the Winnebago was heavier than a coastal fog. I felt the chill in the air."

"They're cute boys," Barney added.

"The little barbarians will wear out the two adults just like that," Floyd said, snapping his fingers. "Those two don't have children of their own. They'll crack under the stress.

Add to the mix a fool cat that doesn't know how to shut its mouth and a dog ready to rip it apart, and we have the makings for a great scenario."

"What do you mean, Boss?"

"No one across the country gives a damn about a happy couple in a Winnebago, but a story about two people who hate each other, traveling with the kids from hell, now that has journalistic appeal."

"I'd like to make a little wager," Barney said, pulling out his wallet. "I'm betting Karen wins."

Floyd laughed, a deep boisterous sound that reverberated through his office and into his showroom. Once he'd caught his breath, he looked into his salesman's vacant blue eyes. "If I wasn't such a nice guy, I'd take your money."

"Are you saying you expect Thomas to win?"

"I'm telling you there will be no winner."

Chapter Four

A half hour later Thomas pulled off the Maine Turnpike into the Burger King parking lot. "I have a phone call to make. We'll be at Old Orchard in about forty minutes." He hopped down from the motor home.

Karen didn't trust him for one instant. For all she knew, he might be working for Floyd so she decided to keep close tabs on him. "Come on boys." The three stampeded toward her.

"I want fries."

"I wanna shake."

"I wanna burger."

"Me too, me too."

As much as she dreaded going inside the fast-food chain with the children, she couldn't allow Thomas to get the best of her. She dashed a wet paper towel over their faces, grabbed their hands, and hurried into the franchise. Thomas was talking on a cell phone in the lobby with his back to them. The small hairs in the nape of her neck stirred. Before she could get close enough to hear what he was saying, he flipped the phone shut and tucked it in the pocket of his L.L. Bean jacket. She cleared her throat. He turned and gave her a cursory glance.

"It strikes me as odd you'd come in here to make a call."

"Since this is a competition, I plan to use everything in

my power to win. And I can see by your tactics," he nodded to indicate the children, "you're playing by the same rules."

"What's that supposed to mean?"

"A woman with three children will have an easier time catching the press's attention. Let me warn you; in this game, there are no rules."

She wanted to slap that damnable know-it-all look from his face. She planted her hands on her hips and to regain her composure, counted slowly to ten.

"Anything goes," he continued.

This time she counted to twenty. She ran her fingers through Charlie's sticky hair. "Did you hear that boys? With your help, I'm going to win."

One corner of his mouth hiked up before he turned away. She ignored his disarming smile and the slight elevation of her pulse. They were opponents. Only one of them would win. Second place would walk away with nothing.

He got in line and gave his order to a young woman who seemed taken by his charm. Gripping the boys' hands tightly, she got in line behind Thomas. Peter nudged her. "Can I have fries?"

Charlie followed suit. "I want a cheeseburger."

"Drink too."

"No a shake."

"Me too."

"I wanna pie."

Overwhelmed, she glanced from one child to the other. "Growing boys should eat a healthy breakfast." Peter stuck out his tongue. Charlie pretended to gag. Byron made a rude noise. Thomas took his order and turned to Karen. For a moment his intense blue eyes caught her off guard.

"I'll meet you outside," he said, off-handedly.

She regarded him with what she hoped was a self-assured smile.

"I think that's them," a man in line said.

"Are you the children we saw on television this morning?" someone else asked.

"Yup, that's us," Peter said, air escaping between the gap in his teeth.

"Me too," Charlie said.

Byron grinned. "You're a poop head."

Karen handed the children sticks of gum.

"So you're the little lady who's going to do all the cooking."

Before she could dispute this nonsense, another man wiggled his eyebrows. "From the sound of things, if Thomas gets his way there'll be lots more cooking than a couple of steaks."

Was he insinuating—sex? The crude comments didn't deserve a reply. Besides, this was her chance to earn points. "Yes, we're the people in the motor home from Floyd's RVs, located on upper Lisbon Street in Lewiston, Maine," she said in a loud voice.

A woman behind her squeezed Karen's shoulder. "I don't envy you being cooped up with that man."

"Though he is a hunk," the woman next to her said.

Another woman elbowed her good-naturedly and whispered in her ear. "It's a good thing those children are along or you might use up the entire gross of 'you know whats.' "

Before Karen could ask the woman what she meant, a teenage boy behind the counter asked, "Can I help you?"

"Yes, I'd like four orange juices, four orders of scrambled eggs and English muffins to go," she said over the children's protests. A moment later she took their order and had started out the door when she spotted a group of men tapping

Thomas' back and giving him thumbs up as though he'd already won.

Thomas sauntered to the table inside the motor home and bit down on his breakfast sandwich. He tried to ignore the deafening meows coming from the bedroom. Karen, he noted, already looked as though she'd put in an eight-hour day on a construction site. Her short stylish brown hair was slightly disheveled. Soft wisps fell over her forehead, making her look as though she'd just fallen out of bed.

Lust zinged through him. Shocked by his reaction, he tried to shake some sense into his head. But as he admired her trim waist and shapely behind, he realized he'd rather have her for breakfast than whatever he was eating. Fortunately, the children were around to run interference.

Bear sighed and rested his paw on Thomas' knee. Realizing he was undoing months of training, he coaxed the dog to hop onto a chair next to him. Thomas broke off a piece of his sandwich and set it on the tabletop in front of the drooling dog. The animal scarfed up the morsel and left behind a puddle of saliva.

"Good boy," Thomas said, stealing a glance toward Karen. He knew by her mortified expression, he'd scored himself a point. "Is something wrong?" he asked.

"I hope you plan to clean that up."

He ran a napkin over the drool. "There, are you satisfied?"

Her eyebrows winged upward. "That's disgusting. Think of all the germs you've left behind."

Peter pushed his brothers aside. "My mom says a little dirt never hurt anyone. And she says a few germs won't kill you either."

Karen frowned.

"I think your mom is a smart woman," Thomas said.

"She is," Peter replied.

Charlie nodded and hugged his plastic dump truck to his chest. Karen rested her hands over Peter's shoulders. "Some germs can make people very sick."

"My mom knows everything about germs and boys," Peter added with certainty.

Thomas sipped his coffee. "Your mother is absolutely right. The shots the doctor gives you have a few germs in them to keep you guys healthy."

"I know that," Peter said.

Thomas persuaded Bear to hop down and lie at his feet. "You're a smart kid."

"Yup."

"Me too," Charlie said.

"Damn straight," Thomas said, finishing his sandwich.

Byron grinned. "You're a poop head."

Karen let out a frustrated sigh. "What have I told you about saying that bad word?"

He stuck out his hand. "Gum."

"First, showers."

Peter glanced down at his shirt stained with orange juice. "My mom says a little soap and water never hurt anyone."

"Finally, something I can agree with." Karen threw back her head and laughed. Though a bit loud for Thomas' taste, her laugh still had a nice ring.

"Before I shut the door, I want you to know I'm going to be listening. The person who's the quickest will get his name on my incentive chart," she said, looking down at the youngsters.

Thomas noticed a poster board on the couch with the names of the three boys. He chalked it up to another of her harebrained ideas.

48

"How come?" Charlie asked.

"Because I see great potential in you boys, and I'm sure with a little effort you'll accomplish much during the short time we're together."

To Thomas, four weeks did not seem like a short time, but he kept his opinion to himself.

Looking confused, the boys shrugged. "Does that mean we get gum?"

"No, you'll earn a star next to your name. It's not necessary for you to receive a reward every time you do well. Doing well just for the sake of it should be reward enough." Three pairs of blue eyes stared up blankly at her.

"And I'll be monitoring your language."

"Why?" Charlie asked.

"I believe in letting you know in advance what to expect from me. This way there are no hurt feelings later because of any misunderstanding."

The boys exchanged confused glances.

"I'm trusting you. I figure you'll want your privacy. Remember I'm waiting right here." She shut the door and folded her arms across her chest as she stood in the narrow hall between the living space and the bedroom.

Thomas sipped coffee from the Styrofoam cup and eyed her skeptically. "Do you think it's wise to leave those three hellions unsupervised?"

"Children will live up to our expectations."

"Where did you get that malarkey?"

She planted manicured fingers over her hips. "In books."

A low chuckle escaped his lips. Her eyebrows winged upward. "I've taken extensive courses in dealing effectively with people."

"I see." He nodded and did his damnedest to look serious.

"Children are not that different from adults."

49

"You really believe that?"

"Absolutely."

From inside the bathroom came the sounds of running water. A moment later the door slammed open and out dashed Charlie, stark naked, hair covered with shampoo, water dripping on the floor. As he reached for the chart, water from his arm drizzled over the lettering, which ran on contact.

"I'm first, where's my star?"

"You have to finish your shower."

"I'm done."

"You need to rinse off."

"If I do that, I won't be first."

"Just for this time, I'll let everyone put a star behind their names."

"Really?"

"Yes, so go back in there," she said, opening the door and guiding the child back inside.

Loud voices echoed from the bathroom.

"You're stepping on my feet."

"Am not."

"Stop touching me."

"You pushed me first."

"Did not."

"Did too."

Karen exhaled a deep breath and closed her eyes. "Boys remember my chart."

The children giggled. She knocked on the door. "If you want to stick stars behind your names, you have to act accordingly."

"If I remember correctly, everyone is getting a star," Thomas reminded her. She pierced him with a disgruntled look. "You shouldn't give them a star unless they earn it."

"I'm merely encouraging them," she said.

"I think you're making a mistake, but what do I know?"

"Precisely. What is it you do for a living?" she asked, her tone nearing the breaking point.

"I work construction," he said, for a moment losing himself in the pools of her deep brown eyes.

"How would you deal with someone who wasn't performing his duties?"

"I'd cuss and warn that person to shape up."

"Those children certainly don't need more colorful words to add to their vocabulary." Her lips thinned into a straight line.

"A swat on their behinds might do more good than your charts and your chewing gum."

"Fortunately, I'm in charge of those boys and you aren't."

"We finally agree."

A moment of silence ensued. Someone shut off the water in the bathroom. Relief skittered across Karen's face.

"See," she said, sounding sure of herself. "Before long, my chart will be brimming with stars."

"Stop it!"

"Butt head."

"Poop head."

"Your wee wee's wrinkled." More giggles. Karen's cheeks glowed a delicate pink. Thomas hid his smile behind his coffee cup.

As they pulled into a parking lot at Old Orchard Beach, Karen noticed the gathering crowd and a huge sign advertising Floyd's RVs in bold red lettering. Thomas pulled the motor home to the side of the curb. "Impressive, don't you think?"

"That's yours?"

His mouth curved into a cocky smile. "All it took was three four by eight sheets of plywood and a little paint to put me in the lead."

"Don't be so sure of yourself. You don't know what I have in mind," Karen said, absolutely clueless.

From around the corner came a marching band, led by a cigar smoking turkey, pumping his arms and strutting his stuff. Thomas opened the door to the motor home, hopped down, and threw her a glance over his shoulder. "You should quit now. You don't stand a chance."

Karen gritted her teeth and groaned. "Hurry boys." When she helped Byron undo his seatbelt, she noticed he'd wet himself. "I thought your brother was potty trained." She directed her comment at Peter.

"You need to remind him or he sometimes has accidents."

"So I see."

"Mom says Byron shouldn't feel upset. Everyone has accidents once in a while."

Karen slipped clean underwear and pants on the toddler. "When we go outside, I want you boys to promise me you won't say any bad words. Do you understand?" The three nodded. "Charlie and Byron will hold my hands, and Peter will stand by my side." Again they nodded. "If you see any reporters or men with cameras, I want you to shout *Floyd's RVs* in your loudest voices."

"My mom says if we holler in public, people will think we're wild barbarians," Peter said.

"Well . . . yes, I agree with that." She hated to lead them astray, but she glanced out the window and saw Thomas shaking the turkey's wing. "We're playing a game so it's all right to be loud."

"How come?" Charlie asked.

"Because we won't win if we're quiet."

In the few seconds that remained, she taught them to shout out the praises of the winged marvel.

Floyd caught a glimpse of Karen when she stepped down from the motor home with the three children who were waving their arms and saying something. The loud speaker blaring an advertisement for his business drowned out their voices.

"How's the little lady doing?" he asked, as a chorus of gobbles rumbled from the speaker to his left.

Karen's smile looked strained, like someone about to abandon ship. *One down, one more to go.* He wondered whether she'd go for his kind—sixty inches tall, balding, and filthy rich. Lots of women dug wealthy men.

If he did say so himself, he wasn't bad on the eyes, just a bit shorter than he'd have liked. The padded insoles of his penny loafers helped a little. Anyway, his attitude more than made up for his short stature, as did his charisma and sex appeal. Floyd removed his headpiece, gave her a killer smile, clamped the cigar in the corner of his mouth, and dabbed his forehead with his handkerchief. "Let's go inside where we can talk privately and have something cool to drink. I'm sweating like a swine at a pig roast."

Peter tugged at Karen's elbow. "I want to ride the merry-go-round."

"I want fries," Charlie added.

"I wanna play in the sand."

"Me too."

Karen nodded at the boys. "We'll do all that in a little while, but first, don't you have something to say to the people?"

Floyd swung the microphone in front of the boys' mouths. Charlie and Byron tucked their hands under their arms and flapped their elbows. "Squawk, squawk."

Peter added, "Talk like a chicken at Floyd's and get a good deal."

"That's turkey," Floyd corrected.

Looking flustered, Karen grabbed the mike. "Be assured you won't find any dumb clucks at Floyd's RVs."

Karen had gumption. He liked that in a woman.

"The little lady is right. Come to Floyd's and see for yourselves." He raised his wings and smiled into the crowd. "Because of this contest, we're running a special promotion so fly on down to Floyd's and see for yourselves."

That said, he turned on his charm and climbed aboard the motor home, one wing tucked beneath Karen's elbow, followed by the children and the other unsuspecting so-called-winning-ticket holder.

Chapter Five

Karen sat on the couch and wondered who was in the lead. Would Thomas' plywood sign be worth more than three cute children shouting about chickens instead of turkeys? Had her quick thinking saved the day? Floyd crammed his bulky feathered frame next to her, flicked a quick glance at her chest, and winked. "You sure have pretty eyes."

She wanted to turn away and ask him what color they were. Since he'd ultimately decide the contest winner, she smiled demurely.

"In case you haven't heard, I mentioned your business at Burger King this morning."

"I'm sure you did, but I need proof. Who would I believe if you told me one thing, and Thomas told me the exact opposite?"

Jaw rigid, Thomas leaned in close to Floyd. "She is telling you the truth, you slimy piece of s . . ." He glanced at the boys and cut his sentence short. "So go ahead and give her credit for advertising your business."

Karen looked into Thomas' stormy blue eyes. That was a generous gesture, she thought, her heart skipping a beat. "Thanks, that was very nice of you."

"No thanks necessary. I'm going to make sure I get credit for the sign my crew constructed."

So much for being a nice guy.

Floyd cleared his throat and ran a shaky finger inside the collar of his shirt. "No need to get your dander up, Son. You're taking this the wrong way. The press is going to keep tabs on our little contest so I need a way of scoring that'll prove I'm not favoring either side. There's a lot at stake here, and I want to be fair to you both and not find myself in a heap of trouble. So I've come up with a plan that's damn clever if I do say so myself. Also, I've added a small stipulation to our deal."

Thomas' eyes narrowed to slits.

"Since the purpose of this trip is to advertise my motor home, I think you should have to stay inside at least ten hours a day. That includes the time you spend eating and sleeping. If one of you is even one minute short of the ten hour minimum, then you lose."

If Thomas hadn't looked as though he was about to explode, Karen would not have agreed so quickly.

"I have no problem with that."

"Not so fast, Karen," Thomas said, raising his hand in protest. "Floyd doesn't have a right to add any conditions now. He should have stated all the rules before the contest began."

"I think we should give Floyd a chance to explain," Karen said, thinking that agreeing with Floyd might boost her odds of winning.

"Thank you, Karen," Floyd said, tapping her hand approvingly.

Thomas frowned. "You should decide who's ahead at the moment."

Floyd yanked his cigar from his mouth. "Not to worry, my plan takes everything into consideration." He unzipped the front of his costume and pulled out a small tablet. "When you see what I've worked out, I think you'll agree that my plan is more than fair. Also, if you want to add anything, I'm open to your suggestions." Floyd paused and glanced at the children. "Before I get into the particulars, I've got good news for the boys. The Winnebago will be staying right here for three to five days."

"Yippee," chorused three voices.

Floyd turned his attention back to Karen and Thomas. "The press coverage has been damn good. I'm hoping the folks from nearby communities want to drive on by and take a peek at the Winnebago. There's big money in the Portland and Falmouth area. I'd just as soon empty a few deep pockets before leaving town."

"When we gonna go to the beach?" Charlie asked.

Floyd flapped a wing at the boys. "Soon, soon. Now take the remote and watch satellite television while we adults talk. And keep the volume down so we can hear ourselves think." Peter aimed the remote at the television. The hum of voices filled the room. "As you can see, I've set up a point system. You earn one point if my business is mentioned in the local paper due directly to something you've done. Ten points if the local paper prints a picture along with a short story. Twenty-five points for front-page coverage. Fifty points for air time on television."

Charlie elbowed his brothers. "What are those?"

Peter covered his mouth and whispered in his brother's ear. Before Karen could check to see what the boys were watching, Floyd handed out printed pieces of paper.

"I made copies for both of you. If you manage to get my business mentioned on the national news, it'll be one hundred points."

"Is that the entire scoring system?" Karen asked.

"Well, yes, unless you think of something I've left out."

"If there's one thing I've learned, it's never to underestimate anyone's abilities. What if by some wild stroke of luck one of us is responsible for getting Floyd's RVs world-wide attention?" Karen asked.

Floyd smacked his lips together. His gunmetal gray eyes brightened. "I like the way you think, Karen. If news of my business reaches the eastern hemisphere, that person earns two hundred and fifty points and probably cinches the game."

Thomas grunted disapprovingly. "You're both out of your minds. There's no way in hell either of us can get Floyd's RVs national or world-wide press coverage."

"Where there's a will, there's a way," Floyd replied, grinning at Karen. "Maybe the little lady will figure something out with help from her troops. Right boys?"

No one answered. Mesmerized, they stared at the television, giggling and whispering. Charlie nudged Peter and pointed at the screen. "That man sure has a big wee wee." Karen sprang across the room, grabbed the remote, and as she snapped off the television, caught a glimpse of two naked adults.

Charlie grinned and cupped his hands in front of his chest. "That lady sure had big boobies."

Karen grabbed his arm and pulled him off the couch. "I didn't realize it was so late, let's hurry and go to the beach."

"Yippeeee," the three shouted, scurrying toward the bedroom. She blinked away the tears springing to her eyes, and turned away so Thomas wouldn't notice. How could she have been so careless? Abby had trusted her, and she'd betrayed that trust by allowing the boys to watch pornography. She bit back a cry and dashed away a tear with the back of her hand. Why couldn't she have inherited her parents' ability to face disappointment without crying? Maybe because she cared so much.

Over the years, she'd never seen her parents cry. Then too, she'd never seen the love she so desperately craved in their faces. Nothing she'd ever done was ever good enough or bad enough to warrant a second glance. She knew she needed to stop being so hard on herself. She needed to toughen up, stiffen her upper lip, pull back her shoulders, and force a smile. Otherwise, Thomas and Floyd would think her an emotional wreck. No one liked a weepy female. Least of all her parents.

Thomas stood, walked across the room, and grabbed the manual for the satellite system. "I'll put a block on the set so this doesn't happen again."

She wanted to thank him, would have if the lump in her throat hadn't prevented her from speaking. Inhaling a calming breath, she nodded helplessly and hurried from the room.

A few minutes later she and the boys dashed out the door, leaving her at a disadvantage because Thomas and Floyd would now be alone to conspire together.

As they marched across the street, Karen's arms felt as though they were being pulled from their sockets. Byron had refused to walk so she held him in her right arm, his chubby legs straddling her hips. Wearing his favorite striped shirt, Charlie was holding onto her fingers from which dandled a beach bag and a towel. From her left hand hung a picnic cooler, life preservers, and a plastic bag filled with beach toys. Peter carried hats, sunscreen, and Charlie's dump truck.

She'd been so absorbed in listening to what Floyd had to say about the contest she'd ignored her duties as the children's guardian. From now on, the boys would come first. With a bit more organization, she'd be able to care for the boys and plan her next move.

"Can I give you a hand with that?" Thomas asked, his deep voice startling her.

She spun around. The cooler slammed into his knee. The lines around his mouth deepened.

"Did I hurt you?" she asked, bending over to check on the damage she'd done.

He looked down, his head butting hers. The impact caused her to lose her balance. He rescued Byron and caught her around the waist. For a few seconds she stood there, caught in the warmth of Thomas' sea-blue eyes, her bare legs against his hairy ones, their torsos joined at the hip, her breasts flatted against his muscular chest. Her breath stilled, her pulse roared.

He blinked, shook his head as if to break the spell, and released her. "You all right?"

It took a moment for his words to register. "Oh . . . yes, I'm fine. How about you?"

"I have to remember to be on my guard when you have something in your hands," he said, a crooked grin hiking one corner of his mouth as he absently rubbed the small bruise below his right eye. He set the toddler down.

"Byron, you're too big to be carried around like a baby. I need your help. Here," he said, shoving a beach towel at the child. "Carry this and we'll get there faster. Peter, you take the cooler and follow me. Charlie, carry your own dump truck."

They marched over the hot sand and stopped a few feet from the surf. Thomas doled out orders like a drill sergeant, and though Karen wasn't sure whether she approved of his firm tone, she noticed the boys listened to his directions. Within minutes they'd spread out a blanket and opened an umbrella for shade. The boys grabbed their toys and started constructing roads. Karen dropped down onto her hands and knees, poured red Kool-Aid drink into cups, and took out peanut butter and jelly sandwiches for their lunch.

Thomas ducked under the umbrella. Their eyes locked. She grabbed hold of the picnic cooler to steady herself. She couldn't trust him. For all she knew he and Floyd had conspired together to make her lose. She didn't need this man in her life. But she couldn't ignore his eyes or the way he made her body tingle. When she won the motor home, she'd win her parents' respect. They'd finally see her as a success. Until she'd met her goal, she couldn't afford to befriend Thomas. She knew by her pounding heartbeat and quivering limbs her traitorous body would never be satisfied with being just friends.

Thomas had helped her, and she couldn't let him just walk away. Common courtesy, she thought, doubting her motives.

"We have plenty," she said. "If you'd care to join us."

"Thanks, maybe some other time."

Her insides clenched in disappointment. He balled his fist and knuckled her jaw playfully. "Good luck, you're going to need it."

"Are you referring to the boys or the contest?"

"Both," he replied, his cocky grin in place, liquid fire in his eyes.

She watched him stand, amble over the sand, and plunk his towel about one hundred feet away, next to a large-breasted blonde. Bleached blonde, she wanted to shout at him, and those boobs were probably fake too. *What did she care?* If Thomas wanted to be seen with that bimbo, that was up to him.

Ashamed of herself, she inhaled a calming breath. She wasn't being fair to the woman. For all she knew she had a PhD. *Fat chance.* Again, she chastised herself but seemed unable to control her feelings.

"Miss Implant USA," she mumbled under her breath, sending the blonde a telepathic message, wishing for the implants to burst under the hot rays of the sun. Jealousy ran rampant through Karen's body, tightening her stomach in knots and bristling the short hairs at the base of her skull. What was wrong with her? Struggling to set her priorities in order, she called the boys. "Let's have lunch, then you can put on your life jackets and we'll go swimming."

They ran toward her, kicking up sand and giggling.

"I'm starving."

"Me too."

"Can I have a drink?"

Charlie attempted to jump over his cup. He missed and kicked the container in the air. Its contents splashed over Karen's face and dripped down her neck and over her white bathing suit.

"Gee, I didn't mean to," Charlie said, eyes wide and his hands over his mouth.

Peter grabbed a paper towel and handed it to her. "Mom says . . ."

Karen interrupted. "Let me guess, everyone has accidents once in while."

"Yup, but she also says, there's no sense crying over spilt milk."

As Karen dabbed at the liquid, she looked at their serious faces and smiled. "Your mother is right. Let's have our lunch and enjoy ourselves." *Easier said than done.* Thomas had since slid over to the blonde's blanket.

Charlie pulled his sandwich out of a baggie and sat next to Karen. "I learned a new word today . . . boobies."

"That's not a nice word."

"How come?"

"Because it isn't."

wasn't wearing a robe. "Let me go get dressed . . ."

"You look dressed to me," he said, his slow gaze traveling from her open-toed slippers to her face. "That nightgown covers you more than the red bikini you wore today."

"My bathing suit is white."

"The Kool-Aid turned it red." He paused, his pupils widened in appreciation. "Except for the silver belly button ring."

She was pleased he'd noticed.

He ran his tongue over his lower lip. The provocative motion sent a jolt of electricity up her spine.

Bear stretched under the table and eyed his master. Thomas grabbed a dog bone from the cupboard. "Here boy, come." The dog pranced to his side and sat at perfect attention. "Good boy." Thomas gave Bear the treat and patted the dog's head approvingly.

A meow blasted from behind the bedroom door. Karen stood and dished up a small portion of cat food. She then disappeared in the bedroom and returned empty handed a moment later.

"Luce was hungry," she said. "He should be all set for a few hours."

The cat was a royal pain in the butt, but since Thomas wanted a chance to get to know Karen, he kept his observations to himself.

"What will you do with the motor home if you win?" she asked.

"I'd sell it and take the cash. What about you?"

"I have something very special in mind." Without elaborating, she glanced down and combed her fingers through the fringe on a pillow.

"Have you got your game plan all figured out?"

"Not yet," she said, looking at him with sad eyes.

"Then what do ya want me to call those things?"

His question surprised her, left her speechless. After a moment, she said, "I wish your mother were here for this discussion, but since she's not . . ." She inhaled a deep breath. "They're breasts, but young boys shouldn't talk about women's bodies."

"How come?"

"Because it's not polite."

"Can I tell you one more thing?" An impish smile crinkled his face.

"Go ahead."

"That lady on TV had big ones, but the lady with Thomas has the biggest boobies of all."

Karen frowned, but she agreed wholeheartedly. "What you saw on television was inappropriate for young boys," she said, squinting at the blonde *bimbo* and detesting the adorning way she ran her fingers along Thomas' muscular chest. He was lapping up the attention like a lovesick schoolboy.

"Now let's stop staring at Thomas' bim . . . friend and finish our lunch." When Karen stole another glance in Thomas' direction, what little appetite she had left vanished as he started massaging sunscreen over the woman's back and worked his way down to her shapely thighs.

Thomas had figured the best way to forget about Karen was to concentrate on another woman. So he'd strolled toward a good-looking blonde lying on her stomach. When he spread his towel next to hers, she turned over and smiled. His eyes nearly fell from their sockets. A chest-man would have thought he'd died and gone to heaven. But Thomas preferred breasts that fit in the palm of his hand. For an instant his gaze traveled to Karen. He returned his attention to the woman before him.

They introduced themselves. "I'm Cherie," she said, her voice a soft purr.

This beat playing ref for three unruly children. Thomas wanted to live happily ever after without the constant bickering, the constant power struggles. *Never again,* he reassured himself.

He turned to his companion. They were deep in conversation when he heard screams. Thinking one of the boys was drowning he jumped up and ran toward the commotion.

Byron was digging a hole with a shovel. Peter had wrapped an arm around Charlie's shoulder while Charlie sobbed. Karen was knee deep in water, shouting for the boys not to move as she ran anxious hands through the breaking surf.

"What's wrong," Thomas asked, running to her side.

"The tide carried out Charlie's dump truck, and I can't find it anywhere."

"Go wait with the boys, and I'll have a look." He dove into the frigid water and ran his hands along the bottom. He found an empty sea urchin shell and a sand dollar. He stood up and looked into Charlie's expectant face. The odds of finding the child's toy in this current were very slim. But he needed to give it one more try. He dove in again but couldn't find the plastic truck.

"Sorry, Charlie," he said a moment later. He opened his hand and showed the child the sea urchin and a few shells. "Would you like these?"

Charlie puckered his lips and wailed.

Later that night, when Karen entered the bedroom, she saw that Peter and Charlie had fallen asleep on her bed. Byron was curled up in a sleeping bag on a foam mattress on the floor. The sound of him sucking his thumb pulsed in the

room. She pushed the two older boys aside and climbed between them. Within minutes Peter and Charlie were sn gled next to her. Peter's bent knee pressed against stomach, Charlie's foot dug into her back. After tossing turning for half an hour, she decided to get up and have a of hot chocolate.

She slipped her feet into her slippers, padded out to kitchen, and poured water into the kettle. According to clock it was after midnight. Thomas was still out gallivant with his buxom babe. Some time later Karen sat on the cou and was sipping hot chocolate when a silver sports car pul in next to the motor home.

Had she not peeked between the closed curtains, wouldn't have seen Blondie throw her arms around Thom neck and she wouldn't have seen him hug her back. He kiss the woman's cheek and hopped out of the vehicle. "That for everything, Cherie."

Everything? Thomas watched her drive away. Whistli he entered the motor home a moment later. "It's been a l time since anyone's waited up for me," he said, coming cl and looking down at her, the warmth of his eyes leaving weak kneed and breathless.

"Is that what you think I was doing?"

"It's one possibility."

"I was having some hot cocoa."

"It's a little warm for that, don't you think?"

"I find it comforting, regardless of the temperature o side."

"I'll get myself a beer and join you. Since we're going spend the next few weeks together, we should sit down get to know each other."

As she rose from the couch a gentle breeze stirred fabric of her nightgown. Until now, she'd forgotten

He wanted to wrap his arms around her and chase away the hurt look on her face. He needed to keep the battle lines clearly drawn. She was his opponent.

"We need to understand each other. I want the motor home, and I don't plan to back out."

"Neither do I."

"I aim to do everything in my power to win. Even if it means I have to be a conniving, underhanded bastard."

"Same here."

By her short burst of laughter, he knew she didn't believe him, which might work in his favor. He was one hundred percent serious. As the competition wore on, she'd crumble under the pressure. And he'd push until she did. Too bad they hadn't met under different conditions. Maybe in time they could be friends, close friends. No way. This contest would get ugly, and once they parted ways, they'd never see each other again. He opened the refrigerator. "Can I get you anything?" he asked over his shoulder, taking a long glance at the woman sitting on the couch that would soon be his bed. Visions of naked bodies with tangled arms and legs skittered through his mind. Maybe she hated kids, he thought, knowing better. He'd seen the way she treated the three boys. Someday she'd be a wonderful mother.

"Are your troops bunked down for the night?"

"I hope so."

He uncapped his beer, sat next to her, and anchored his right ankle over his left knee. "I bet you're anxious to have babies of your own."

"Yes, how did you guess?"

"Just a hunch."

"I'd like two girls and two boys, not that I have a choice."

"That's a large family."

Her brown eyes deepened a shade. "I was an only child."

67

"I should have been so lucky," he said, grinning. "I got saddled with two brothers and a sister."

Worry skittered across her features. "The way you said that sounds awful."

"They know I love them. I just like to give them a hard time." He changed his mind about her hair. The sleek, short cut looked very feminine on her. If he didn't have a brain in his head, he'd have run his fingers along the sides of her head. He wanted to capture her mouth in a dizzying kiss guaranteed to steal their breath. Most of all, he wanted to kiss the tanned flesh around her belly button ring, a piece of jewelry that had taunted his mind most of the afternoon.

"Growing up as an only child can get awfully lonely . . ." Sadness crept into her voice as she looked across the room, seemingly deep in thought. Her eyes grew misty. She cleared her throat and blinked several times. "How many children would you like?"

"None, zilch, zero."

"That surprises me. You have a way with the boys. I bet you'd make a good father."

"Not in this lifetime. I raised my brothers and sister. I've done my time."

"You make it sound like a jail sentence."

"It can be. Children take and take, until there's nothing left to give."

"It doesn't have to be that way."

"And you know?"

"I've read a lot. Children can enrich a couple's life."

"Hah," he laughed, his tone humorless. "Throw out your books. That's a crock of bull."

Chapter Six

That night Thomas punched his pillow and turned over for the hundredth time. According to the brochure, the motor home was capable of sleeping six comfortably. Whoever had written that nonsense had never reclined on the pullout sofa. The full-size mattress was too short for Thomas' six foot two frame. With each passing hour, the metal bars underneath the thin mattress jabbed painfully into his lower back and behind his knees.

The image of a sterling silver belly button ring added to his distress and made sleeping on his stomach damn near impossible, giving him lots of time to think. By dawn, battle plan in place, he rose and showered.

A little later he poured himself a cup of black coffee and ran a strip of silver duct tape down the center of the Winnebago.

"What ya doing?"

"What's it look like?" Thomas glanced down at Charlie, holding a seashell and wearing a grimy striped shirt.

"You're sticking tape."

"Smart boy."

"How come?"

Thomas winked. "It's part of my game plan."

"I like games."

"Can I play too?" came Peter's voice from behind them.

Charlie clapped his hands. "Me too, me too!"

Thomas couldn't turn them down, especially when it served his purpose. "Sure, I'll cut the tape, and the two of you can help to divide everything. Now remember this side is mine," he said, pointing to his left. "The other is Karen's. So try to be fair."

"I put your name on Karen's chart," Peter said, pointing to a poster leaning against the wall. Thomas saw his name in bold, crooked lettering, six stars trailing behind. "What did I do to deserve all those stars?"

"It's 'cause you dived into the water to save my brother's dump truck."

"But I didn't find the toy."

"My mom says that don't matter a wit as long as you try really, really hard."

"Thanks," Thomas said, cupping his hand over the boy's shoulder, feeling a strong connection.

The boy scrunched up his face. "When you got out of the water, you looked like this."

"That bad, huh?"

"Yup, I could tell by your sour expression you did your bestest."

Thomas laughed. "My mother used to call me her little sour puss when I looked grumpy." Even after all these years, the loss of his mother left a raw ache in his gut.

"I can see why," Peter replied with a nod.

Charlie ran a curving line of tape into the bathroom. "Karen says you're a grumpy old man."

"She said that?" Thomas asked.

"Yup."

Peter chuckled. "My mom says if she got a nickel every time Charlie fibbed, she'd be rich."

That pleased him. "So Karen didn't call me a grump?"

"Charlie didn't fib about that. I heard Karen tell my mom you was the hunkiest grump she ever saw."

"Hummm." Thomas crossed his arms, pleased she found him attractive. Maybe Karen didn't approve of his attitude, but she hadn't seen anything yet.

"Is this good?" Peter asked about to adhere the tape in the exact center of the walkway.

Thomas curled his finger. "Pull it over this way a little. My feet are bigger so I'll need more space."

Karen awoke to find Byron cuddled next to her, his blanket tucked under his arm, his thumb deep in his mouth. Her maternal instincts surfaced as she hugged him by her side. Some day she'd have her own family and lots of children. The short time she'd spent caring for Abby's brood had opened her eyes. Children were loads of work. They did not always listen. In this case, they rarely listened. They could be rude, demanding, but deep down, always loveable.

Of course, Karen's children would be better behaved because she'd dole out lots of attention. She'd set a good example, and she'd always put their needs before her own. Her children would never doubt she loved them. Their childhood would be perfect. *Unlike hers.*

A familiar longing surfaced. Forcing herself to think brighter thoughts, she brushed a wisp of downy hair from the toddler's forehead, kissed his brow, and filled her lungs with his sweet scent. Big mistake! A rancid, pungent order permeated her nostrils. She'd never changed a soiled diaper. *Her luck had run out!*

She planned to put off the unpleasant task as long as possible. Unfortunately, Byron picked that moment to wake up. A moment later between gags, she removed the disposable diaper, used a box full of wet wipes, and managed to help him slip on clean underwear without throwing up. Trying not to breathe through her nose, she tossed the mess into a plastic bag and knotted it closed. At least, her day could only improve. *Wrong again!*

"What's going on here?" she asked, taking in all the duct tape over everything.

"We're playing a game with Thomas," the boys said happily.

An off-centered zigzagging line ran along the floor from the front to the back of the motor home and into the bathroom. Tape divided the toilet seat, the shower stall, and the sink. Every chair had tape running down the center, as did the couch, the television, and the toaster. Tape divided the windows, the microwave, and the front windshield. Even the steering wheel sported a band of gray. As she swung open the cupboard, she discovered every glass and dish had tape down the middle.

"Stop this instant," she shouted; according to her books, an inappropriate tone to use with children. If children became accustomed to raised voices, they'll soon tune out that adult. She peeled the tape from the cup she removed from the cupboard. "I'm sorry, I shouldn't have spoken so loudly."

"That's all right," Peter said. "Mom hollers at us all the time."

That didn't surprise her. "Where's Thomas?" she asked, ready to slap a strip of tape down the middle of his face.

"Dunno, we was doing such a good job he left us in charge," Charlie said proudly, giggling.

"Don't you tell about Bear," Peter warned.

Karen was ready to insist they confess what they'd done when Thomas climbed into the motor home. She knew by his shocked expression he was surprised. He ran a hand through his hair.

"I see you guys have been busy."

"Yup, we divided everything we could find just like you said. Do we get paid now?"

Guilt flashed across his face as he handed the boys a dollar.

"This isn't fair, you're using the kids to do your dirty work."

"No rules, remember," he said, sparing her an innocent look.

"What's all this tape supposed to mean?"

"I think you already know."

"Surely you don't expect me and the boys to stay cooped up on one side of the room?"

"It's only fair."

"How can you say that?" she asked with a swing of her arm. "There's one of you and four of us; five if I count Luce."

"Regardless, I've spoken to Floyd and he thought this was a good idea."

"When did you see Floyd?"

"We had breakfast earlier this morning."

She saw red! "Why wasn't I included?"

He struck a casual pose. "Floyd invited you, but I explained you'd be exhausted after caring for the children so we decided to let you rest."

"How considerate of you!"

"Thanks. Oh, before I forget, Floyd and I have made a few changes to our itinerary."

"Why wasn't I consulted?"

"Since you slept late, I figured I'd relay any important messages."

"And I'm supposed to trust you to tell me all the important details?"

He shrugged nonchalantly. "You don't have a choice."

She gritted her teeth.

"Floyd has changed his mind about us touring all the New England states. He wants us to restrict our travel to Maine, New Hampshire and Massachusetts. He figures anything farther won't help his business."

"I should have been there for that discussion. When did you first hear about the breakfast with Floyd?"

"I guess I forgot to tell you I saw Floyd at a bar last night. He said for us to meet him this morning because he wanted to discuss more contest changes. Since you were so gung-ho about his other changes when he was here yesterday afternoon, I figured you wouldn't mind."

She planted her hands on her hips. "You miserable, damnable piece of pond scum."

Peter cleared his throat. "You want to know what my mom says?"

Karen turned to him. "No."

Thomas nodded, "Sure, go ahead."

"My mom says if you can't say nice things you should say nothing at all."

Thomas winked at the boy. "Too bad Karen doesn't hang around your mom more often, she could use some of that wisdom."

Karen's pulse pounded in her ears.

"We both hold a winning ticket that gives us an equal share of the Winnebago," Thomas continued calmly. "In time it'll all be mine, but for now, I'm taking my half."

"Which side is mine," she asked, staring down at the uneven line that ran from front to back.

Peter pointed to the larger section. "Thomas said he needed more space 'cause he has bigger feet."

"You put them up to this?"

"I may have mentioned my shoe size, but they took over from there."

"You can't be serious," she said ready to rip the hair from his head one follicle at a time.

"I am."

She fisted her hands by her side and groaned. "Are you nuts?"

He glanced around the room and nodded. "Personally, I think the boys did a great job."

"Don't you think they got carried away a little?" She hated her high-pitched tone.

"Nope." He threw the boys an approving glance. "They deserve a bonus."

His cocky grin vanished when he looked over her shoulder. She followed the direction of his gaze and spotted Bear ambling toward them. A strip of gray tape ran from the animal's forehead, down his back and onto his tail.

Thomas soon regretted his decision to divide the motor home. He stretched a cramped leg, and every sore muscle in his body cried out in pain. Unfortunately, he hadn't taken into account the foldout bed inside the couch, which he couldn't open because two feet of the mattress would extend beyond the duct-taped border. For the last three nights he'd tried to sleep with his body pretzeled within the confined space.

Also, he couldn't use the table, microwave, stove, or the refrigerator. He was forced to order out all the time. By the fourth morning, he was sitting on the couch, every inch of him on his side of the taped line, watching Karen and the children eating breakfast: juice, home fries, scrambled eggs, bacon, whole-wheat toast. He bit into his breakfast sandwich. The muffin was dry as cardboard, the egg rubbery. "Yum," he said, hoping to cause a stir. "You don't know what you're missing."

Peter and Charlie turned. "Tomorrow we get pancakes. The day after that we get waffles, and the day after that . . ."

Karen tapped her spoon against the tabletop. "What did I tell you boys about talking with your mouths full?"

"Sorry."

"That's all right. Finish your breakfast. We'll be leaving soon."

When Karen carried her plate to the sink, she slid Thomas a look that confirmed his suspicions. She knew he was suffering, and she was enjoying herself. Determined to get even, Thomas stood and leaned into her air space. "I have something for you." He reached down, curled his fingers over her hand, and slapped the keys into the palm. Her pupils widened in surprise. "It's your turn to drive," he said, turning away to hide his satisfied grin.

"Well, I've never . . . that is, I . . ."

"You gonna drive Karen?" Peter asked.

"Wow!" Charlie added, before she could answer. "When I'm grown like you, I'm gonna drive giant dump trucks and bulldozers. This is really, really big, but I bet not as big as the giant dump trucks, huh?"

"Of course, she's going to drive," Thomas said, swinging around, pleased to see Karen's shocked expression. "And I agree with you, Charlie, this motor home is tiny compared to the rigs hauling dozers to the construction sites."

Karen frowned at him.

"It's only fair," he pointed out in a reasonable tone guaranteed to ruffle her temper. "Everything in the Winnebago is split right down the middle, and that should include the responsibilities of driving and maintaining this vehicle."

Her eyes narrowed; manicured fingers clenched into tight

fists. Her breath puffed from slightly opened lips like a runner about to reach the finish line. Only she'd lost this race, and Thomas was ready to claim his prize. Beneath her bravado he saw indecision and fear. Though Thomas wasn't a demonstrative guy like his brother, Joe, he was ready to pump his arms in the air and shout out a victory whoop until Karen threw the keys in the air and caught them mid flight.

"I sure hope this buggy is fully insured. Buckle your seatbelts, boys. We're going for a ride."

Chapter Seven

Karen recognized the look on Thomas' face, the one that said she didn't stand a chance. Well, he was in for a surprise, and so was Floyd if they thought she was going to back out now. She was more convinced than ever the two of them were working together. Why else had they excluded her from their breakfast meeting? They wanted time alone to regroup and to think up ways to make her quit. *Well, think again!*

No doubt, Floyd, the despicable man, had had no intentions of parting with the motor home. So he'd planted a so-called winner in his showroom. Thanks to a computer virus, Karen's luck and her life were about to change. Meanwhile, she turned to the children. "Byron, honey, finish your cereal. Boys put away the tape and find a book or game to amuse yourselves. Charlie, take off your favorite shirt and put on a clean one."

"But I love this shirt."

"Do as I say, and I'll buy you something special."

"Me too?" Peter asked.

"Yes, I'll give everyone a surprise."

"Does that include me?" Thomas asked, his gaze locking with hers. Eyes bluer than the clear summer sky held her captive a moment as she noticed the hazel specks ringing his black pupils.

Against her will, her heart skipped a beat. She raised her fist. "How about a knuckle sandwich?"

The boys laughed and for a moment she was pleased with herself.

"Very interesting," he said, taking her hand and stroking her fingers. "What did you have in mind for dessert?"

Tiny electrical shocks zapped their way along her arms and settled where they had no business. Images that had nothing to do with sugary confections flashed through her mind. She yanked her hand away. Thomas leaned against the counter and crossed his legs at the ankles. She glanced at his feet over the taped line. "You're on my side."

"Not for long," he said, not budging an inch, insinuating she was about to lose the competition.

Though the idea of driving the enormous motor home frayed her nerves, she steadied her voice. "We'll see about that."

"Do you honestly think you can drive this Winnebago?"

She cast Thomas a confident smile. "I could drive this baby with one eye closed and one hand tied behind my back."

Granted, her idea of parallel parking was pulling into a parking lot and lining up with the next car. She drove a Toyota for heaven's sake, and that small car was enough for her to handle. But Thomas didn't know that, and she wasn't about to tell him. So with a force of will, she buckled the children onto the couch. After feeding her cat, and closing the bedroom door, she settled into the bucket seat opposite the wheel.

She studied the expansive control panel and the video monitor allowing her to see the Volkswagen hooked to the back. Calculating approximately sixty feet total, she gulped in a breath, stuck the key in the ignition, and prayed she didn't flatten everything in her path.

Thomas gave Karen a point for having some guts as she inched out of the parking lot like a snail. She was a lot tougher than he'd originally thought.

"Take it easy," he said, gripping the seat as though they were traveling at breakneck speed, sending her another grin guaranteed to churn up her quick temper. She slid him a look that might have maimed a lesser man, but since he'd raised teenagers, he was immune.

"Hold on boys," he said, tipping his head to the side, keeping one eye trained on Karen. "Looks like we're in for a wild ride."

"Yippee, I like to go fast," Charlie said, missing Thomas' sarcasm.

"Me too," Peter added.

Karen hit the brakes, which brought them to a complete stop, not much slower than her driving. A small unintelligible sound crept up from her throat, but she didn't even spare him a glance as she bit into her lower lip and waited a millennium to make her turn.

"Floyd won't be happy if we spend the rest of the month here," Thomas pointed out in his most helpful voice.

Her eyebrows shot up. "You and Floyd can take a flying leap."

Thomas lifted a hand in peace. "You needn't go berserk on me just because I'm telling it like it is." His brother Joe's familiar expression wrung a smile from his face. Putting up with his mouthy siblings was finally paying off. "Why are we waiting?" he asked, fascinated with the way her brown eyes darkened several shades.

She opened and closed her fingers over the wheel. "For enough space to pull into the traffic."

"Huuuumph," he craned his neck from one side to the other. "I could have pulled a freight train into that last space you passed up."

Ignoring him, she checked the mirrors, maneuvered the motor home onto Route One, and they were on their way. On the sidewalk an elderly man in a battery-powered wheelchair zoomed past them.

"Poop head." Byron stuck out his hand. "Want gum."

Flicking a quick glance in the rearview mirror, Karen groaned. "I'm out of gum, but if you behave, I'll let you put a star behind your name."

Byron's lower lip protruded like a small shelf. "Gum, gum!" His shriek a second later blasted Thomas' eardrums like a jackhammer.

Thomas would have called a stop to the commotion had he not seen the sweat beading Karen's forehead, her white knuckles gripping the steering wheel. He could almost hear her frenzied heartbeat. For a moment he considered offering to do all the driving. *But only for a moment.* Thomas intended to win, and his strategy didn't allow for compassion. Instead, he scratched Bear's neck and whispered in the dog's ear, "Kitty, kitty." Bear's head shot up. The animal sprang to his feet, barreled down the length of the motor home, and positioned itself at the closed bedroom door. Getting down on its haunches, it sniffed under the crack of the door and barked.

Bear had endurance and a deep voice capable of driving sane men mad. Add to that, the resulting sharp meows, Byron's wails, and Peter and Charlie arguing. Thomas leaned back in the passenger seat, certain this happy family would soon crumble under the stress. Yes, he thought, stretching and popping in a CD to add to the din, soon he'd be on the road by himself. Karen and the children would leave, and he'd enjoy the peace and quiet.

81

He rested his right foot over his left knee, puckered up, and whistled along with the CD he'd borrowed from his sister, which wasn't easy because it didn't have a distinctive beat, just loud drums, guitars, and a high-pitched garbled voice that sounded like someone who'd struck his thumb with a hammer. Karen looked as though she was about to crack.

Thankfully, caring for his siblings had rendered him able to drown out background noise. His unplanned parenthood had given him great fortitude. Something Karen lacked. Thomas turned to the boys. "Do you kids know how to whistle?"

After a few miserable attempts, they joined in and clapped along with the racket. He smiled to himself. Bear would soon be rid of the pesky feline, and he'd be rid of the pesky female and her brood of kids.

A pounding headache started at Karen's temples and radiated along the top of her skull. Her heart rate had hit warp speed when she'd sat behind the wheel of the mammoth vehicle. Every muscle tensed from the strain, and she wondered how she'd manage to drive the Winnebago for several more hours.

"Oh, I almost forgot," Thomas said. "Floyd wants us to stop at Scarborough Downs Racetrack for a couple days."

"I bet you forgot," she muttered through clenched teeth, itching to slap the damnable grin from Thomas' face only she didn't dare release her grip. "I don't want the boys exposed to horse racing and gambling."

"That's up to you. Just don't place any bets around them."

Every cell in her body clenched in fury.

"I'll try to control myself."

"I'm relieved to hear that." Another cocky grin.

Another strong urge to do bodily damage. Given the

choice, she preferred his scowl. She didn't trust him, not one bit. She would have told him that except she needed every bit of gray matter to concentrate on her driving.

She pulled into a space at the back of the parking lot, away from other vehicles. From a distance, she spotted cameramen gathering and another large wooden sign announcing their arrival and paying tribute to Floyd's RVs. The satisfied look on Thomas' face said it all. He expected to win. He'd take credit for the advertising, and he'd rack up more points for his efforts, unless she thought of something—fast.

With a foxy smile, Floyd led the pack of reporters toward the motor home. Before the boys could spring themselves loose, she leaped up, charged out the door, grabbed hold of Floyd's arm, and leaned in close to his ear.

"If you don't want me screaming foul play you'd better listen up, or I'll tell the reporters how you and Thomas are running a scam. I'm sure they'd be interested to learn I wasn't included in your little breakfast chat."

Floyd's face flushed, and his arm circled her waist. "Now, now, little lady, don't go getting your dander up."

"Then you'd better treat me fairly."

"Fair is my middle name," he whispered with wide-eyed innocence before turning to the crowd. "If you'll excuse us a moment, Karen and I have some business to attend to." As he took her elbow and led her out of earshot, Karen was happy to see that Thomas' scowl was back in place.

"Don't blame me because you wanted to sleep late," Floyd said.

"If I had known about the breakfast, I'd have been there."

Floyd shrugged. "Thomas seemed so sincere when he said you'd had a rough day with the boys. He convinced me you wanted to catch a little shuteye. I'd seen those three kids in action so I believed him."

"You were wrong."

"I can see that now," he said sincerely. "Let me make it up to you."

"How do you intend to do that?"

"I'll take you out for dinner tonight. Just the two of us. I'll go over every detail I discussed with Thomas this morning, along with a few new facts."

Karen started to feel better until she thought of Peter, Charlie, and Byron. "Who'll take care of the boys?"

"You women are a tricky lot. I'm sure you'll find a way to persuade Thomas to baby-sit."

She ran her tongue along her lower lip. "That won't be easy. I don't think he likes the children."

"He doesn't need to like them. All he has to do is let them eat junk food and watch TV while you and I have a little one-on-one."

Desperation clouding her judgment, she ignored the glint in his beady eyes. He looped his arm over her shoulder and escorted her toward the cameramen. "You do what you can with Thomas. I bet he'll come around."

Thomas flashed a grin at the reporters and tried to act as though he didn't have a care in the world. Out of the corner of his eye he'd seen Floyd and Karen, their heads butted together, deep in conversation.

"How's it feel to be in the lead?" a reporter asked.

"Great," he said, pleased with the news. Until now he wasn't sure of the score.

"Your sign made the Old Orchard Gazette, page three, and there's a picture of you standing next to it."

"Was there any mention of Miss Brown or the children?"

"Nothing in the local paper."

"That's a shame," Thomas said, not meaning one word and glancing behind him to check on the children. The first chance he had, he'd set Karen straight. They were her responsibility, not his.

Floyd arrived with Karen and released his hold on her. Barney handed Thomas a bundle of newspapers, and looked at his boss for approval.

"Barney's in charge of collecting all the data on the contest, and he's doing a damn good job of it," Floyd said before turning to Thomas and pumping his hand.

"You're ahead, son, by a substantial margin. But the little lady has some points, too. When you two have a chance, you can scour the papers and tabulate the numbers for yourselves. I hope to have a final score later tonight."

The children tumbled out of the motor home. Peter led the way, holding a peanut butter and jelly sandwich, a bit heavy on the jelly oozing onto his pants. Charlie had put on a clean T-shirt with his favorite striped shirt on top. The baby looked as though he'd rolled in peanut butter and jelly. Thick strands of hair spiked over his ears and on top of his head.

"Aren't they cute?" someone behind them said.

"The baby's adorable."

Thomas would have laughed at Karen's horrified expression except he feared the children would steal the show. That meant pictures in the newspapers. That meant points. He liked being in the lead, which was where he intended to stay. So he slipped an arm under the baby's legs and swung him into the air. The child giggled. "Tiger, it's time you took a bath."

"Swing me too," Charlie said, yanking on his arms.

"Me too," Peter added.

"Shower duty for everyone," he said, rounding up the boys before the cameramen could do any more damage.

85

"We'll play after everyone is cleaned up."

When he saw the relief on Karen's face, he knew she didn't suspect his motives. She smiled at him gratefully, "Thanks."

He herded the children into the motor home and was surprised to see Floyd follow behind him.

"I told the little lady to wait outside so we could have ourselves a man to man conversation."

"Sure, suit yourself," Thomas said, nodding to the coffeemaker. "Would you like a cup?"

"This early in the day, I prefer to limit my drinking to whiskey or beer," he said with a raucous laugh.

"There's a Bud in the fridge if you're interested."

Thomas stripped the sticky clothing off the boys and pushed the children into the bathroom. With effort he insisted Charlie part with his favorite shirt, and when the child wasn't looking, he heaved the shirt along with the other dirty clothing into the washing machine. Once he heard the shower start, he sat at the table opposite Floyd.

"What's up?"

Without questioning the gray tape stuck to everything, Floyd lifted the bottle of beer and took a swig. "You know how women are. Always yacking and making a fuss about fairness."

A commotion came from the next room. Thomas raised his voice and inched open the bathroom door. "You three better behave, or I'm coming in there."

"What's gonna happen if you come here?"

"You don't want to know."

"Yup, we're gonna be good," chorused three voices, followed by childish giggles.

"You were saying?" Thomas asked Floyd.

"Karen pitched a fit about not being included in our breakfast conversation."

Not that he blamed her because if it were him he'd have been madder than hell.

Floyd's Adam's apple bobbed up and down his fat neck. "To pacify her, I said I'd take her out for dinner tonight."

"I can't trust either of you alone," Thomas said, shuffling his shoe along the tape on the floor. "I can't have you two ganging up against me."

Floyd chuckled. "We men stick together. If I have to give away the Winnebago to anyone, it might as well be to you."

"There's no *if* about it. You're giving away this motor home."

Floyd's eyes shrunk to pinpoints. "All I'm saying is I'd rather go to the poor house knowing another man had benefited from my loss."

According to rumor, the man was loaded. His pathetic attempt to draw sympathy didn't faze Thomas. Thomas wasn't worried about Floyd taking Karen out for the evening. With the children around, the adults wouldn't be able to get a word in. "Where are you going to eat?"

"I haven't decided, but I was thinking somewhere nice with music and candlelight. I figure after a drink or two, I'll be able to smooth her ruffled feathers."

Thomas doubted Karen could be easily pacified. Since that was Floyd's problem, he didn't bother to state his opinion.

"I'd think twice about taking the boys to a fancy restaurant."

"I'd have to be nuts to take those hellions anywhere."

As if on cue, shouts came from the bathroom.

"Stop pushing me!"

"You shoved me first."

"Did not."

"Did too."

"Poop head."

"You got boobies." Lots of giggling followed the last comment.

Thomas cracked the door open. "You have one minute to finish up, or I'm coming in there."

"We'll be good."

"If you aren't taking the kids to the restaurant, who's babysitting?"

The weasel lifted his chin and flashed a sly grin.

"You."

Thomas laughed. "Right, tell me another joke."

Buck naked, the boys scampered out the bathroom and made a beeline for the bedroom. Hissing, the cat charged out of the room, leaped over the table, and perched above the cupboards. A deep growl rumbled from Bear's throat.

Floyd frowned and covered his ears with his hands. "How do you stand it?"

"Bear, go lie down," Thomas ordered. The dog hesitated a moment before doing what it was told. "I don't have much of a choice if I want to stay in the game," Thomas said.

Floyd raised the bottle of beer to his mouth. "It won't kill you to be a nice guy for one crummy evening. Karen could sure use the break."

"No way."

"Humph," Floyd said with a roll of his eyes. "All this time I had you pegged for being smart. Now I find out you're nothing but a dumb son of a bitch." Floyd inched away and raised his hands. "Listen up, and I'll explain. If you do a favor for the little lady, she'll appreciate your efforts. She'll start to trust you." Floyd tapped his fingers along the amber beer bottle. "Besides, if you decide to take the kids for a couple of hours this evening, I'll fill you in on any new developments tomorrow."

"Does Karen know you're in here pleading her cause?"

"No way, the little gal doesn't have a clue what's going on."

Thomas could barely stomach looking at Floyd, but he schooled his features to look agreeable.

Floyd continued, "You want to stay in the lead, you do what you can to befriend Karen. The little lady thinks with her heart. If you win her over, it'll be a hell of a lot easier to become the proud owner of this Winnebago." He pointed a stubby finger at Thomas' chest. "Remember this, once you gain a woman's confidence, you can get away with almost anything."

Chapter Eight

Floyd left a moment later, and Karen entered the motor home, looking as though she had something serious on her mind. Thomas had already decided he'd baby-sit, but he figured he'd let her broach the subject. *Besides, he wanted to see her squirm.*

"The boys are in the bedroom. They were clean a moment ago, but who knows what you'll find."

A nervous smile lifted a corner of her mouth. "I really appreciate what you did."

His intentions had been purely selfish. Guilt revisited his conscience as he dismissed her praise with a wave. "It wasn't anything."

"I'm grateful my parents won't be seeing a picture of the boys in that condition."

"There's nothing wrong with kids getting dirty. It shows they're having a good time. I'm sure your parents would understand."

She shook her head. Worry clouded her eyes. He stepped forward and rested a hand on her shoulder. "If you decide you need someone to talk to, I'm a good listener."

"Sometimes I think I'm waging a losing battle," she said, her eyes tearing before she rested her head against his chest. Instinctively he knew she wasn't referring to the children or the Winnebago. He wanted to question her, but Charlie ran into the room, wearing one sock and nothing else.

"I can't find my favorite shirt, and I don't got no more underwear."

Karen hid her shock well. She pulled away, and Thomas' arm dropped to his side.

"You boys packed enough clothing and toys to last a long time."

"Yup, we did, but you told us to put some boxes back 'cause everything didn't fit in the car."

"But I assumed . . . well . . ." A blush crept up her neck and settled on her cheeks.

Thomas laughed. "No chart is going to fix this. You can't trust children to pack for themselves."

"I know that. At least, I know it now," she said, directing a smile at him that went straight to his groin.

He temporarily forgot she was the enemy. "If you'd like, I'll take the Volkswagen off the hitch, and you can go shopping for the boys. I'll stay with them."

Thomas realized his error, but it was too late to back out. He was making life easier for Karen. He should have walked out of the motor home and allowed her to deal with the situation alone. She threw him another grateful smile, and he discovered he didn't have any regrets.

Karen returned ninety minutes later with clothing for the boys and gifts for everyone. She'd also picked up the fixings for a meal guaranteed to bribe the pants off Thomas. Wrong wording! Big mistake! The image of Thomas wearing nothing but a smile lodged in her mind and lingered long enough to render her speechless and spike her temperature.

The boys greeted her at the door, towels secured with duct tape at their shoulders and waists. Poster board armor covered their chests. Peter swung a cardboard sword. "We're gladiators."

"Me too." Byron mimicked his brother and slashed the air with a paper dagger.

Charlie growled. "I'm a dragon." He raised gloved hands and dropped to the floor. Triangle foil cutouts were fastened to his back. Charlie raised his head and pulled at the red bandana taped to his chin. "Look real fire comes out of my mouth. Grrrrrrrr!"

Seemingly no worse for wear, Thomas sat on the couch, watching a quiz show on television.

"I really appreciate you taking the boys."

He didn't spare her a glance as he flicked through the channels. "Think nothing of it."

Is that what he'd say when she asked him for a repeat performance?

"To show my gratitude, I've bought a thick T-bone and all the trimmings. I'm going to cook you supper."

"I never turn down a meal," he said, aiming the remote at the set.

"Do you enjoy cooking?" she asked him, crossing her fingers behind her back.

"Not particularly. I cook only because I have to."

Yes! She shouted to herself, mentally pumping her hand in the air. "I'm making strawberry shortcake for dessert."

He set the remote down and faced her. Disbelief streaked across his features. "That's my favorite."

Yes! The glow in his eyes said she'd hit her mark. The way to a man's heart . . . she thought, remembering the familiar adage. In this case it wasn't his heart but his childcare services she was after.

"Did you remember to get us something special?" Peter asked.

"Definitely." She dug into the paper bag and handed each child a coloring book and crayons. Three small faces frowned. Karen understood. Coloring couldn't compete with swords, armor, gladiators, or fire-breathing dragons. She led them into the bedroom and put their new clothes on the bed. "Get dressed and then I'll get your meal ready."

"Can we have cheese macaroni?"

"Sure, but I want you to be especially good."

"How come?"

"I want Thomas to see how well behaved you boys are."

"Thomas likes us just the way we are," Peter said, slipping on new shorts.

"He says boys are s'pose to get dirty. Ya know what? He said his brothers was noisier than us." Charlie eyed his new striped shirt skeptically.

"I want my favorite shirt."

"You'll get it back first thing tomorrow after I do the wash."

"Ohhhh . . . all right."

"I bet you boys had a great time this afternoon."

"Yup, we had lots of fun."

"So behave and maybe Thomas will decide to take care of you again this evening."

Peter pulled the tags off his shirt. "I already asked him if he'd play gladiators with us tonight. He said he had plans."

Karen's heart nose-dived toward her knees.

Thomas stole an occasional glace at Karen as she fed the boys and went about preparing the shortcake. Wonderful smells saturated the interior of the motor home. As he inhaled deeply, his mouth watered, and his stomach rumbled with hunger. His thoughts wandered south when she turned her back to him. He wanted to cup his hands over her firm rear outlined by her tight jeans. Suddenly, strawberry shortcake was not his first choice for dessert.

"How come Thomas gets to eat later?" Peter asked.

Karen shot Thomas a quick glance. "Because I thought he'd enjoy a moment of quiet." *Then she'd drop the bomb and ask him to baby-sit.*

It was clear to him Karen excelled in the kitchen. It was also clear why she'd gone to all this trouble. He wondered when she'd asked him her loaded question and suspected the subject would come up shortly after dessert. Thomas chuckled to himself. Karen was a conniving female, with a great behind, he added after another long appreciative look. He'd make the most of this opportunity.

"How do you like your steak?"

"Huh?"

"Do you want your steak well done?"

"Medium." He realized the boys had finished their meals and had disappeared from sight. Her short haircut flattered her and pulled his attention to her expressive mahogany eyes, a small nose, and a pretty heart-shaped face. He studied the outline of her lower lip, bowing just so and begging to be kissed. Although the complete package appealed, her butt won out by a landslide.

"Where are the children?"

"I told them to give you a break and go color in the bed-room."

"How thoughtful," he said. *Add to that—shrewd and cunning.*

She set the table, poured a glass of red wine, and removed a thick steak from the under the broiler. On a plate sat a large baked potato, topped with sour cream and butter. Tossed salad completed the feast.

"Mmmm," he said. "Too bad the meal's on your side of the Winnebago."

"Just for tonight, we'll forget about the barriers. Come sit down and enjoy." She turned to remove fresh asparagus from the stove, once more sending his thought out of kilter.

He wanted to indulge in a lot more than what she was offering. Resisting the urge to reach out and trace the contours of her well-shaped behind, he studied every inch of her lush curves. Lust hit him hard and fast, settling in his groin. When he was able to walk, he sauntered to the table. "Aren't you eating?"

Guilt flashed across her face. "Oh, me, that is, no, I thought I might catch a bite later."

"I see," he said, locking gazes until she looked away. "Are you sure? I don't mind sharing my steak."

She waved away his offer. "No, I'll eat later."

"Oh gee, I almost forgot." She jumped up and slid a CD in the player. "I wanted to buy you something you'd like and I remembered the CD you played while I was driving. I don't know anything about heavy metal music, but the teenager at the store assured me you'd love it."

Grinding noise blasted from the speakers. He hated the sound, hated the CD he'd played for her. His intent had been to distract her and to add to the commotion.

"Thanks."

She looked pleased. "Maybe some evening you can explain to me the difference between speed and trash metal."

"Sure," he said, not having a clue. He cut a piece off the T-bone, and bit down on the tender morsel. "Done to perfection. A man could get used to eating like this."

"I've been thinking about just that. It seems a pity for both of us to go through the bother of preparing meals." Her face flushed crimson.

He tried the potato and moaned. "This is great."

"I scooped out the inside and beat it with a little milk and spices. It's called twice-baked potatoes. You like it?"

"Your cooking skills beat mine."

Once he finished eating, she put a generous serving of strawberry shortcake heaped high with whipped cream in front of him. Thomas doubted he could eat another bite but discovered he'd soon cleaned his plate. He leaned back in the chair and stretched out his legs under the table. "I owe you one. If you'd like, I'll take you and the children out to eat."

"That's not necessary. After all you've done with the boys, you don't owe me a thing."

"I guess you're right," he replied, biting back a laugh.

She chewed her lower lip nervously. He watched her clench and open her fingers several times. "How would you like me to cook more meals for you?" she asked in a wavering tone.

"Beware of people bearing gifts," he said with a wink that reddened her face.

After a lengthy pause, she sucked in a deep breath. "I have a business proposition for you."

"Sounds interesting."

"Well . . . it could be in both of our best interests if we helped each other out."

He cupped his chin and pretended to consider what she'd said. "How so?"

"I could cook for you in exchange for you watching the boys once in a while."

He let the silence stretch between them. "Will you prepare all my meals?"

Her eyes widened in surprise. "I hadn't planned on cooking every meal."

"I guess for lunch I could make my own sandwich," he said, barely controlling his laughter. "We might be able to work something out if you agree to cook for me, let's say . . ."

Another pause. "Once a day."

He was pushing his luck, but since he'd planned to baby-sit anyway, he figured he couldn't lose.

"How often will you baby-sit?"

"I'll watch the boys every day while you prepare supper. It's the least I can do."

Her eyebrows angled sharply. "How generous of you."

"I'll throw in one evening, but that's my final offer," he said, raising his hands. "Take it or leave it. It's the best deal you're going to get."

She issued a frustrated sigh. "All right, I'll do it. Only I need you to watch the boys this evening, and Peter said you already had plans."

"That's not a problem. I told Floyd this afternoon I'd take the boys to Funtown."

"You made me go through all this for nothing!"

"I wouldn't call your agreeing to cook for me nothing."

Floyd had reserved a table by the window at the Salt Water Grill. For two hours Karen had brushed off his advances with polite smiles. She'd managed to keep up a steady conversation about the weather and the boys, but she was quickly running out of things to say.

"I'm glad you agreed to come to dinner with me this evening," Floyd said, his eyes bright in his flushed complexion. He slid his chair closer to hers. "The view is breathtaking."

Instead of looking out at the star-studded sky or the boats in the harbor, he was staring at her, stealing occasional glances at her chest. Uneasiness crept up the back of her throat as she turned away from him and glanced out the window. "Yes, the view is magnificent." She pushed back her chair a little. "When I agreed to eat dinner with you, I thought we'd discuss the contest, but each time I bring up the subject, you talk about something else."

An easy smile creased his plump cheeks. "There's not much for me to say. At our meeting this morning, Thomas brought up a very good point when he suggested I restrict the motor home's itinerary."

"Wasn't that your idea?" she asked, surprised to hear this new development.

"I wish I could take the credit, but that stroke of genius was Thomas' alone. There's no point you two gallivanting too far from my dealership. It makes good business sense for me to keep the Winnebago near my home base."

"How convenient for Thomas," she said, her stomach knotting with anger.

"How so?"

"This makes it easier for his construction company to deliver billboards to our destinations."

"That never entered my mind." Floyd raised his glass of whiskey to his lips.

Apprehension tickled her nerve endings. The thought that Thomas might be working for Floyd again resurfaced. Were they conspiring against her? She drew in a deep breath. "I don't have time to waste so if this is a game you and Thomas are playing, tell me now."

Looking hurt, Floyd reached for her hand. His smooth fingers stroked her knuckles. "It disappoints me to hear you say that. I would like for you to trust me. As I told you before, and I'll say it again, this contest is legit. When the month is up, either you or Thomas will own the motor home. You have my word."

"I hope you're telling me the truth."

He placed his hand over the left side of his chest. "You wound me. I want us to be best of friends."

He looked so upset, she squeezed his arm. "I'm truly

sorry if I've hurt your feelings."

He scooted his chair a little closer. "Now that's more like it. You know my mother had a saying that could apply in this case." He paused, his eyes narrowing to pinpricks. "One hand washes the other. Just say the word and I'll tip the scales in your direction."

"I hope you aren't suggesting I do anything underhanded."

"No, of course not, I was just offering my moral support along with strategic assistance. A little gal like you doesn't stand a chance against someone like Thomas. You need my sharp crafty mind on your side."

"What can you do for me that I can't do on my own?"

"You'd be surprised."

She could just imagine. "What would I have to do in return?"

"You're a suspicious gal. I like that in my women."

"I'm not one of your women," she said, making sure there were no misunderstandings.

"It wouldn't hurt for us to exchange favors. You scrub my back, I'll scrub yours."

Taken literally, his words turned her stomach.

"Mistakes happen all the time. It would be beyond my control if Barney were to lose track of some important newspapers or if the computer virus screwed up the final score." Floyd tossed back the contents of his glass and grinned. "You just can't trust technology."

Chapter Nine

Karen was relieved when Floyd pulled into the Scarborough Downs parking lot. For what seemed like the hundredth time, she pushed his fingers away from her knee.

"Sorry, I'm trying like the devil to behave, but when I'm around pretty ladies, I suffer from poor muscle control." He chuckled under his breath.

"Touch me again, and I'll break every bone in your hand," she said, tired of discouraging his advances.

"I like women with spunk. And I love a challenge."

"There is no challenge. I'm not playing hard to get. I'm not playing at all."

"Women have been known to change their minds."

She groaned in frustration.

"Anyway, you think about our little discussion. And ask yourself this, would Thomas refuse my help?" He pulled in front of the Winnebago, and before he could again slide his hand to her side of the front seat, she'd opened the door and leaped out. "If you come to your senses, let me know. We could have lots more fun together."

"I'm not interested in your idea of fun."

He laughed. "When you change your mind, I'll come calling."

Ready to confront Thomas about lying to her, Karen bolted into the Winnebago to find him stretched out on the couch, sound asleep with Byron snuggled in the crook of his arm. The baby's eyes were closed, and he was sucking his thumb. The fingers of one small hand were wrapped around a water pistol, the evidence of their battle in the wet spots on Thomas' shirt and pants. She'd arrived ready to have it out with him, to tell Thomas exactly what she thought of his lies. Instead her heart turned over with emotion at the scene before her, and she wanted to wrap her arms around Thomas and absorb his warmth, his strength, and his passion.

She realized he was her competitor, and he'd do whatever was needed to win, including lying to her. So why was she standing here thinking about kissing him instead of pounding her fists against his chest? She took a moment to appreciate his wide shoulders, thick neck, and the hair curling over the V of his unbuttoned shirt.

Byron stirred and whimpered in his sleep. The water pistol slipped from his grasp. She picked him up and carried him into the bedroom. After slipping off his clothes, she dressed him in a disposable diaper and a T-shirt and covered him with his sleeping bag. His brothers were curled up on her bed, looking innocent and sweet. She enjoyed the peaceful scene, knowing that tomorrow would bring new challenges. As she looked down at the sleeping boys, she yearned for babies of her own. She'd be a good mother. *Unlike her . . .*

She refused to finish the sentence, assuring herself that her parents had done their best, and they loved her. Deep down she was certain they cared deeply. *Did they? Then why did she still feel the need to prove herself to them?* This time she managed to shove aside the doubts going through her mind. She didn't need to prove anything. She was merely giving her parents the motor home as a gift.

Shaking her head, she turned her thoughts to the matters at hand. The break had done some good, and she was back on track as she marched into the living room, ready to confront Thomas. He'd stretched one of his long legs onto her side. With the tip of her shoe, she pushed his big foot over the duct tape. Slowly he opened his eyes. His sleepy smile temporarily weakened her resolve.

"Did you and lover boy have a good time?" he asked in a teasing tone.

"You sure have a way with words," she replied sarcastically.

He sat up and rolled down his shirtsleeves. "So were your efforts worth it? Did you and Floyd plot against me?"

"Hummph, you should talk!"

The lines around his mouth hardened. "What's gotten into you?"

"I know this is a contest, and I realize only one of us can win, but I don't like being lied to."

His back stiffened. His eyes turned a stormy blue. "I don't lie. I say what I mean. I conduct both my business and my life with that code of ethics."

She raised her chin defiantly. "Tell your story to someone who'll believe you."

Thomas shot to his feet, grabbed her wrist, and brought his nose inches from hers. "If you're going to accuse me of lying, then you sure as hell better tell me what I supposedly said."

He towered over her. His size dwarfed the interior of the motor home. She felt his anger pulsating from his body, yet she didn't fear him. She'd seen how gentle he was with the children and even with his dog, Bear. Though he hid behind a frown and a deep voice, she knew he wasn't a violent man.

"You told me Floyd suggested we tour only Maine, New Hampshire, and Massachusetts. Now I find out it was your idea."

"That's a crock of bullshit. Floyd came up with that plan on his own."

"Just last night you told me you'd do everything in your power to win."

"That's right, and I will. But that does not include lying."

Karen didn't know whom to believe, and she might have said more, but she thought she heard a familiar meow in a distance. *Luce?* Her body tensed. Now that she thought about it she hadn't noticed her cat sleeping with the boys on the bed. Looking from one side of the room to the other, she checked the interior of the motor home, hoping to see Luce. Her heart clenched with fear as she ran into the bedroom and back out again.

She bent to look under the table and chairs. When she straightened and turned quickly, she bumped into Thomas.

"When I went out this evening my cat was in the bedroom. The boys must have left the door open."

Guilt clouded Thomas' eyes. "I'm to blame. We were running around shooting at each other with the water pistols, having so much fun. We left the door to the Winnebago open so we could reload our weapons."

"Luce isn't an outdoor cat. He doesn't know how to defend himself."

Panic crept up her throat and stole her breath.

"Try not to worry. I'll find him."

Tears rimmed her eyes and rolled down her cheeks. "I hope he's all right. I love that cat."

She expected Thomas to laugh at her for falling apart over an animal, but the compassion on his face said he understood. At that moment she felt a strong bond with her competitor and a deep sense of gratitude. He put his arm around her shoulder. "Trust me, I'll do everything I can to find your pet."

His words comforted her. He grabbed a flashlight from inside the cupboard and hurried outdoors with her at his heels. As they searched the parking lot and a nearby wooded area, she kept an eye trained on the Winnebago in case one of the boys woke up.

"Luce," she called out, her voice cracking with worry.

Luce was more than just a cat. He was her trusting companion and the one constant thing in her life. For the last fourteen years, she'd whispered her problems to him at night before falling asleep. As she stroked his fur, he'd purr and curl up by her side. He loved her unconditionally.

Karen pulled a tissue from her pocket and tried not to cry, but she failed. Unbidden visions of her cat trying to cross the heavy traffic on Route One added to her concerns. Thomas arced the flashlight beam into a stand of tall hemlocks about fifty feet from her. "I think I see him."

Her heart stilled when she heard several frightened meows from high in a tree. She ran to where Thomas stood, craned her neck, and spotted her cat on a thin branch about twenty feet up. Relieved, she hollered, "Luce, come down. Luce, come." A piercing screech rent the night.

"Here, kitty, kitty," Thomas called, which started Bear barking inside the Winnebago.

She turned and saw Peter poking his head out the door. "Where's everyone?" he shouted, sounding frightened.

Though Karen wanted to remain with Thomas, she knew her place was with the children. "Stay inside with your brothers. I'll be right there."

She threw Thomas a glance over her shoulder. He had tucked the flashlight in his shirt pocket and had swung his leg over a low branch.

"Be careful," she said.

"If I break my neck, the Winnebago will be yours," he reminded her with a soft chuckle. "For all I know you and Floyd put Luce up to this."

"Just be careful."

"Don't worry about a thing, I don't mind heights, and I've climbed lots of trees."

"Luce is probably scared to death. He'll claw you if he's frightened."

Tree boughs rustled. "Just what I wanted to hear."

Karen hurried toward Peter who looked relieved to see her. "We would never leave you boys alone."

"I got up for a drink of water, and I couldn't find Thomas or you anywhere."

She wrapped her arm around the boy's shoulder and kissed his forehead. "Let's go make some hot chocolate."

"I miss my mother," he said a moment later as she filled the kettle with water.

"We'll call her tomorrow, and you can talk to her on the phone."

"I'd like that." He took down two cups and removed the gray duct tape dividing them in half.

"After we have our hot chocolate, maybe you can help me peel the duct tape off everything."

"How come? Thomas said you and him were fighting a battle. He said you two are enemies."

She heaved a weary sigh. "I thought so too, but after to-night, I no longer want us to quarrel about petty things."

"How come?"

"Thomas and I are competitors, but I like him, and he deserves to have the run of the motor home."

"I like Thomas too. We had a really good time at Funtown tonight. We went on lots of rides. Thomas bought us water pistols. We ate cotton candy, and fries, and pizza, and do you know what?"

Karen poured boiling water into two cups. "No, why don't you tell me."

"Charlie went on the merry-go-round, and he puked all over the place. Then we came back here, and Luce threw up his supper on Thomas' shoes."

"It sounds as though Thomas had a rough evening."

"Maybe, but he still said he liked being with us. I think you should put more stars on your chart after Thomas' name 'cause he's the best babysitter we ever had."

"I'll keep that in mind."

An hour later she tucked Peter in bed and again peered out the window. Barely able to see the hemlocks in the distance, she put her ear against the screen and listened. Several explicit swearwords bounced off the surrounding trees, assuring her Thomas was still alive and well.

Some time later she spotted the silhouette of a man approaching. She recognized Thomas' large build dashing toward the Winnebago. Bare-chested, sporting several deep scratches, he rushed inside, hugging his ripped shirt in his arms. The cat poked its head out of one sleeve. As Thomas handed her the bundle, Luce sprang free and leaped on top of the cupboard, where it arched its back and hissed.

"The next time Luce escapes, I'm wearing chain mail when I go after him."

Relieved her cat was all right she swung her arms around Thomas' neck. To show her appreciation, she intended to give him a quick peck on his cheek, but he turned his head, and her lips grazed his. The feather-soft touch was barely discernable, but she felt its effect deep inside. Somewhere in her heart a tiny flame flickered to life.

Like steel bands his arms wrapped around her waist. Their gazes locked, his sapphire eyes hypnotic and filled with desire. His nostrils flared. She noticed the way his upper lip bowed, and how a day's growth of beard shadowed his jaw. As his breath fluttered against her cheek, she inhaled the smell of hemlock boughs and spice and something totally masculine. She moved her hand over his chest and felt the rapid beat of his heart against her fingertips.

She swept her tongue over her dry lips.

With a moan, he captured her mouth in a kiss that liquefied her bones. One second she was standing, the next, he'd swept her up into his arms, and she found herself sitting on the couch. He was leaning over her, his hands cupping her shoulders, his tongue tracing the seam of her mouth. She opened her lips and his tongue darted inside, tangling with hers. Ribbons of light flashed behind her closed eyelids. Then one hand landed on her knee, the other on her breast. Her nipples pebbled under his touch. A small voice in the back of her mind warned her to slow down.

She ignored the voice, and instead arched her back and welcomed his advances. From the bedroom, Charlie shouted.

"Ya better hurry. I'm gonna throw up again."

When Karen entered the bedroom, the smell gagged her. Peter had already hopped out of bed and was standing next to his brother, holding a box of tissues under his head. Vomit covered the pillow, the floor, and a corner of the sheet. She knew she'd have to take care of the mess, but first she needed to help Charlie shower. Her stomach roiled as she scooted Charlie into the bathroom, helped him wash up, and change into clean clothes. She rinsed out the soiled shirt and underwear.

"I was gonna run to the bathroom, but everything just came up."

"It's not your fault," she said, but that didn't make the

task ahead any easier. Thinking of the mess awaiting for her, she felt sick as she took Charlie's hand and stepped out of the bathroom.

Peter ran up to her. "Did you know the table comes down and has cushions that go on top?"

She noticed the table in the dining area had been transformed into a bed.

"Thomas fixed everything up," Peter informed her. "And he got rid of the yucky sheet and pillowcase. He even lit a candle in the bedroom to kill the stink."

"Where is Thomas?"

"He said if he didn't go outside for some air, he'd be barfing his guts out, too."

A short while later Thomas came inside and sat on the couch. He picked up the remote and clicked through stations.

"Are you sure you don't mind the boys sleeping in here?" she asked.

"A smart person told me he helped you peel off the duct tape because it was time to stop arguing about petty stuff." He directed his gaze at Peter before turning back to her. "There's no sense all of you being cooped out in the bedroom while there's an extra bed out here."

"Thanks."

He turned back to the television. She tucked the boys in and kissed them goodnight before dimming the lights.

When she entered the bedroom to check on Byron, she saw that Thomas had also put clean sheets on her bed. For the second time that night, her heart twisted with emotion. Planning to thank him, she went back into the other room, checked on Charlie who'd already fallen asleep, and grabbing her chart and envelope filled with stars, she sat on the couch beside Thomas. Thomas shut off the television. "What are you doing?"

"Peter informed me tonight you deserved more stars behind your name. The red one is for saving Luce's life."

He examined the scratches on his arm and hands. "You're lucky I didn't strangle the damn fool while he was swatting at me in the tree."

"You'd never hurt an animal."

"Don't bet on it," he said, his tone gruff.

She ignored him because she knew better. "I'm giving you a blue star for being so nice to the boys, and this silver star is for cleaning up after Charlie. I owe you," she said, hoping he knew how much his kindness meant to her.

"If it'll make you feel better, you can cook me breakfast tomorrow," he suggested, one corner of his mouth lifting.

"I'll cook breakfast all week if you want me to."

"If you insist." He looped his arm around her shoulder.

She leaned into him, feeling as though they'd known each other a long time. "You're so good with the boys, you'd be a wonderful father. It's hard for me to believe you don't want children of your own."

For a fleeting moment a tortured look twisted his features. "I was nineteen and a sophomore in college when my parents died in a car accident," he said, heaving a steadying breath and focusing across the room at nothing in particular. "Late one night I got a call telling me to come right home." His fingers dug into her arm, his eyes clouding with the painful memories.

"I'm sorry," she whispered.

"It was a long time ago. I left school never to return. A friend packed up my belongings, and I took over the job of being both a mother and a father to my two brothers and my sister."

"How old were they?" She reached up and rested her hand over his.

"At nine, my sister was the baby, and she needed her mother, not a big brother who didn't have a clue what he was doing. My brothers were eleven and twelve and a handful. They understood I was doing my best, but they resented me when I forced them to do chores and homework. They challenged me every step of the way."

She finally understood why he didn't want a family.

"Enough about me, why are you doing this?"

"I want to give the motor home to my parents for their thirtieth anniversary."

"There has to be more to it than that. Why not send them flowers, a gift certificate. Hell, even take out a loan and send them on a trip, but this," he raised his hand to indicate the Winnebago. "Why would you feel the need to give them such an expensive gift?"

"I want to prove to them how much I love them."

"I would think they'd have figured that out a long time ago."

His words struck hard. An imaginary hand tightened around her heart and squeezed until she feared she'd cry out in pain. Fortunately, Thomas picked up a large smiley-face sticker from the envelope on her lap. "What are your plans for this one?"

"I'm saving it for when the boys do something really special."

"In that case." He peeled the sticker from the sheet and stuck it on the chart behind her name.

"What did I do to deserve this?" she said, forcing a smile so he wouldn't see how much his questions had hurt. His face turned serious; his eyes glowed with lust.

"It's for the kiss you gave me earlier tonight."

Chapter Ten

Late that night Floyd was working with his audio equipment in his office when he was aware of someone behind him. He looked over his shoulder to find Barney staring down at him.

"What are you doing, Boss?"

"Taking out an insurance policy."

"Huh?"

"You wouldn't understand." He waved dismissively.

"I thought I heard Karen Brown talking to you so I got curious."

"You heard right. Listen up," Floyd said, especially pleased with himself. He pressed the play button on the recorder.

"Touch me again, and I'll break every bone in your hand."

"Did Miss Brown know you were taping her?"

"Of course not."

"Oh."

"I tape lots of conversations. What people say might later come back to bite them in the ass."

A light flickered in Barney's blank eyes. "Boss, I don't think Miss Brown likes you very much."

"Maybe not, but I can make her warm up to me. Do you want to hear?"

"Sure, Boss."

"Pour us each a drink and give me a little time to make a

few adjustments. You'll be surprised how quickly the little lady changes her attitude."

Barney dropped ice cubes into glasses and added a splash of Jack Daniels. He pulled a chair near Floyd and studied the state of the art recording equipment. Floyd picked up his glass and tossed back the contents. A while later he pressed the play button and listened to the new version.

"Floyd, I'm your woman. Touch me again."

Barney and Floyd shared a laugh.

"How'd you do that?"

"It's easy. I just take out a word or a phrase and rearrange the sentences. Pretty soon Karen is saying exactly what I want to hear."

"That's really something."

"With a little more tweaking and the help of my computer software, I can soften her tone of voice until she's purring like a kitten."

Barney looked at him in awe. "You're the smartest man I know, Boss."

"Yeah, sometimes I even amaze myself."

Karen woke up and stretched. Without the boys in her bed, she'd slept right through the night and felt more rested than she had in days. Thanks to Thomas, she thought, her heart somersaulting. The sun streaming between the closed blinds in the window promised a great day with new opportunities. She also felt a warm glow in her chest when she thought of the kiss they'd shared last night. Her stomach quivered as she closed her eyes and remembered soft but insistent lips, a lush tongue, strong arms, a pine smell all his own, and his erection straining against his trousers, pushing into her belly as he molded their bodies together.

"Hmmm," she murmured, slipping her legs over the side

of the bed. Thanks to Thomas she'd walk around all day with her spirits buoyed and her stomach fluttering.

Though Thomas was still her competitor, she saw him as a man of integrity. She believed him when he'd told her he hadn't lied to her.

Unfortunately, she was attracted to him. Big time. She'd need to keep a cool head and an equally cool heart, or she'd lose. Since she was behind in the scoring, she needed to come up with a strategy. She considered using the children to gain media attention and thought how surprised everyone would be when she had them remove their shirts and expose their chests with Floyd's RVs printed in water-soluble paint. More important, no one, especially Thomas, would suspect her advertising ploy hidden under the children's clothing.

When she remembered how good he'd been with the boys and how he'd cleaned up after Charlie, she felt guilty for contemplating such sneaky tactics. Using the boys to her advantage seemed unfair, but she wouldn't win if she allowed her softhearted nature to influence her decisions.

Instead of guilt for using the children in such an underhanded way, she felt an immense sense of satisfaction. After breakfast she'd call the newspaper and the television station to be sure she racked up lots of points. Feeling confident, she flipped opened the blind and came face to face with a stranger.

She screamed.

With a paintbrush in one hand, a man jumped off a stepladder and raised startled eyes toward her. Through the window she spotted the boys, their faces and arms splattered with paint, smiling for the reporters who turned their cameras on her. She ducked and gritted her teeth. Her nails dug into her palms. Determined to find out what was going on, she dashed out of the bedroom and through the living quarters.

113

Too late she realized she hadn't worn her robe but quickly dismissed the thought. Her mid-calf white cotton nightgown covered her well. She leaped down the few stairs onto the ground. She saw *red!*

Bold red letters spelled *Floyd's* on the side of the Winnebago. Standing tall and proud, Peter put the finishing touches on a crooked *R*. With Floyd's help, Charlie drew a *V*, while Byron pointed to a backwards *S*.

When the boys removed the paint-splattered smocks, she noticed their matching shirts with a picture of the Winnebago on the front and Floyd's RVs printed on the back. Writing on the boys' chests did not compare to Thomas' publicity stunt. Everywhere they traveled, he'd get credit for the advertisement on the motor home. His score would mushroom until she no longer stood a chance of winning. She frowned at Thomas.

"The boys offered to help," he said, his voice blameless.

She saw the gathering crowd, the reporters taking notes, the boys looking pleased with their accomplishments, and it took a moment to find her voice.

"How dare you stoop so low as to use innocent children for your own selfish purposes."

Using the children was despicable and devious. Damn the man for beating her at her own game.

Thirty minutes later Thomas planted himself on the chair at the table and waited for her to cook him breakfast.

"I'm so hungry, I could eat a horse," he said, hoping to defuse some of the tension between them.

She slammed the frying pan on the stove. "Oh, wait a minute while I go shoot one for you."

He chuckled. "I don't think the owners of the race track would appreciate that."

Her eyebrows angled sharply. "Humph. You're mighty chipper this morning."

"I'm in a good mood if that's what you mean."

She cracked an egg into a bowl and started to beat the life out of it.

"I don't know why you're so upset. The boys wanted to help. I couldn't turn them down."

"How thoughtful of you." She picked up another egg. "I'd love to crack this over your thick skull."

"Go ahead, if you dare," he challenged.

"I should probably get the children to do it for me."

"Now why didn't I think of that?"

The boys came out of the bedroom wearing their Floyd's RVs shirts. Thomas knew the instant Karen spotted his name above the dealership, praising the business, making it clear who would rack up points when the children wore the shirts. Her eyes darkened. "Get those off this instant."

Peter looked down at what he was wearing. "Get what off?"

"The shirts."

"How come?" Charlie said. "It's my new favorite shirt. Thomas bought it for me last night. And I love it."

Realization streaked across her face as she turned to him. "Did the boys wear those at Funtown while they were out with you?"

"Of course. Personally, I like the shirts."

"I do, too," Peter said.

"Me, too," Charlie added.

She groaned and rolled her eyes. "Keep them on for now. After breakfast I'll find you boys something more suitable to wear."

"Floyd likes our new shirts," Peter said, looking confused.

"That doesn't surprise me."

"Floyd said we've been a big help, and he's gonna buy us each a toy."

"I told him I want another dump truck," Charlie said.

"I want one of them Water Cannons that blasts water fifty feet," Peter added.

Thomas elbowed Peter. "You get one of those, and I'll have to invest in a more powerful weapon."

"Nothing can out fire the Water Cannon." Peter sat on the couch and turned on the television. "You won't stand a chance against me."

"We'll see about that," Thomas replied with a grin.

Byron hopped onto the chair next to Thomas and wrapped his chubby arms around Thomas' waist. "I love you."

Something deep inside Thomas stirred as he looked down at the boy and ran a finger over the downy hair. He was a cute kid, wide eyes, ruddy cheeks, a bowed mouth, and the look of a cherub. He was the type of child who could make unaware men yearn for children of their own. Fortunately for Thomas, he was very much aware of what childrearing entailed, and he'd taken precautions to insure in a weak moment he wouldn't make a huge mistake.

Charlie inched closer. "Are you gonna play with us again today?"

"Maybe later."

"Boys, don't pester Thomas."

Thomas glanced up at Karen. "They aren't pestering me."

"I just don't want them to be disappointed," she whispered, out of the corner of her lips.

"I'm not planning to disappoint anyone."

"I was simply trying to make a point. To a child, 'maybe later' means just that. I don't want the boys waiting all day for something that might never happen."

"I said maybe and I meant it," he replied with a hard edge to his voice. Couldn't she get it through her head he was man of his word? His anger vanished when he saw the hurt in her eyes. For a brief moment, compassion swelled in his chest for his opponent.

Karen poured the pancake batter onto the skillet and contemplated what Thomas had said. *Maybe later.* Those two words wrenched her insides and awakened painful memories. How often had she heard that phrase? Her parents had always been too busy with work, with friends, or with each other to pay attention to their daughter. Instead of giving up, Karen had followed them around, waiting for her big moment.

Was she still waiting? Was the Winnebago just another ill-fated attempt to gain their attention?

As she bent to remove the blueberry muffins from the oven, she caught a glimpse of Thomas' lecherous grin, his gaze focused on her behind.

"Is something wrong?" she asked with enough sarcasm even he wouldn't misunderstand.

"No, just the opposite. I was thinking you deserved another smiley sticker," he said with a damnable grin.

"How come?" Charlie asked.

"Yeah, we saw the sticker this morning and Thomas wouldn't tell us how you earned it," Peter added.

Byron clapped. "Karen's a good girl."

"Precisely," Thomas said, winking at her.

Her stomach turned over. Damn the man.

A short while later Charlie joined his brother on the couch. His eyes widened with fear. "A mommy and a daddy are crying. The man on the TV said someone stole their little boy, Tommy."

"There's lots of police and reporters on the news," Peter

added, his gaze glued to the screen.

Before Karen could stop what she was doing, Thomas had crossed the room and sat between the boys. "That's why it's very important for you three to stay close to Karen or me when we're out in public. Remember the talk we had last night?" The children nodded.

She was again taken by surprise by the gentle and caring way he spoke to the boys.

"Will the police find the bad man?" Charlie asked.

"We hope so."

She appreciated that he hadn't lied to the boys or made empty promises he couldn't keep.

"The newscast is far away from here," Karen said to calm their fears.

Peter traced the flower pattern on the sofa before looking at her. "If someone kidnapped me, I'd take my Water Cannon and shoot him in the face. Then I'd run away."

"If anyone ever approaches you boys, yell at the top of your lungs." Abby had entrusted Karen with the major responsibility of caring for her children. What if something were to happen to one of the boys? A shiver raced down her spine.

Thomas took the remote and shut off the television. "The broadcast will be aired all over the United States so that law enforcement officers everywhere will be on the look out for the missing child and the bad person who has him. I don't want you guys to worry. Karen and I are here to protect you."

Thomas threw her a look that said they were in this together. Byron pushed himself off the chair and hopped onto Thomas' lap. As Karen rested a reassuring hand around Peter's arm, Thomas' steady gaze pierced right through her. Gooseflesh pebbled her arms. She liked Thomas a lot, maybe too much for her own good. When she glanced away and spotted the newspaper on the arm of the couch, her heart skipped a beat. Bold headlines: *Stick 'em up partners!*

On the front page were the boys' smiling faces, water pistols drawn, all three in matching Floyd's RVs shirts. Thomas wore a cocky grin she both loved and despised.

Chapter Eleven

Karen could no longer ignore the facts. Thomas excelled at gaining media attention for Floyd's business, and he had no qualms about using the boys to his advantage. After breakfast, she brought the children into the bedroom. Her cat, Luce, curled around her legs.

"Do you guys understand that Thomas and I are playing a game and the winner gets to keep this Winnebago?"

Peter shrugged.

"Nope," Charlie said.

Byron extended his hand, his mouth curving into a wide grin. "Want gum."

Pleased that he hadn't said the forbidden phrase, she smiled at him. "Byron, honey, I don't have any gum, but if you're a good boy, we'll go buy some later this morning."

The baby nodded, scrambled onto the floor, and leaped over the cat. Not long ago, he'd have pitched a fit. She congratulated herself at her slow but steady progress with the child. She directed her next question at Peter and Charlie. "I bet you two play lots of games together?"

"Mama doesn't like us to play games."

That struck Karen as strange. "Why not?"

Charlie planted his hands over his knees and rocked back and forth. " 'Cause we fight." He cupped his hands and slicing his fingers through the air, growled.

"Mom says we shouldn't play games 'cause we don't like to lose. She says we act like barbarians. If we don't stop fighting she's gonna collect all our games, throw them in the back yard, and start a big bonfire," Peter added with a lisp, his tongue poking through the gap in his teeth. "Mom says she's never seen brothers fight like we do. She's saving every spare cent to build herself a tree house so she can escape and get some peace and quiet once in while." Peter smiled. "Me and Charlie are big enough to climb so we're gonna borrow mom's tree house."

Even though her friend allowed the boys to run amok, and she didn't discipline them as often as she should, Abby was a great mother, Karen decided. The children knew they were loved. Nothing mattered more.

Now that Karen had had the boys for a week, she saw fewer faults in Abby's child-rearing skills. Granted her friend ignored the advice in books written by leading children's psychologists. But how would those authors fare taking care of these three boys? Would they shred the pages from their books in frustration? Would they rip up the charts and throw away the good incentive stickers? *Would they buy gum by the truckload?* Karen turned to Peter and Charlie. "As I started to explain, Thomas and I are playing a game. Only one of us can win, and I was hoping I could count on your help."

"Thomas said we're the best helpers he's ever seen," Peter said.

How to word her request? *Stop helping Thomas* seemed too harsh. Besides, she didn't want to confuse the boys. She'd already told them to follow Thomas' instructions. After listening to the news report about the abduction of the small child in California, she trusted her instincts. To tell the boys not to listen to Thomas would not only be selfish, it could be dangerous.

Stop helping that devious, lower than the belly of a snake, son of a slimy . . . Too strong, especially since she had lots more adjectives to add to her growing list. She blew out a breath. "Since I'm your mother's friend, I was hoping you'd start to help me?"

"How come?" Charlie asked.

"Because I really want to win this Winnebago, and I can't do it without your help. Thomas already has lots more points than I do."

"I got an idea," Charlie said, bouncing on the mattress. "I'll tell Thomas he has to give you some of his points."

Peter's face brightened. "Mom makes me and Charlie share our stuff. Thomas should share too."

"Mention that to Thomas when you have a chance," she said with a smile. "And tell him I thought it was a good idea."

"I want you to get lots and lots of points," Peter said, for a moment wrapping his arms around her waist.

"Me too," Charlie echoed, hugging her.

Her heart constricted. When she'd offered to take the boys on this trip, she'd done it out of obligation to Abby. She'd dreaded the responsibility of caring for three unruly children. She'd been right. The boys hardly ever listened. They misbehaved, and they were lots of work. But the perks of having children far outnumbered the disadvantages. She hugged both boys against her. She kissed Charlie's forehead and smiled down at Peter. "Thanks. Even if I end up losing, at least I've had the opportunity to spend some time with you boys."

"What can we do to make you win?" Peter asked.

She sucked in her lower lip. "I don't know yet. If only I could think of a way to make national news." She chuckled. "I'm getting carried away. I'll be lucky to make the front page of the local paper."

"We got our pictures on the front page in this morning's paper," Peter pointed out.

"I know that. I'm getting further behind every day. I need to think of ways for us to make the television news. The more publicity I earn for Floyd, the more points I accumulate."

Peter raised his forefinger. His eyes twinkled. "Me and Charlie will think of something. You just wait and see. We're gonna get you lots and lots of points."

Feeling a bit guilty, she clasped her hands. "I don't want you to worry about the contest. As the adult, it's my job to come up with the ideas. This is not your problem."

"Yup, but as Miss Driscoll, my teacher says, it won't hurt for us to put on our thinking caps." Peter settled an imaginary hat on his head.

Charlie mimicked his older brother's actions. "But I still wanna help Thomas 'cause he's my friend."

Peter made a face. "That's real dumb. He's on the wrong side."

She considered trying to discourage Charlie but quickly dismissed the idea. "I'm glad Thomas is your friend."

"It's okay if I help Thomas too?" Peter asked, looking confused.

"If you want to help him, that's fine with me."

Her stomach convulsed. With this attitude, she'd come in second place and leave empty-handed. But there was no way she'd pit the boys against Thomas or each other. She desperately wanted to win, but not at the children's expense.

Charlie broke into her thoughts. "When are we gonna call mama?"

"As soon as we get to a phone," Karen replied.

"Thomas has one," Charlie said. "I saw him talk on it this morning 'bout wood for a sign."

Damn that shifty, conniving man! He'd ordered the

materials for his next project.

"I bet Thomas would let us borrow his phone," Peter suggested. "I'll go ask him."

"Me too," Charlie added.

"Poop head, poop head," the baby chanted as he followed his brothers out the bedroom door.

Karen frowned at the back of his retreating head. The children returned a moment later and handed her Thomas' phone. An idea popped into her mind. Did she dare? *Absolutely.*

"I'm going to change my blouse so I'd like you boys to wait in the other room."

"Hurry. I really, really miss my mom," Peter said.

"Me too," Charlie added. "I miss mama a whole bunch."

Byron's eyes rimmed with tears. "I want my mama."

With a persuasive shove, she escorted them to the door. "I won't be long. We'll call your mother in just a minute."

She shut the door, clasped Thomas' phone in her left hand, and pressed redial.

Ten minutes later, expecting the boys to rush toward her, Karen opened the bedroom door and heard cheers along with the voices on the television.

"The police found Tommy," Peter said, swinging his arms above his head and dancing around.

"Yippee." Charlie ran in circles.

Byron jumped on the couch until Thomas caught him and swung him in the air.

"Why all the commotion?" she asked.

Thomas anchored Byron against his hip and strode toward her. As if it were the most natural thing in the world, he looped his arm over her shoulder. She felt safe, as if she'd arrived home after a long journey.

"The police found the kidnapped child unhurt. He's been reunited with his parents."

Tiny sparks zapped where his fingers touched.

"The bad man is going to jail," Peter added.

"Tommy's safe with his mommy and his daddy," Charlie said, relief washing over his young features.

Byron freed himself from Thomas' grasp, ran across the room, and took a flying leap onto the couch. Thomas squeezed her shoulder. His smile warmed her heart. When his eyes locked with hers, she lost herself in his heated gaze.

"When we gonna call mom?" Peter asked.

She pulled away; the fog slowly cleared from her mind. Thomas was her opponent. If she didn't watch her every step, he'd use his charisma against her. Under his spell, she'd lose focus on the contest. Until he drove away in his Winnebago.

"Where are we going next?" she asked, pretending she didn't already know.

"Floyd dropped by early this morning to drop off our itinerary." Thomas handed her a piece a paper from the countertop.

Orono, Maine was first on the list, a college town north of Bangor, a couple hundred miles north. Second was Cape Cod, Massachusetts. "Why Orono?"

"I was surprised, too. I'd expected us to head south and hit the wealthy tourists traps. According to Floyd, the University of Maine is having their freshmen orientation this weekend. The students come from all over, and some of their parents are loaded. So it's not up to me. Floyd's the boss," he added with a cocky grin.

As Karen's fingers tightened around his phone, her heart drummed against her ribcage. She was eager to see his smile vanish. It would once they arrived in Orono. She wanted to celebrate her impending victory by shouting for joy. Instead she inhaled a calming breath. "Boys, let's call your mother."

As Thomas drove the motor home along Interstate 95, he stole a glance at Karen. By her smile, he knew she had something planned. He wasn't worried. This time he'd outdone himself. When they arrived at the Orono campus, his carpenters would have constructed an archway with Floyd's name along with painted turkeys and the words, "The dealership that talks turkey."

Every vehicle driving under the archway would receive a pamphlet showing off the features of the thirty-nine foot Winnebago and inviting them to meet them at one o'clock where each person would be given a chance to win a one thousand dollar gift certificate to use toward merchandise at Floyd's. The idea had been his brother Joe's. This promotion would set them back some money, but once word got around about the gift certificate, the crowd would grow rapidly. Though Thomas was taking a chance, he'd decided to go with his instincts. Anyway, he felt sure of the outcome.

He'd earn lots more points, lessening Karen's chances of ever catching up. Thomas pulled into the next rest stop. "Does anyone want to get out and stretch their legs?" he asked, peering into the rearview mirror at the boys already undoing their seatbelts.

Karen eyed him skeptically. "We stopped just half an hour ago."

He struck his chest with a fisted hand. "Indigestion."

"At this rate, we'll never get there."

"What's the big hurry?"

She glanced at her watch. "I guess we still have plenty of time."

"Floyd said we could get there any time before four."

Worry skittered across her features.

He knuckled her jaw. "I'm guessing you're up to no good."

Any remaining doubt vanished when a blush crept onto her cheeks.

"Maybe, maybe not," she said, in a tone drenched with guilt.

"I'm not worried."

"We'll see about that." She uttered a low chuckle before turning her back and grabbing hold of Byron's hand. "You're coming with me to use the bathroom before you have an accident."

Peter jumped out the door with Charlie at his side. "We're going in the men's room. We'll be right back."

She shot Thomas an anxious look.

"Don't worry, I'll keep an eye on them."

Thomas followed the boys into the bathroom.

"I don't need to pee," Charlie pointed out.

"Me neither," Peter said.

"Let's wash our hands anyway," Thomas said, turning on the hot water.

"How come? We haven't done anything," Peter said. "No sense wasting soap and water."

Thomas grinned. "You make a good point. But we can't always see germs."

"My mom says a few germs never hurt anyone."

Thomas cupped his fingers over his chin. "I say germs don't mix with candy. If you boys wash and dry your hands really good, I'll let you choose something from the candy machine in the parking lot."

Charlie and Peter dashed to the sinks and turned on the water. Keeping one eye on his watch, the other on the boys, he managed to blow fifteen minutes inside the bathroom before the boys' hands passed his inspection.

As they were leaving the men's room, Charlie pointed across the parking lot. "I bet that's the Boogie Man."

Thomas glanced at a shifty character, leaning against an older model, white Dodge pickup. He wore a fake black beard, a loose cap that fell over his ears, and was covered neck to ankles in a long black trench coat. When the stranger caught him watching, he jumped into his pickup and drove away, giving Thomas a parting glance over his shoulder. Although Thomas had never seen anyone in that disguise, something about the man looked familiar. Uneasiness wedged itself in the pit of his stomach.

"You let me know if you see that man again," he said tightening his hold on the boys.

"He was at Funtown too," Peter said as he studied the display in the candy machine. "I can't decide what I want."

"What was he doing there?" A chill settled in Thomas' heart.

"Eating cotton candy," Peter said with a shrug. "I still can't decide what I want."

"There's no hurry," Thomas said, again glancing at his watch. Was it coincidence or was the man following them?

Karen walked up to them and put Byron down next to his brothers. "What took you guys so long?"

Peter shrugged. "We had to wash our hands 'bout a hundred times."

Charlie elbowed Peter aside. "Now we get to pick out our reward."

Byron pounded on the glass. "Gum."

Karen speared Thomas with a disapproving look. "You know the boys aren't supposed to eat candy in the morning." Turning to Peter and Charlie, she suggested, "Wouldn't you prefer juice?"

"No way," they said in unison.

"Sorry, I forgot," Thomas said.

"Yeah, I bet." Her eyebrows arched as she again checked her watch.

Thomas smiled innocently. "It's almost eleven. I'm not in a hurry. If you'd prefer, we'll stay a while and play with our water pistols. Once noontime arrives, we'll buy the candy and leave."

"Damn it," she said through clenched teeth in a low voice only he heard. She tapped each boy's shoulder. "Just for this once. But you better hurry and choose your candy because I'm leaving in three minutes."

"I have the keys," Thomas calmly pointed out. Karen frowned and started to tap her foot impatiently. Thomas nodded toward her. "Would you like me to get you something?"

"I know what you're doing. You're wasting time so your crew can finish your project."

He covered his heart with his hand. "Your words wound me."

"I bet."

He leaned forward and whispered in her ear. "You're a sneaky woman. I know you're up to no good. And I'm going to delay our time of our arrival as much as I can."

When the boys weren't looking, she stuck out her tongue at him. He threw back his head and laughed.

Chapter Twelve

As the Winnebago neared the campus entrance, Karen's heart leaped. From deep in her throat came an excited "whoop."

Thomas mumbled, "What in the hell?"

Behind her the boys shouted, "Look at all the turkeys!"

"Are they dead?" Charlie asked, craning his head to get a better look.

"I think they're taking a nap," Karen replied, waving frantically toward the drama students stretched out on their backs like stuffed birds on a Thanksgiving platter. "Toot the horn at them," Karen ordered, waving her arms and laughing uncontrollably.

"Not on your life," Thomas replied as he made a sharp turn onto the University grounds.

Karen rolled her window down and hollered, "We're here!"

One of the feathered creatures lifted its head and jumped to its feet. The others followed suit and were soon dancing around the Winnebago. Reporters arrived with notebooks and the cameramen snapped pictures. A crowd gathered as the turkeys kicked up their heels and sang a ditty about Floyd's RVs. Thomas raised a quizzical brow. "What happened to my archway?"

"Beats me."

She turned toward the boys. "Let's go have some fun."

"Are you winning yet?" Peter asked.

"I'm on the right track."

As she undid Byron's seatbelt, she wondered how many points she'd racked up. Before hopping down from the motor home, she glanced at Thomas through lowered lashes. *If looks could kill!* The last semblance of control slipped away. She raised her chin, flashed a victory smile, punched the air with her fist, and gobbled at the top of her lungs. He shook his head in amazement and followed her out the door.

The students had assembled on a makeshift stage and were handing out helium balloons printed with Floyd's name and a silhouette of a turkey. She rushed forward with the children who each got two balloons and lollipops that were supposed to be turkeys but looked more like bears. Karen examined the candy.

"Sorry," one of the turkeys said.

Karen recognized Becky's voice.

"You called too late, and since I didn't know how to reach you, I decided you wouldn't mind if I substituted black bears. They're the college mascot, and it was all I could get on such short notice."

Gobbling echoed from nearby speakers. Karen was disappointed. "At least you got the turkey costumes."

"Yes, but I couldn't get Clint to play Floyd."

Karen's stomach dropped. According to Becky, Clint was a gorgeous hunky, super athlete, a ladies' man, everything Floyd saw when he looked in the mirror. "Oh no."

Becky waved her wing. "But don't worry. I saw Floyd on the newscast, and I picked out a dead ringer."

Karen moaned. She didn't want a dead ringer. She was out to earn points, not emphasize Floyd's faults.

"This guy does a great imitation. You'll love him," the

turkey said, adjusting her beak.

Karen handed her an envelope with the money she'd promised. "You did a good job, considering . . ."

Becky snatched the payment from Karen and waved at the musicians. A short plump turkey hopped onto the stage. He had a bottle of Jack Daniels tucked under his right wing, a microphone in one hand, and an oversized cigar in the other. Much like Floyd, he strutted across the stage. When he removed the head of his costume, Karen's jaw dropped open. Thomas and the boys cheered him on.

"No deal too small," the balding young man said, taking a swig of whiskey, raising winged arms, and sticking out his paunch. He then puffed on the foot long cigar and blew smoke rings at the gathering crowd. "At Floyd's we talk turkey."

He had beady eyes, thin lips, and a double chin. A remarkable likeness. *Floyd's clone.*

"Did I point out the Winnebago has two sliders?" He paused and looked over the crowd, his lips molded into a carbon copy of Floyd's foxy grin. "It's big enough for a family, a dog, a cat, two healthy adults . . ." He wiggled his eyebrows and speared Karen with a smart-ass grin. "And a gross of condoms."

Karen gasped. Laughter rang out. Students jeered. Charlie tugged at her arm. "What are condoms?"

Karen stuck a lollipop in the child's mouth.

"Where did he get such an idea?" she asked no one in particular, ready to jump onto the stage and ring the turkey's neck when Thomas grabbed her arm and held her back.

"College humor," he whispered. "Don't let them know they got to you." He squeezed her fingers. "Smile for the cameras."

Karen gripped Thomas' hand. With an act of sheer determination, she threw back her head and forced a laugh that sounded hollow to her ears.

Once Thomas had parked the Winnebago away from the crowd, he loaded the boys' water pistols, tucked his weapon in his waistband, and warned them to stay near the motor home.

"When you gonna play with us?" Charlie asked.

Peter stepped closer. "You promised, remember?"

"I said, 'maybe later'."

Peter frowned. Charlie stared him down. Byron stuck out his lower lip. Thomas grinned at their pathetic faces. These kids were good but not nearly as good as his siblings who were masters at inflicting guilt.

"Be patient. I'll take on all three of you in a few minutes, providing you do as I say and stay right here."

"My water pistol is already empty," Charlie said, squirting the last few drops into his mouth.

Thomas filled a bucket with water. "Here's plenty of ammo for your guns."

Charlie dunked his arm up to his shirt sleeve. "Thanks, we'll be good."

Thomas entered the motor home. Looking shell-shocked, Karen sat on the couch, twisting a napkin between her fingers. She glanced up at him silently.

"What happened to the feisty woman who gobbled at me earlier?"

"You must think I'm stark raving mad."

"It's crossed my mind," he said, smiling and looking out the window at the boys.

She sniffed. "Everything was going so well . . . until Clint canceled out and was replaced by Floyd's double."

Thomas stepped over a matchbox truck. "The kid did a great imitation."

Her deep brown pupils narrowed. "I wanted tall, handsome, and savvy. Not short, balding, and sleazy."

"He looked enough like Floyd to be his son."

"Precisely," she replied, blowing out a long breath. "I wanted to flatter Floyd, not insult him."

"What difference does that make?" Thomas asked.

Her cheeks glowed a rosy pink. Her eyelashes fluttered down. "I was hoping he'd give me a few bonus points."

Thomas held her hand and ran a finger along her palm. His heart rate increased. "Do you think that's fair?"

She shook her head. "I'm beyond fair." She looked at him skeptically. "For all I know you and Floyd are a team."

"I'd rather be stripped naked, tarred and feathered than to have my name mentioned alongside that shifty bastard's."

She looked at him for a while as if making up her mind. "Sorry."

"We're even. I accused you of being in cahoots with Floyd the day we drew the winning tickets."

"I would never side with that man," she said, her tone sincere. "I can't imagine what would inspire that drama student to spout off about condoms, especially in front of the children."

Guilty as hell, he cleared his throat. Remorse would not undo his earlier comments to the tabloid paper. "At his age, his mind is preoccupied with sex." Lately, Thomas' mind fell into the same category.

"I suppose you're right." Her eyes clouded with worry. "I hope my parents don't get wind of this. They have an image to uphold."

"It's only a college prank. Your parents will probably laugh."

She grimaced. "Chances are this fiasco won't reach Massachusetts."

"You're probably right. What is it your parents do?"

"They're professors at Boston University. They watch very little television, and since they live on the outskirts of Boston, I think I'm safe."

"I'm sure you're right."

He stretched his arm along the back of the couch and lowered it around her shoulder. Smooth move and a perfect fit, he thought, leaning in closer to fill his senses as he brushed a silky wisp of hair from her forehead.

"Someone's following us."

The muscles in her shoulder tensed beneath his fingertips. "Are you sure?"

"I can't be certain, but I noticed a bearded man staring at the boys at the rest stop. Charlie referred to the suspicious-looking character as the boogie man. The children said they'd seen him at Funtown. After we arrived at the Orono campus, I saw him again among the crowd. When he spotted me looking at him, he jumped into a white pickup and took off."

Karen shivered. "He could be a pervert or a kidnapper."

Thomas agreed. "He could be dangerous. Otherwise why hide his identity?"

"This gives me the creeps. I should take the children home."

"Good idea," he said with a wink. "Then I'll win the Winnebago." But he soon realized by her expression she was serious. "Hey, that's not necessary. I'll help you watch the kids. I won't allow anything to happen to them."

She relaxed a little. "If I find out this guy is stalking us, I'm taking the boys home to Abby."

Now the truth comes out. "I thought their mother wasn't able to take care of them."

135

"She can't, but I can. There's no way I'll endanger the children's life for any amount of money."

Not only did Karen appeal to him physically, he liked what he saw inside. She was a woman with scruples, a woman willing to abandon her goals to ensure the boys' safety. She was one hell of an amazing lady. A lot like his mother, he realized as a rush of warmth flooded his chest.

"We're always with the boys, and we won't allow them out of our sight. I promise," he said, taking her hand.

She eyed him skeptically. "I thought you'd encourage me to leave so you could claim your prize."

"I want to win but not this way."

"You surprise me."

"I surprise myself."

For Thomas, the contest had changed. When he'd packed his bags, he was ready for a battle of wills, a dirty fight to the finish, no holds barred. Nothing would deter him until he'd won the Winnebago. He still planned to win, but he didn't want Karen to abandon ship because of some jerk in a beard and a long trench coat. And he wasn't yet ready to say goodbye to her. That frightened him. "If you spot the creep, don't go after him alone. You stay with the boys, and I'll chase him down."

"Thanks. I didn't want to have to give up this soon. I'd like to compete until the end."

"You're going to lose," he reminded her, his cocky grin firmly in place.

"Maybe you'll regret persuading me to stay." Her eyes danced with mischief.

Karen looked like a kid, all smiles and a bubbly personality. Although she'd irritated the hell out of him when they'd first met, he liked the child hidden within the woman. And he liked what he saw on the outside a lot, too. Looking vulnerable, she sighed. Thomas wanted to wrap her in his arms and make love to her. But he wouldn't. No good would come of forging a relationship. Karen wanted a husband and babies. *Lots of babies,* he reminded himself as his stomach knotted. So instead of nibbling on her mouth, he drew from an inner strength and asked, "What happened to my sign?"

At first she looked repentant. He'd make her suffer a little before accepting her apology. She lifted her chin and met his gaze. Tiny lines crinkled around her sparkling, non-repentant eyes. Her lips twitched before she burst out laughing. Once she could speak, she pointed her finger at him.

"I wish you could have seen your face when we first arrived and you saw my turkeys instead of your sign."

"How'd you do it?"

"When you lent me your phone, I punched the redial. I explained to your secretary that I was a friend, and you'd asked me to call. There'd been a change of plans and you were on your way to Bates College in Lewiston instead of the Orono campus."

Worry skittered across her features. For a fleeting moment, he was furious. But it was difficult to remain angry while sitting this close to Karen with her warm flesh beneath his fingertips.

"I gave my secretary a password to safeguard against someone calling with fake orders."

"When she asked me for the password, I was stunned. I blurted out your dog's name. It was the only thing that came to mind."

Grinning, he stood and aimed his water pistol.

As Karen changed out of her wet blouse and slacks, she looked out the window at the boys playing with Thomas. Their shirts were drenched. Between shouts of joy, they taunted each other with dares. Thomas dashed from one tree to the other, firing off several shots before charging at full speed toward the boys. Water dripped down his face and over his nose. He swiped at it with the back of his arm. Thomas was easy on the eyes, a man of character. Any woman could easily lose her heart. But not a woman who wanted a family. Karen wanted to hold her babies in her arms, and that would never happen with Thomas.

Ignoring the disappointment squeezing her heart, she sat on the bed and dialed her parents' number. Thomas had agreed to lend her his phone only after he'd called his office to change his password. Out of curiosity, she wondered what word he'd chosen. Before she could ponder the matter, her mother answered.

"Brown residence, Madeline speaking."

"Hi, mom, I wondered whether you'd been keeping track of the contest."

"What contest is that, dear?"

Karen would have normally been disappointed that her mother hadn't paid attention to her earlier conversation, but in this instance, she was relieved. "Don't you remember my telling you about Floyd's RVs and the two winning tickets for a Winnebago?"

"That does ring a bell, dear."

"Anyway, we'll be heading to the Cape next, and I thought maybe we could stop in for a visit." Karen hated her tone, like a child pleading her case. The phone slipped from her sweat slicked hands and bounced on the carpeted floor.

"Sorry." Why was she always apologizing to her parents?

"I can't say for sure. Your father and I were planning to take off for a few days. Not that we wouldn't love to see you. It'll depend when you head our way."

A vise tightened around Karen's chest, cutting off her

airway. "I'll call. I expect to be in Massachusetts in a couple of days." A pause and a fortifying deep breath. "I love you," she said into the phone, her tone wobbly.

"Love you, too," her mother said before hanging up.

Love you, too. Just once Karen wanted to hear emotion in her mother's voice.

Chapter Thirteen

Later that evening Floyd arrived carrying a couple of large bags. "I just happen to have toy trucks and five Super Duper Water Blasters in case everyone decides to battle it out."

Small hands lunged for the bags and tore them open.

"Wow, just what I wanted," Charlie said, hugging a yellow plastic dump truck with Floyd's logo to his chest.

Peter chose a backhoe. Byron grabbed the bulldozer, all imprinted with Floyd's name.

"Don't you ever give away gifts just for the fun of it?" Thomas asked, his jaw rigid.

Floyd chuckled. "Why would I do that? This way, everyone's happy, including me."

Charlie ripped the bright red and green turkey-imprinted Water Blaster from the container. "What's it say?" he asked, pointing to the bold print on the box.

Thomas picked up the box. "This gun holds a pint of water and can strike big game over two hundred feet away."

Charlie sighted down the barrel. "If the boogie man comes 'round here, I'm gonna blast him to bits."

A shiver raced down Karen's spine. Should she take the children back to Abby where they'd be safe? As if reading her thoughts, Thomas rested his hand on the small of her back.

"They'll be fine," he said in a low tone.

"I'd have been here sooner, but I had myself some free

hotdogs and drinks at Bates College," Floyd said.

Thomas looked pleased. "I wondered whether anyone would show up."

"Lots of people were there, thanks to your brother, Joe, who paid the local radio stations to advertise the shindig, complete with live music, free food, and a thousand-dollar gift certificate for Floyd's RVs. People were dancing in the parking lot. The guy who won is going to use the gift certificate as a down payment for a popup camper."

Karen stepped away from Thomas and tried to make eye contact, which was impossible because he avoided looking at her. The corners of his mouth twitched. "I'm glad to hear it was a success."

"That little get-together must have cost you a bundle."

"I considered it an investment toward winning the motor home," Thomas said.

"But I thought . . ." Karen's voice trailed off.

Their eyes locked. "When I found out you'd relocated my archway to Lewiston, I called my brother. Since it was too late to move everything up here, we decided to have the party in Lewiston and make the most of an unfortunate situation."

Floyd shook his head. "You're one hell of a sly bastard."

Karen cleared her throat. When she had Floyd's attention, she pointed toward the children. "Watch what you say."

"Sorry," he replied. "Slip of the tongue."

Karen glanced at the boys preoccupied with carving a road through a pile of oyster crackers they'd dumped onto the floor. "No harm done."

When she thought of the points Thomas had racked up, she wanted to shout in frustration. Instead, she turned to Floyd and spoke in a moderated tone. "The drama club put on a wonderful performance that's certain to get lots of publicity for your dealership. Too bad you missed it."

"Oh, I saw it. The turkeys did a good enough job, but the bozo playing me was way off his mark."

"There was a last minute cancellation," Karen explained. "The guy I chose to play you was a handsome devil with broad shoulders, charisma, and enough sex appeal to drive women wild."

Later that afternoon with Floyd's praises still ringing in her ears, she slid behind the wheel of the Volkswagen.

"Can I come?" Charlie asked, running toward the car.

Pretending she hadn't heard the child, she put the car in gear and sped away. She felt guilty for ignoring Charlie, but she didn't want Thomas to know where she was going. None of the boys could be trusted to keep her secret. She drove past Luiggi's and continued on Route One until she spotted a hardware store. As she hopped out of the vehicle, she caught a glimpse of a white pickup. The truck slowed, then sped on its way. A shiver racked her body. She decided to keep a watchful eye when she drove back to the motor home.

Meanwhile, there wasn't time to waste. Since she didn't want Thomas to suspect what she was about to do, she planned to buy her supplies and hurry back. She dashed into the store. Cans of paint were lined up in the aisles to her right. After spending a considerable time sorting through the different types, she realized she'd need help to choose the right brand.

She saw an elderly clerk at the counter, talking to an old man with bushy gray eyebrows and tufts of hair sprouting from his ears. She went to stand in line behind him. Checking her watch, she was shocked to see thirty minutes had passed.

"This'll take a few minutes." The clerk eyed the computer screen.

The old man wrapped gnarled fingers around his suspenders. "Take your time. Unlike today's young folks, always rushing 'round like headless chickens, I'm not in any particular hurry."

The clerk exhaled a deep breath. "Darn computer takes longer to load every day. I expect it to draw its last breath any minute."

"In the good old days, we used a paper and pencil and got by damn well," the old geezer said, his face twisted with disgust. "Computers, I wouldn't trust 'em as far as I can spit."

The clerk nodded while the computer ground out several suspicious noises. "You may be right."

"You can be damn sure I'm right." The old man scratched his whiskered chin. "Saw you at the church supper last night. Did you happen to sample Alice Courbron's blueberry pie?"

"Can't say that I did."

"You're damn lucky. That had to be the toughest damn dough I ever sunk my choppers into. And bitter, it curled my tongue into a tight knot."

The clerk peered over the bifocals perched low on his nose. "That vain woman can't accept she needs glasses. So the rest of us pay the price when she leaves out half the ingredients. Me, I don't touch anything she brings in."

"You're damn smart."

When Karen glanced at her watch, she saw that forty minutes had slipped away. What if Thomas decided to come look for her? She could have crawled on her knees to Luiggi's and have returned with supper by now. "Excuse me, I hate to barge in, but I'm in kind of a hurry."

Both men turned disapproving stares on her.

"You'll have to wait your turn," the clerk said, exchanging knowing glances with the customer.

"Everyone is always in such a damn hurry," the old man said, "and getting nowhere fast."

Karen glanced at her watch ten minutes later. The old man was right. *She was getting nowhere.* She considered leaving, but she'd invested too much time to give up now.

The old man waved his hand at the clerk. "You might as well go ahead and help her. I don't have a big date this evening."

The clerk slapped the counter top and chuckled. "Clyde, you haven't had a big date since our high school prom."

"You're a damn kidder, that's for damn sure," he said, choosing a candy bar from the display. "Add this to my tab."

As she followed the clerk to the paint display, the old man mumbled, "I'll be right back."

The old geezer drew a breath. "Willis, don't hurry none on my account, I just might stay a while and shoot the breeze."

Finally, Karen had what she needed. After waiting for what seemed like an eternity for the temperamental computer to accept her order, she left the store and hid her purchases under a blanket behind the driver's seat. Ninety minutes after she'd left, Karen returned with a bucket of spaghetti and meatballs.

"Luiggi's is only a mile away. What took you so long?" Thomas asked.

"I had to wait in line," she replied and added, "I picked up a dozen chocolate chip cookies for dessert."

The boys cheered.

"Can I have a cookie now?" Peter asked.

"Me too," Charlie said.

"Me too," Byron echoed.

Karen frowned down at them. "No, you have to eat your meal first."

Byron extended his arm. "Want cookie."

She patted his head and eyed Thomas askance. When he caught her glancing, Thomas smiled, raised his Water Blaster to his right cheek, and aimed the weapon at her. He wouldn't be smiling much longer. Now all she had to do was tiptoe past him tonight while he slept. With the boys at her side, she rested her foot onto the step leading to the motor home. A steady stream of water zinged past her head.

"You don't intimidate me," she said with a smirk, assuming his gun must be empty.

Splat. Her backside took a direct hit.

"You no good, low life . . ." Her sentence trailed off when she caught the boys staring up at her with wide-eyed innocence.

After midnight, Karen slowly opened the bedroom door and peeked into the living room. A small light under the cabinets illuminated the interior enough for her to see the outline of Thomas' long frame stretched out onto the extended couch. Peter and Charlie were sound asleep on their stomachs on the mattress covering the table. Byron had made a habit of joining his brothers during the night. She couldn't see the baby, but she assumed he was hidden beneath the covers.

Bear raised his head and sniffed. Luce jumped off Karen's bed and dashed forward. Before the cat could escape, she managed to shut the door. Unfortunately, the dog started scratching on the other side. He was sure to ruin her plans if she didn't think of something quickly. She grabbed her cat and opened the door. Bear charged inside. The cat leaped from her arms onto the top storage unit where it arched its back and hissed. Hoping Bear didn't eat Luce, or vise versa, she shut the door and tiptoed across the living room.

As Karen neared Thomas, she was surprised to see Byron tucked in the crook of his arm. Her heart skipped a beat. Unexpected feelings churned inside. *Thomas was a natural father.*

The baby sighed and stuck his thumb in his mouth before cuddling closer to Thomas. For a moment, she wanted to trade places with Byron. Thomas was everything she wanted in a man, except . . . *he didn't want children.* Her heart wrenched with disappointment.

With a backward glance she went out the door and hopped onto the pavement. She dug her flashlight from her pocket and continued toward the car. After looking around to make sure no one was watching, she opened the door to the Volkswagen and reached behind the driver's seat for the small stepstool, the can of paint, and the brushes she'd purchased earlier. She placed the stool against the Winnebago and wedged the metal opener under the lid of the can. With the narrow beam of her flashlight directed at the paint, she stirred the thick mixture for several minutes. She dipped her brush into the paint and climbed onto the stool. From here she could look through the window at Peter and Charlie sleeping on the mattress.

Careful not to wake anyone, she gingerly swiped her brush over the F in Floyd's name, pleased that Thomas would no longer score points everywhere they traveled. Finally, her fate was in her hands. No more being *Miss Nice Gal.* No more allowing Thomas' touch to weaken her resolve. From this moment on she would stay on her guard. As her brush slashed over another letter, she felt a deep sense of satisfaction. She might not have as many points as Thomas, but there was still plenty of time to catch up. She batted at a mosquito and accidentally tapped the windowpane.

"It's the Boogie Man!" Charlie shouted as she ducked out of sight.

Thomas jerked awake. All three boys were huddled next to him, eyes filled with terror. Peter clenched tight fingers over

Thomas' arm. "Charlie saw the Boogie Man."

"He was right out there," Charlie said, pointing a shaky hand toward the window.

"I'm sure you're mistaken." Clad only in his boxers, Thomas leaped to his feet. "Stay with Karen while I look around." As he wrenched the door open and flicked on the outside light, he caught a glimpse of someone dashing around the back of the motor home. Thomas went the other direction and tackled the culprit as he rounded the corner.

"Let go of me."

It took a moment for the voice to register.

"Karen?"

"Yes, it's me," she said, sounding annoyed.

"What are you doing out here this time of night?"

"I was painting, of course."

She sounded innocent, as though painting at two in the morning was an everyday occurrence. "Oh, now I understand."

"Let me go."

"Not until you explain what you've been up to." A moment later Thomas scrutinized her paint job. "What ever possessed you to do this?"

"I kinda like it," Peter said.

"Me too," Charlie added.

Byron was sleeping inside the Winnebago, so that was one less opinion for Thomas to contend with. "I hope you used water-soluble paint."

"Of course not. That would have washed away during the first rainfall. I used the best automotive paint on the market."

"All you needed to remove Floyd's name from the Winnebago was a bucket of water and a sponge," Thomas explained and saw her eyes widen with disbelief.

"Oh, oh," Charlie said.

"As my mom would say, I don't like the sound of this," Peter added.

"Gee, I didn't know." Looking contrite, Karen bit down on her lower lip.

Thomas shook his head and frowned. "Don't worry about it. I'm sure we'll think of something."

Karen wouldn't have blamed Thomas if he'd shouted and called her names. Instead he wrapped his arm around her shoulder and gave her a comforting hug. His chest was impressive, wide with a dusting of curly hair. Had the boys not been there, she might have traced the contour of his muscles with her fingertips. When she slid her gaze downward to admire his flat stomach, she noticed he was only wearing a pair of dark colored boxers. *The man was almost naked!*

Her heart somersaulted at the discovery. She jerked her head up. Heated gazes collided. Charlie wedged himself between them and put his arm around her. "Tomorrow morning I'll blast that paint to bits with my Water Blaster."

Peter stepped close to her and touched her arm consolingly. "It's all right. My mom says everybody makes mistakes sometimes."

As naughty as they were at times, the boys were sweet and loveable. A knot formed in her throat when she thought of having her own babies.

"Let's go inside, and I'll make you a cup of hot chocolate," Thomas said.

Her insides jiggled like Jell-O. He'd remembered she drank hot chocolate during stressful times. Thomas had to be the most thoughtful, wonderful man she'd ever met. *Whoa, slow down, Karen. The next thing you know, you'll be falling in love with the guy.* Never, she told herself, fearing it might already be too late.

Chapter Fourteen

While Thomas heated the water for hot chocolate, the three boys stretched out on their bed and fell asleep. Karen sat in the chair opposite the stove and tried not to stare at Thomas' boxers. Briefs hugged a man's body leaving little to the imagination. Karen preferred boxers because they only hinted at what lay beneath. *Just like a present waiting to be unwrapped. Had she completely lost her mind?* She twisted her fingers together on her lap.

A short while later Thomas turned with two cups of chocolate. He handed her one and sat opposite her on the corner of his bed. Karen kept her gaze riveted on his face and tried to ignore other areas of his anatomy.

"Do you think the paint will come off?" she asked, her voice tight.

"No."

Karen set her cup on the shelf by the window. "I'll check at the hardware store tomorrow. I bet there's a solvent that'll do the job."

"Maybe, but I doubt it." He lifted his cup, took a sip, and looked at her over the rim. His eyes deepened a shade and ignited embers deep inside her. With effort she glanced away. When Charlie kicked the blankets, she saw part of his plastic dump truck peeking out from under the covers.

"The boys look so cute and innocent when they're asleep," she said, thinking of a time when she'd be tucking her own children to bed.

A soft laugh rumbled from deep in Thomas' chest. "But looks can be deceiving."

She loved the deep timbre of his voice. Leaning forward, she brushed the silky hair from Byron's brow. "I can hardly wait to have a baby."

"You'll be a great mother," he said, his tone edged with disappointment.

"I plan to be." Hoping he'd had a change of heart, she said, "You're wonderful with the boys. I can't believe you don't want children of your own."

"Believe it." He turned his head and focused on the cabinets across the room. She watched his Adam's apple bob up and down twice. "You don't know what it's like to give up your dreams and spend every spare minute of your time raising kids." He shook his head and cast a saddened glance her way. "I could never go through that again."

An imaginary hand squeezed the breath from her lungs.

"If I hadn't stepped up to the plate, my brothers and my sister would have been parceled out to relatives. I couldn't allow that to happen. At first, I considered running away and hiding where no one would find me. But in the end I came to my senses. I couldn't abandon my family. We'd already lost too much. We needed to be together."

Any remaining doubts fled. Blinking back tears, Karen admitted to herself that she loved Thomas with all her heart and soul. He was everything she wanted in a man, and more. But when the contest ended, they'd walk away from each other and never look back.

Needing some time to herself or she'd start sobbing, Karen stood and headed toward the bathroom. When she approached the bedroom door, she remembered leaving the cat and the dog alone together. Panic clawed at her throat as she ripped the door open and spotted the dog sleeping on the bed. She searched for signs of her cat. "Luce, where are you, baby?"

Granted the animal never came when called, but that didn't matter. Karen feared something awful had happened to Luce. "Here Luce, come on, Luce."

Still no cat. She tried to remain calm; horrendous thoughts crept through her mind.

Thomas came up behind her. "What's the matter?"

She eyed the dog suspiciously, its long pink tongue lolling to one side. "Bear's eaten my cat."

"That's ridiculous. Bear wouldn't hurt another living creature. Maybe Luce escaped when the boys went outdoors to look at your painted masterpiece."

"I'm sure I shut the door when I went outside." She looked around the room and dropped down onto her knees to check under the bed.

"One of the boys might have opened the bedroom door."

"I hope not. I hate to think of Luce lost somewhere." She checked the dresser drawers and the closet but still no cat. As she searched frantically, she pictured her loving animal squished in the road. Hot tears flooded her eyes. Thomas stroked his dog's ears. With a sigh the animal craned its neck and rolled onto its back.

"Well, I'll be damned." Thomas pulled Karen next to him and nodded toward the bed. Karen stared in disbelief at her sleeping cat curled in a tight ball against Bear's side.

The next morning Karen awoke to a loud pounding on the door to the Winnebago.

"Hold your horses," Thomas shouted from the next room.

"It's Floyd," came the boys' excited voices. "Maybe he has more toys for us."

She heard running footsteps and Floyd's no-nonsense voice. "I've called the cops. They should be here any minute."

She threw on her robe and hurried into the living room where Floyd stood, his face beet red and his eyes about to pop from their sockets. Karen wondered whether his anger had anything to do with the man in the white pickup following them. Floyd must have seen the confusion on her face because he cast an icy glare at her. Like a scarecrow in a field, Floyd extended his arm at a right angle from his body and pointed at nothing in particular outside the window.

"Hoodlums have vandalized my property, and they're going to pay!"

His loud voice reverberated through the interior. All three boys ran to stand behind her.

"About the damage," Thomas started to say and was interrupted when a police cruiser skidded to a stop near the Winnebago. Floyd rushed outside with Thomas at his heels. In case reporters came along, Karen decided to get dressed but changed her mind when she heard Floyd's outraged voice.

"Find the son of a bitch who painted over my name. I'm pressing charges. No one screws me over and gets away with it."

"Stay here," she told the boys and hurried outside.

One policeman ran his hand over the damage, which Karen noticed looked worse in the daylight. The white paint had mixed with the red water-soluble paint. Several shades of pink streaked over what had once been Floyd's name. Only the apostrophe remained intact. The other policeman removed a pen from his shirt pocket and jotted notes on a small tablet. "Did you see or hear anything suspicious during the night?"

Floyd's lips thinned. "I wasn't here. You'll have to ask them."

Three pairs of eyes focused on her and Thomas, but as the guilty party, she felt their piercing gazes the most. A warm flush rose from her neck and settled on her cheeks as she lifted both hands and ran trembling fingers through her short hair. Thomas moved next to her and settled a comforting hand on her shoulder while her heart pounded out of control, and a bead of sweat slid between her breasts. Thomas directed his comment at Floyd. "For all we know the paint will come off with soap and water."

Floyd shook his head. "Not a chance. I already tried a little spit and rubbed at the mess with my thumbnail."

"Maybe the hardware store has a solvent that'll remove the paint," Karen said, grasping at a very slim chance.

Floyd's nostrils flared. "Any chemical strong enough to remove that paint will damage the finish. The entire side of the motor home will need to be repainted."

Karen was ready to confess when Thomas stepped forward. "Floyd, technically, the motor home will soon belong to either Karen or me. Let us worry about repairing the damage."

"Son, that's all fine and dandy and mighty generous, but what happens if neither one of you wins?"

"Not a chance, Floyd," Thomas replied, grinning. "In two weeks, be prepared to sign over the Winnebago."

After the police left and Floyd had calmed down, he sat inside the motor home, his usual charming self, smiling at the brats, making small talk with Thomas while eyeing the curve of Karen's boobs beneath a cotton robe and a white nightgown. She was a good-looking dame, if you liked your women young and sassy. The sassier the better suited Floyd. Unfortunately, she didn't have the good sense to encourage his advances. Every once in a while she stole a glance toward him, and he returned the favor tenfold by turning on his million-dollar smile. She made him feel like a randy teenager again. What he'd give for a chance to fondle the goods—a little squeeze—a touch here, another there. Like his father and his grandfather, he was a breast man. Along with their exceptional good looks, he'd inherited their wealth and the ability to judge a woman's bra size from across the room.

B, he decided until she sucked in a breath that made him lose his train of thought. He ran a finger inside the collar of his shirt and undid the top button.

"Did you turn on the furnace? It's hot as . . ." He almost said hell in front of the kids, but he came to his senses in the nick of time when he spotted Karen's frown. "Hot as the dickens," he finished, and was rewarded with a slight smile.

A step in the right direction. In no time at all, he'd have the wench eating out of his hand. He set his notebook on the table. "This is the latest on the contest. As far as I can tell, Thomas has a considerable lead, but the numbers aren't all in yet."

"How much of a lead?" Karen asked, chewing her lower lip and hiking his temperature another notch.

Floyd flipped through his tablet. "Says here, Thomas has two hundred and ninety eight points to Karen's sixty five."

"That much?" Karen looked as though she could cry.

"There are still lots more opportunities for you to win. This score isn't official. People everywhere have been checking newspapers and calling to report the mention of my dealership and our contest in their local newspapers. Someone's started a contest website with a chat room.

You two are very popular."

The baby ran a sticky hand over Floyd's pant leg. Floyd cringed but somehow managed to smile down at the kid. Big mistake. The baby gave a watery grin, his mouth filled with graham crackers, opened wide. A thread of brown glistening drool ran down the front of his pants. Floyd moved as far away as he could from the child.

"There's more money being placed on the two of you than on the horses at Scarborough Downs. Meanwhile, I'm making a few bucks on T-shirts and hats. You're celebrities. It wouldn't surprise me if some big shot Hollywood producer showed up here wanting to do a movie about us." He smiled and cocked his head to one side. "At first I considered having Paul Newman play me, but he's a bit old. Brad Pitt might be better." Dead silence greeted his comment. "Anyway, I figured I'd drop in this morning, and we could watch the news together."

Byron handed him the remote, encrusted with mushy tan guck. Floyd grabbed a napkin from the table and gingerly pushed the power button. By an act of sheer determination, he didn't press his lips together in disgust.

"Kids," he said to Thomas and Karen. "You gotta love 'em." He wondered what fool had penned those asinine words. He adjusted the volume and heard the announcer say,

"A gaggle of dancing turkeys invaded the Orono homecoming yesterday . . ."

Karen let out a deafening screech.

"That's fifty more points for me." She did a little dance, led the children in a victory march, and kicked up her heels, exposing nice knees but nothing more. Damn, if only she'd worn a shorter nightgown!

Chapter Fifteen

Later that week Karen both dreaded and looked forward to the visit with her parents. When she'd called, her mother had made up some excuse about meeting them at the Needham shopping mall on the outskirts of Boston to save Karen the bother of going out of her way. Karen knew her parents didn't want three young boys running loose among their antiques and expensive Dedham pottery.

Karen swept the floors and washed the windows. She put away the children's toys and took out the ingredients for peanut butter cookies, her father's favorite. Side by side she and the boys worked for over an hour until the last cookie was cooling on the rack. Karen smiled at her helpers. If the perfect cookies were an indication of the rest of the day, her visit with her parents would go smoothly. Clinging to that thought, she gave each child two cookies and went into the bathroom to shower.

As the hot water sprayed over her tense muscles, she started to relax. *What was the big deal? For goodness sakes they were her parents.* Her throat convulsed. She wanted everything to be just right. Trying to keep her mind on a positive track, she smiled to herself and reached for her favorite herbal shampoo. The bottle was empty. Byron liked the smell, and she'd caught him washing his hands with her shampoo. Normally she wouldn't have minded. But why today of all days?

The boys' pink Bubblegum Shampoo stood on the corner shelf in the shower. Having no other choice, she poured a liberal amount in the palm of her hand and worked the sweet smelling gel into a thick lather. Maybe the scent awakened her inner child, or maybe the stress had sapped the last of her commonsense, but the next thing she knew she'd molded her hair into thick spikes the way she did Byron's.

A freeing sensation flowed through her body. It was difficult to cling to adult worries while acting like a child. She decided to sneak a peek in the bathroom mirror. She shut off the water, stepped out of the tub, and wiped away the moisture from the mirror. Pink tinted bubbles clung to short horns protruding from her head. She chuckled, climbed back into the shower, and shut the glass door. Still laughing, she turned on the tap and was about to rinse her hair when the pipes shuttered. The stream of water slowed and then stopped.

She wrapped insistent fingers around the cold and hot water spigots. No amount of twisting in either direction produced even one drop of moisture. She hopped out of the shower and tried the faucets on the sink. Same results. As she looked up, she saw her reflection. She resembled a hairy wad of cotton candy. *She'd drained the water tank!* Refusing to admit the obvious, she cast one last disparaging glance at her image, covered herself with a towel, and opened the bathroom door a crack. "Thomas, could you come here please."

She heard the scramble of quick footsteps tripping over themselves. A wedge of his face appeared in the narrow opening. Looking confused and pleased at the same time, he grinned. "Do you need my help?"

"You were supposed to fill the water tank yesterday," she said, her voice sharp, her anger rising.

"I did."

"There's no water," she stated firmly, sticking out her

head enough for him to see. "My parents are due to arrive soon, and I look like a punk rocker."

"You've got to be mistaken. I filled the tank just last night." He shouldered his way into the small room and tried the sink and the shower. "I don't understand. There's no way we've used up 100 gallons."

She pointed toward her head and groaned. "Apparently, you didn't fill the tank."

He checked his watch. "Relax, they aren't due for another forty minutes."

"They're usually early. What will they think when they see me with pink hair?"

"It's not that pink," he replied, eyeing her hair and grinning.

"Thanks. I feel much better." She sent him a scalding look.

He inhaled a deep breath. "A bubble gum flavored woman is damn hard to resist."

And she'd have ordered him to wipe that damnable grin off his face had his heated gaze not rendered her speechless. He ran his fingers through his hair and slid an appreciative glance at her towel-clad body before jerking his gaze at her head. "Nice hairdo."

She hauled the towel up an inch. "I don't have the time for your wise-ass comments. I need a solution."

"I'll be right back," he said, returning a moment later with a glass of ice water. "Lean over the sink and I'll pour this slowly over your head."

"Is that all the water we have?"

He scooped out the ice. "The boys drank the rest, and there isn't a drop left in the kettle. Maybe I should heat this up a little."

"We don't have time. So hurry and get this over with," she

said, bending over the sink.

"Yikes," she shouted a moment later when the frigid water struck the back of her head.

"Sorry," he replied.

She squirmed to one side and water splashed onto the floor.

"Hold still." He worked his fingers over her scalp and massaged a small amount of frigid water through her hair.

She enjoyed the feel of him against her, and though sizzling thoughts invaded her mind, she shivered when he drizzled a small stream of icy water over her head.

"Let me warm you up," he said, his voice lowering an octave.

She felt his warm lips at the base of her neck. Goosebumps peppered her arms and legs. Her heartbeat thundered in her ears. As she stood and turned into him, she didn't feel the icy droplets of water that fell onto her shoulders. For a moment she forgot about the boys. She forgot about everything except Thomas.

When he claimed her mouth and slipped his tongue between her lips, she pressed herself against him. He widened his stance and pulled her between the V of his legs, held her against him until all reason fled. Sliding his hand beneath the towel, he cupped her right breast. Just when she was ready to allow the towel to fall to the floor, he broke off the kiss and looked down at her with regret. "I shouldn't have done that," he said, his voice deep, his breath ragged. "I'm sorry."

"Well, I'm not." Another shiver raced up her spine. "That kiss was incredible." She felt like a fool for blurting out her thoughts. The blue of his eyes reminded her of a stormy sea. He cleared his throat and dropped his hands to his side. He looked as though he was about to say something when a shrill voice came from the other room.

"Byron stuck his toes on the cookies!"

Thomas threw Karen a quick glance. "Get dressed, and I'll make sure the boys don't stomp on any more cookies." Needing to escape before he made a complete jackass of himself, he opened the door and dashed toward Byron who had removed his shoe and held a cookie between his toes. Bear was licking the baby's feet while Byron giggled and squirmed. Charlie pulled off his socks.

Thomas swung the boy in the air. "No way, buddy. You worked too hard on those cookies to let Bear eat them all."

Peter cast a disapproving look at his brothers. "I told them to behave, but they don't listen to me."

Charlie pointed a finger at Peter. "You helped Byron take off his shoes."

"Did not."

"Did too."

Charlie's eyes filled with mischief. "I'm gonna tell Thomas you stuck your wee wee on a cookie."

Thomas slammed his opened palm against the table. "Enough of this foolishness." Three pairs of startled eyes stared up at him. "Good, now that I have your attention we need to get a few things straight. There'll be no bad words while Karen's parents are here. I want you three to be on your best behavior. Byron, you aren't to call anyone a poop head." He looked at the boys and waited a moment. "There'll be no more mention of wee wees or other body parts. Do you all understand?"

No one made a sound, just sat on the floor with wide eyes and opened mouths.

"Want gum." Byron extended his hand.

"No, I'm not paying you to behave." He conjured his deepest scowl. "But I'll tell you this. If you say the forbidden words on Karen's chart, you'll be sorry." For effect he arched his eyebrows and lowered his head until he was at their level. "Do we understand each other?"

Shock registered across their faces. Peter raised his chin. "My mother says it's wrong for mommies and daddies to spank their children."

"She's right. A parent should never strike a child. Unfortunately for you guys, I'm not your parent." Besides, he'd never said a word about spanking. He wanted to scare them, and he could tell by the startled expressions, he'd succeeded.

"What you gonna do?" Charlie asked.

Thomas shook his head slowly. "You don't want to know."

Hair stiff and wearing a fuzzy pink robe and a frown, Karen sashayed past and pierced him with a stony look. The scent of bubblegum lingered in his nostrils and left him yearning to kiss her again. Visions of Karen wrapped in a towel swamped his mind and left him reeling with desire. When she anchored her hand on her right hip, the neckline of her robe buckled enough for him to catch a glimpse of her cleavage. He wanted to trace the underside of her breast, to feel her nipple pucker under his touch. He wanted to explore every inch of her body.

She spared him another icy glance, which he didn't notice until she cleared her throat. "Don't you boys worry. I won't allow anyone to use heavy-handed tactics on you."

Thomas ground his back teeth. "Give me some credit. I've never struck a child in my life." He'd shouted and threatened his brothers and sister until his voice grew hoarse. They'd ignored him and done as they pleased, leaving him to clean up their messes. Again he was reminded of his inability to care for children.

"If I promise not to pulverize these three, will you go get dressed?"

Karen threw him a warning look and disappeared into the bedroom.

"What's pulverized mean?" Charlie asked.

Thomas lowered his voice. "It means warming your butts with the palm of my hand."

"My mom says smart people talk over their problems instead of using their fists."

Thomas frowned at the boy. "My mom used to say when words fail, get them where it hurts."

Peter eyed him with disbelief. "I bet your mom never said that."

The kid was sharp. Thomas admired his quick wit and the way he protected his brothers. Thomas got down on one knee. "Karen is very excited about seeing her mother and father. You can understand that, can't you?"

Peter blinked. "Yup."

Wrapping chubby arms around Thomas' waist, Charlie rested his head on Thomas' shoulder and sniffed. "I miss my mom wicked bad."

"Karen misses her mom and dad too. She wants this visit to be perfect. I'm counting on you three to act your best while her parents are here."

"We loves Karen." Byron popped a piece of cookie into his mouth. "And we loves you too," he added in a way that tugged at Thomas' heart.

Glancing at Charlie's chocolate smeared cheeks, Thomas loosened the child's arm and stood. "First thing on the agenda is getting you boys cleaned up."

"My mom says a little dirt never hurt anyone," Peter reminded them.

"My gut instincts tell me Karen's mother doesn't live by that sentiment."

The boys dashed to the sink and turned the spigots. "There's no water."

Thomas looked for a substitute. The bottle of ginger ale caught his eye. *Wet, clear liquid!* It would have to do. Although sticky to the touch, the boys looked cleaner a few minutes later. "Who wants to come outside with me and check out the valve to the water tank?"

Byron dropped down on the rug and played with the trucks. Charlie and Peter followed Thomas out the door.

Beneath the motor home was a large puddle and wet footprints leading toward the shopping center. For someone to tamper with the fuel or water, they needed to unlock the utility compartment alongside the Winnebago. Thomas hunched down to check the tank. Peter got down on his hands and knees. "It looks like we sprung a leak."

Thomas slid his fingers along the smooth metal and looked closely for a hole. He straightened and wiped the dirt off his jeans.

"I bet the Boogie Man did this," Charlie said, looking frightened.

Thomas had wondered the same thing. If so, how had he drained the water without the key? Only one other person came to mind. *Floyd.* The crafty son of a bitch would do anything to sabotage their trip.

Peter wrapped his arm around his younger brother's shoulders. "Don't worry. I'm here to protect you."

"That's him!" Charlie shouted, tears welling as he pointed at a white truck leaving the parking lot.

"That's not him, you dummy." Peter rolled his eyes and exchanged knowing looks with Thomas. "That truck's a Ford."

"So what, it's white."

"Let's not waste time arguing," Thomas said as Karen

came up behind them and cast a worried glance at the water puddle beneath the motor home. "Did something puncture the tank?"

"I couldn't find a hole." Thomas studied her sticky clumps of hair and noted she still looked sexy as hell. He needed to clear his mind. He needed someone to knock some sense into his thick skull. There was no point obsessing about Karen. "I don't have time to refill the tank before your parents arrive, but I'll go buy some drinking water."

"Can I come?" Peter asked.

"Sure."

As Karen and Charlie climbed the two steps into the motor home, Thomas said, "Be sure to lock up."

Karen threw him a questioning glance.

"It can't hurt to be cautious," he explained. Holding Peter's hand, Thomas dashed across the parking lot and returned a short time later with a few gallons of water. As they neared the Winnebago, the sound of Karen's scream chilled Thomas' blood. He put the water down and grabbed the handle only to find it locked. Digging in his pocket he dug out his key and opened the door.

He spotted Charlie, pushing a load of cookies in the back of his dump truck. As he drove by, Bear swiped a cookie with his long tongue. Karen wrapped her arms around the dog's neck to keep him from wolfing down another. When Karen spotted Thomas, her eyes narrowed. "You better take care of your dog before I extract its teeth with my bare hands."

Thomas grabbed hold of Bear's collar, and Luce, who'd plunked itself in the middle of the cookie rack. He deposited both animals in the bedroom. The boys scampered onto the couch, grabbed the remote, and flicked on the television. Karen dropped to her knees and scooped cookies from the floor onto a ceramic dish. She lifted panic-filled eyes. "I left the room to try to comb my hair and heard the clang of metal."

She looked cute and damn sexy kneeling there with her shapely behind in the air. He bent and picked up four cookies. "These look fine."

"They may look fine, but when I came out of the bedroom, Bear was licking some of them. I have no way of knowing which ones he's touched."

Thomas brushed a black hair off one cookie. "Your father will never know the difference."

Charlie joined them and lifted a broken cookie to his mouth. "Yummy, dog drool tastes good."

Her eyes widened in shock. "Don't eat that."

Charlie popped the last bite into his mouth. "Too late."

She glanced down. "Look at my pants."

"I've already noticed them," he said, admiring how well the black material hugged her curves.

Pink tinted her cheeks. "The knees are covered with crumbs. I'll have to change again." At the sound of a vehicle she looked outside and gasped. "Oh my goodness, they're here!"

Thomas watched a middle-aged couple climb out of a vintage Corvair, parked diagonally and taking up two parking spaces. He glanced at the front fender inches from the Winnebago. "A little closer and his car would be in our living room."

Karen brushed furiously at the crumbs on her pant legs. "He doesn't want anyone else parking near him." With a cursory glance, she shoved a half-dozen unbroken cookies onto a plate and tossed the rest into the trashcan under the table. "Remember, boys, be polite, behave, and under no circumstances say bad words."

Byron stuck his hand out. "Gum."

Karen didn't seem to notice. Thomas threw the boys a warning look. Bottom lip drooping, Byron lowered his hand.

Karen started toward the door, her shoulders stiff, her smile strained, fingers clenched by her side. Thomas concluded even a man going the gallows would look calmer.

Chapter Sixteen

Karen's mother wore a tailored dress with low heels. Her brown hair was pulled back in a tight bun, giving her a no-nonsense appearance. Lips puckered, she kissed the air on both sides of Karen's head. The gesture irritated Thomas, but he did his best to look cordial. A man dressed in a suit embraced Karen. "Sweetie, how are you doing?"

"Fine, dad," Karen replied, then bit her lower lip.

Thomas stepped forward and extended his hand. "I'm pleased to meet you, Mr. Brown."

"Call me Frank."

Karen's father had a firm handshake, a direct gaze, and genuine warmth in his eyes when he looked at his daughter.

"The boys and I are planning to head out for some ice cream. Would you like me to bring you back anything?" Thomas asked. With the children gone, he'd lessen the odds of one of them doing serious damage.

"Yippee!" resounded in triplicate.

"No thank you, we've already eaten," Karen's mother said, looking relieved to hear Thomas and the boys were leaving.

"Me too, me too," Byron said, waving his arms in the air.

Thomas picked him up and wiped the baby's face with a napkin he took from the counter. Tiny tufts of paper stuck to Byron's sticky cheeks. Peter plucked a piece of paper from his brother's chin. "I guess washing with ginger ale was a bad idea."

Karen's mother winced, but she quickly regrouped and forced a smile. "What a darling baby." She pressed her back against the cupboards to let Thomas pass.

"We made your favorite cookies," Charlie said on the way out the door, directing his comment at Karen's father. "But don't worry none, we dusted off the fur, and you can hardly taste the dog drool."

Karen heated some water for coffee while her parents looked around the Winnebago.

"What have you done to your hair?" her mother asked.

"We ran out of water."

"Oh." The one word rang with disapproval.

"Sweetie, the Winnebago is impressive," her father said, using the pet name she loved.

"With a little luck, it'll be mine in two weeks."

"I'm not so sure of that," he said, reluctantly.

"What's that mean?"

"Your father thinks Thomas is going to sweet talk you into losing your heart and the prize, dear."

"There's no way that'll happen. I know the score."

"I wonder," her mother said, tapping a manicured nail on the table. "It's apparent from the newspaper pictures we've seen that you're infatuated with Thomas."

"No way!"

"He cannot be trusted. If this debacle is allowed to continue, he'll ruin our good name and your reputation."

"It's only for two more weeks," Karen said, wondering why her mother was so upset. "I thought you'd be proud of me."

Her mother unclasped her handbag. "You should hear the jokes going around about you two. It's a disgrace."

"When the contest is over, I'll give an interview to clear up any misconceptions." Karen forced a smile.

Her mother huffed. "If only it were that simple. We can barely hold our heads up among our associates."

"Mom, you're taking all of this much too seriously."

"It's becoming a national pastime. The students and faculty are tuning into their favorite radio and television stations hoping to hear the latest about this contest fiasco." Karen's mother dug in her large handbag and threw several newspaper clippings onto the counter. "These pictures are despicable. I cannot believe you'd go out in public wearing only a nightgown. The sunlight left little to the imagination. To add insult to injury, the look on your face is telling the world you're infatuated with the man."

Karen's heart ached with disappointment at her mother's critical tone. Cringing, she stared at the black and white picture of her in a nightgown, backlit by the sun, outlining her legs and breasts. Her mother shuffled through the articles. "The boys are dressed like homeless waifs. Don't they ever bathe? And I can't for the life of me understand why you'd tolerate their deplorable language."

Looking embarrassed, her father cleared his throat. "Sweetie, some of the students at the University are taking bets on when Thomas will have to replenish his supply of condoms."

Karen was about to explain she and Thomas had no control over what the media wrote when her mother shoved a newspaper article under Karen's nose.

"Look at this!" she said, her high-pitched tone nearing hysteria.

Karen's heart fluttered when she saw the picture of Thomas beaming a smile. She loved the way his eyes crinkled in the corners and how his mouth curved. The tap of her mother's long nails on the tabletop interrupted her reverie. "Well, what do you think?"

Sexy, handsome, the love of her life. Karen turned her eyes to the caption. Her heart skipped a beat and then stopped.

One man, one woman, and one gross of condoms!!!

When asked whether he'd brought along condoms for the trip, Thomas O'Leary winked at the reporters. "I packed a gross in my suitcase."

Karen felt sick. "I didn't know."

Outraged, her mother jumped to her feet. "You should collect your pride and those children and march out this instant."

Tears burned at the back of Karen's eyes when she faced her mother, a raw ache settling in her chest. "I can't do that."

"Is it worth it?" her mother asked, lifting her arms to indicate the Winnebago

"Sweetie, be careful." Her father patted her hand.

Her mother added, "As long as those boys are here, there's a semblance of decency. If it weren't for the children, I'd insist you leave this instant."

When Thomas returned an hour later, he unbuckled Byron's seatbelt and sent the two older boys warning looks. "Remember what I told you."

"We need to be on our best behavior," Peter said, jumping out of the Volkswagen.

"And we shouldn't talk 'bout boobies, wee wees, dog hair, or poop," Charlie added for good measure.

"That about covers it," Thomas said with an approving nod. "In fact, try not to speak unless spoken to."

Peter's eyebrows rose. "My mom said children should say what's on their minds."

"Once Karen's parents go out the door, you can talk all you want." As Thomas carried Byron inside, he admired the silver Corvair parked outside the Winnebago. Karen's father had spent considerable time and money restoring the vehicle into mint condition. He opened the door and put the children down. "That's a sharp looking car you have there," he said and noticed how Karen's father's eyes lit up with pride.

"I found her in a junkyard last year. Little by little I've had everything redone. My mechanic rebuilt the engine, and the leather seats are new. The paint on her is barely dry. As a matter of fact, this is her maiden voyage."

"She's a beauty," Thomas said.

Frank threw an admiring glance through the window. "She's my pride and joy."

Thomas looked at Karen and was surprised when she speared him with cold eyes. Uneasiness tightened the muscles in the back of his neck. He thought she'd be pleased he was getting along with her father. Something was wrong, and he couldn't imagine what.

"What do you think of the motor home?" he asked Karen's mother.

"I can't imagine how five of you live in such tight quarters for weeks on end." Karen's mother indicated the space between the table and the couch.

"Since we're in a parking lot, we didn't open the sliders. But they make a big difference," Karen said, avoiding Thomas.

Charlie started dragging a chair toward the bedroom. Thomas wondered what the kid was up to, but he didn't ponder the matter because his mind was preoccupied with Karen. Whenever he tried to make eye contact, she gave him the cold shoulder. He was ready to check on Charlie when

Luce and Bear charged from the bedroom and settled under the table, knocking over the trashcan. As Bear polished off the cookies, Luce gobbled up crumbs and small bits of dough.

Looking nervous, Karen shooed the animals away. Bear stretched out in the middle of the aisle. Luce jumped onto the arm of the couch near Frank, rolled onto its back, and licked its behind. Frank swatted at the animal. "Dammit, Lucifer, do that somewhere else." The cat blinked its blue eyes, stretched its neck, and puked a crumb-coated hairball onto Frank's expensive suit.

Karen swiped the paper towels from the table and knocked over an opened bottle of ginger ale onto her mother's purse and several newspaper clippings.

"Watch me," Charlie shouted, standing on a chair at the control panel ready to press the button that opened the living room slider.

"Noooo!"

Thomas dashed toward the child, tripped over Bear, and collided with Karen. The sound of grinding metal and Frank's cries echoed inside the Winnebago.

Karen watched the boys scramble into the bedroom with the animals and slam the door. Thomas stood at the control panel, pressing the button to retract the slider. She heard her father's strangled moan and her parents' footfalls as they hurried outside to survey the damage.

"Dad, I'll pay for the repairs," she said a moment later, standing nearby, blinking back tears.

Her father ran a gentle hand over the crumpled metal. "It took months for my mechanic to find the right fender. He may never locate another."

She'd messed up again. Instead of impressing her parents, she'd disappointed them.

"Sorry." Her words were inadequate.

She felt Thomas' presence before she saw him. Against her will, her insides twitched with excitement. From the corner of her eye, she saw him watching her, waiting for her to react. She kept her gaze riveted on the vehicle. Finally, he left her side, walked around the vehicle, dropped to one knee, and inspected the dented metal. "The fender is wedged into the tire thread. If you'd like I can hammer it out so you can drive the car home."

Her father winced and looked at Thomas as though he'd lost his mind. "You needn't bother. I'll call the wrecker."

Wrapping his fingers around the twisted metal, Thomas gave a hard tug. "If your mechanic can't find a fender to replace this one, I'd be glad to have a go at it. Over the years my brothers and I have patched many dents with body putty. With a little sanding and a new paint job, you'll never see the imperfections."

"I'll pass, thank you." Her father inhaled a deep breath and ran a gentle finger over a long scratch. "Until a few minutes ago this Corvair was a work of art."

Thomas threw Karen a compassionate glance over his shoulder. She jerked her gaze away and focused on the dented slider still touching her father's car. The value of the motor home had decreased again. Although he wasn't responsible for damaging her father's car, he'd publicly humiliated her and shamed her parents and had humiliated her with his wisecrack about the condoms. She examined her emotions closely and admitted she still cared deeply for Thomas. But the next time he turned on his charm, she'd remember that same smile aimed at the reporters as he boasted of his future sexual conquests.

Thomas had made a fool of her, but it wouldn't happen again.

Red faced, eyes bulging, sweat beading his forehead, Floyd pounded at the slider with the palm of his hand. "This contest isn't supposed to be a demolition derby. At this rate the Winnebago won't be worth shit." He turned crazed eyes at Karen and Thomas. "It would serve you two jackasses right if I called a halt to the contest this instant."

Thomas leaned in close to Floyd. "According to my attorney, legally you have to allow the contest to run its course."

"If there's a loophole, my lawyer had better find it. It's time he earned his keep. I don't pay the son of a bitch to just sit around on his ass."

"If the contest ended today, I'd win the motor home because I have more points," Thomas said with a cocky grin.

Karen clenched her hands. "That wouldn't be fair."

"Don't get your panties in a bunch, sweetheart." Floyd puffed smoke out of the corner of his mouth. "Neither of you deserve to drive off in my Winnebago."

Thomas moved even closer to Floyd. "You're looking for excuses to renege on our agreement. You never had any intentions of parting with this motor home. I'd bet a month's wages you're responsible for draining our water tank."

"You better not be hinting there's something else wrong with this vehicle, or I'll toss everything you own into the parking lot this second." Floyd threw down his cigar and stomped a foot over the burning embers. "If I don't move fast, there'll be nothing left of my motor home. You two better be prepared to pack up your belongings. I'm coming back with eviction papers."

Floyd studied the smeared white paint. "According to the estimates, it'll cost me a fortune to have someone reputable paint my Winnebago," he said, stressing the word, *my*. "And I intend to wrench every damn cent from your miserable hides."

Chapter Seventeen

That night after everyone had fallen asleep, Karen lay in bed, deep in thought, remembering every disastrous detail of her parents' visit. Before driving away, her mother had said: *people will do almost anything for a large sum of money. If you continue to trust Thomas, you're a bigger fool than those news articles portray.*

She couldn't befriend the opposition. Granted Thomas had enough sex appeal to curl her toes, but she couldn't allow him to get the best of her. He could pose for all the pictures he wanted to with his cocky grin. He could spout off wise-ass comments, but she wouldn't be standing next to him looking like a lovesick female.

She heard a snapping sound outside the window. Every muscle in her body tensed. Heart racing, she spotted a shadowed figure, peering into the dark room. Her heart hammered an unsteady beat. She could make out the silhouette of a man with a long beard. With an act of sheer determination, she reached for her flashlight next to the bed and directed the beam at the intruder who scurried off like a rat. She dashed toward the window in time to see him jump into a white pickup and drive away. She considered waking Thomas but quickly decided against that.

For all she knew Thomas had hired their stalker to frighten her away. He could have deliberately drained the water in hopes of dashing her spirits, thinking she might give up and go home. It was difficult for her to think of Thomas as anyone but the man she loved. And though she tried to refute her emotional entanglement, her foolish heart said otherwise.

Thomas was awake when the bedroom door opened. Out tiptoed Karen with the beam of her flashlight shaded by her hand as she made her way past the couch. He kept his breath even and pretended to sleep. She crept outside in short lace-trimmed pajamas that hiked his temperature several degrees. He waited a few minutes so she'd be fully immersed in whatever crafty scheme she'd conjured. Silently, he climbed out of bed and wrapped his fingers around the doorknob, casting a look over his shoulder at the sleeping boys.

He didn't see Karen right away. Then in the moonlight, he saw the outline of her shapely rear pointing skyward as she knelt under the Winnebago. He grew hard as erotic images washed over him. He saw himself crushing her against him as he toyed with her breasts, trailing a thumb against the turgid peak while kissing the underside of her jaw, and wrenching a moan from her throat.

In the distance a horn tooted, returning him to the present.

"What are you up to now?" he asked, coming up behind her.

She bumped her head. "Dammit." She backed out from under the Winnebago. Outrage crossed her features. "What are you doing out here at this hour?"

"I was going to ask you the same question." He grinned and did his damnedest to keep his gaze above the neckline of the scrap of lace that barely covered her body, leaving little to his overtaxed imagination. In the dim light he could almost make out the dark tone of her nipples through the material.

His throat clogged his airway. He sucked in a deep breath and clenched his fingers together to prevent them from doing something he'd later regret.

"Can't a woman go for a moonlit stroll without playing twenty questions?"

"Not when she's tampering with the underside of the Winnebago."

"I think you're trying to scare me off. You probably hired that guy who peeked in my bedroom window tonight."

Uneasiness clawed the back of Thomas' neck. "What guy?"

"I'm onto you."

Thomas reached for her hand but she yanked her fingers away. "Was it the same bearded man we've seen before?"

"Yes, call him off. Tell him it won't work because I'm not going away."

"You're wrong. I don't want you to go anywhere," he said, meaning every word. He moved closer. She stepped back, until she was leaning against the motor home with no hope of escape. Leaning close, he anchored an arm on either side of her head.

"Leave me alone," she said through clenched teeth.

"No." He could smell her, a mixture of lilacs and spice. She made a feeble attempt to shove him away. He lowered his mouth and brushed her lips. Slowly, she wrapped her arms around his neck.

"Not only can't I trust you, but also I can't trust myself around you." She kissed him, a long sweet joining of their lips that left him reeling for more. "This can't continue," she said, pressing her right hand against his chest, while holding on tightly with the other hand.

"Your protest is as flimsy as your nightwear." He cupped

her buttocks and molded her against him.

A flash went off, blinding them both. Thomas heard the pounding of footsteps. When the spots cleared from his vision, he spotted a cameraman diving into a dark, late-model getaway car.

Thomas followed Karen into the bedroom and shut the door.

"This is all your fault," she said as she put on a robe.

"What happened out there was no one's fault. I'm dammed attracted to you, and I know you feel the same."

"Ha, you wish." Heat rose to her face, refuting her statement. "I hope that picture doesn't end up on the front cover of some well-read paper."

He sat on the edge of her bed and rubbed Luce's neck. "Chances are that cameraman works for a sleazy tabloid paper. You know the kind?"

"An example comes to mind," she said, gripped by another surge of anger.

"You probably have nothing to worry about. Your parents don't strike me as the sort to read that trash."

"They purchase groceries, and those papers are displayed at the checkout lines nationwide." She opened the nightstand drawer and threw the condom article at him. "Here's tabloid press at its finest."

Guilt darkened his features. He lowered his gaze, toyed with the fur on the tip of the cat's tail until Luce batted his hand away with its sharp claws.

"I wondered when you'd see this."

"Is that all you have to say for yourself?"

"I regret that interview. But at the time, I wanted to get rid of you as quickly as possible so I did my best to sound like an ass."

"Congratulations, you gave a stellar performance."

After a restless night, Karen awoke to the sounds of chirping chickadees outside the bedroom window. In the pre-dawn light she remembered how quickly she'd melted into Thomas' arms, forgetting her resolution to remain strong and aloof. She'd pay dearly for her mistake. Her startled face would be splashed on the pages of the tabloid paper along with her partially clad body in a compromising position. Her mother would die of embarrassment when she saw the picture of her only daughter in the arms of her competitor. Karen groaned, closed her eyes and tried to prepare herself for the day ahead when she'd be a laughing stock and a disgrace to her parents. Again!

She slipped her legs over the side of the bed and went to check on the boys. As she tiptoed across the carpeted living room, she saw Thomas propped against the couch cushions, sipping a cup of coffee.

"You're up early," she said, her voice harsher than she'd intended.

"Well, if it isn't Miss Sunshine herself," he replied, his tone no cheerier than hers.

Thomas was bare-chested and clad in a pair of denim shorts, his long muscular legs stretched out on the mattress, the white sheet emphasizing his deep tan. *He looked unbelievably sexy.* She turned her back to him and glanced at the boys sleeping together, arms and legs entwined. A strong wave of longing washed over her. She wanted babies of her own to hold in her arms.

She sauntered toward the coffee pot and poured herself a cup, added sugar, and a liberal dollop of milk. She considered going back into the bedroom, but that would look as though she was too weak to confront Thomas. Instead she sat in the chair next to the couch, tucked her feet underneath her robe and pretended to be preoccupied with something out the window. She heard the creak of the couch springs as he leaned over and cupped his hand over her arm. Tiny jabs of electricity prickled her nerve endings.

"I've already apologized for shooting off my mouth to the reporters. What else can I do?"

"Nothing, you've already done enough," she said, spearing him with cold eyes, while her heart warmed at his contrite expression. Since she needed to appear unfazed, she brushed his hand away and was struck by an immediate sense of loss.

"We have almost two weeks left in the contest. That'll be a hell of a long time if we aren't talking to each other."

"I can take it if you can," she said, admiring the angle of his jaw and the way the stubble of his beard shadowed his face. *No good Karen.* A woman does not ignore a man by listing his favorable characteristics. Instead she'd focus on his flaws, the warts on his personality. By emphasizing his repulsive points, she'd become a stronger opponent.

Pretending to study the filigree design on her cup, she glanced at him through her lowered lashes and detected a small scar above his right eye. *An imperfection.* Unfortunately, the mark only strengthened his features. *Darn!*

"I made a bunch of phone calls last night, hoping to buy off the photographer who took our picture."

Her heart leaped to her throat. "And?"

He shrugged. "By the time I tracked down the newspaper, it was already too late."

"Wake up call!" came Floyd's voice from outside.

"I wonder what he's up to?" Thomas said standing and opening the door.

"He's probably here to evict us."

181

"I checked with my lawyer. Floyd can't bail out now."

Floyd bustled into the motor home. "Good news!"

Charlie sat up, Byron pulled the blanket over his head. Floyd tapped the boy's head. "Charlie, my friend, how would you like to go to an amusement park?"

Charlie nodded and shook Peter awake. "We going on rides?"

"Not so fast." Thomas raised a hand in protest. "Don't get the boys' hopes up until you've told Karen and me what you have hidden up your sleeve."

Karen liked the way he stood up to Floyd. Floyd turned toward Karen. "I've rented a stretch limo. If you accept my generosity, the driver will be here in about an hour to take everyone out for breakfast. I've scheduled a shopping spree for the kiddies, then it's off to an amusement park and later dinner in Cape Cod."

Distrust narrowed Thomas' pupils. "Why are you doing this?"

Floyd threw them a sly grin. "I'm doing it out of the goodness of my soul."

Thomas cast a tentative look at the boys' eager faces. "Somehow I doubt that."

"Can we go?" Charlie asked, jumping to his feet.

Peter climbed out of bed. "Pleeeeeeeeeease."

Chapter Eighteen

Uneasiness crept up the back of Thomas' spine when the late model limousine arrived fifty minutes later. He was certain he'd regret accepting Floyd's offer, but he'd brushed aside his common sense in hopes of spending time with Karen. No doubt he was a fool for trying to get closer to a woman who'd walk away when the contest ended. Karen herded the boys outside and Thomas stayed behind to have a word with Floyd. "You're up to something."

"I don't know why you're flapping your jaws. In all likelihood, you're going to win."

Thomas slid his cell phone into the leather case hanging from his belt. "What's caused the abrupt change of heart since yesterday?"

Floyd's face cracked into a weasel-like grin. "I had a chat with my lawyer. There's no way in hell I can throw your ass out the door." He uttered a humorless laugh. "So I decided to do my damnedest to come out of this contest smelling like a rose."

Thomas wrinkled his nose in disgust. "Impossible." He couldn't figure out how the sleazy businessman would benefit, unless he'd called the media, hoping to make a big splash.

Floyd lowered his bulk onto a chair by the couch. "Anyway, I'm beat. This contest has taken its toll on me. I figure I'll get myself a little shuteye, take the dog for a stroll, and maybe watch the Playboy station on satellite TV."

The door opened several inches, and Peter poked his head inside. "Byron is getting tired of waiting, and Charlie is going out of his mind."

"I'll be there in a minute." Thomas watched the boy skip across the parking lot to the limo. Thomas stepped away and sent Floyd a warning look over his shoulder. "This better not be a trick."

"You need to learn to trust people more," Floyd said. "You might not want to admit it, but you and me are a lot alike. We aren't afraid to go after what we want." Floyd paused for effect and wiggled a bushy eyebrow. "If you play your cards right, I might throw in a free paint job when you win."

Thomas wasn't in the best of spirits when he climbed into the limo's back seat and after three tries managed to shut the door. His mood didn't improve when he saw the ripped upholstery, cracked window, and threadbare carpeting.

"Isn't this great?" Peter said.

"Sure is fancy," Charlie added.

"Fancy," Byron repeated, his chin glistening with drool.

Thomas slid in beside Karen, who didn't spare him a glance.

"I want to go on the Tilt-A-Whirl and the Cyclone and the Merry-Go-Round," Peter said, his eyes bright with excitement.

"I'm gonna eat cotton candy, a caramel apple, and lots of fries at the 'musement park," Charlie said.

Byron bounced in his car seat. "Me too, me too."

"Are you gonna go on rides with us?" Charlie asked Karen.

She smiled at the boys. "We'll see."

"Where are we gonna eat breakfast?"

"I don't know because Floyd arranged everything."

Thomas caught a glimpse of her mahogany eyes. "Doesn't anyone else suspect Floyd's motives?"

Bewildered, Charlie and Peter stared at Thomas as though he'd sprouted a horn in the middle of his forehead. Karen spared Thomas a quick glance. "Maybe Floyd is trying to make amends for being so harsh yesterday."

At least she was speaking to him again, and for that he was grateful. Maybe being cooped up in the limo would force them to mend their fences. When the limo pulled into the Burger King parking lot, Thomas almost swore aloud. "I suppose this is Floyd's idea of a top-notch restaurant."

"Yippee!" the boys shouted, looking pleased.

As she chewed on a breakfast sandwich, she was aware of Thomas looking at her. Her heart tripped against her ribs. Damn the man for having such a strong hold on her.

"Can I throw away the trash?" Peter asked.

"No, me, me." Charlie reached over the booth and knocked a cup of water onto Karen's pants.

Karen jumped to her feet. Thomas grabbed several napkins and dabbed at the moisture with far too much enthusiasm.

"Give me those." She meant to take the napkins but her fingers tangled with his. For a moment their eyes met, and she knew she couldn't remain angry with him.

"Let's declare a truce. Just for today, we'll forget about the contest," he said, his voice and face sincere.

Easy for him to say since he was way ahead.

She stuck one hand behind her back and crossed her fingers. "Yes, that's a good idea."

The chauffeur glanced into his rearview mirror. "Our next stop is a shopping spree at Wal-Mart."

The driver, a short man with a receding hairline, had a familiar look about him. Maybe it was the way he carried himself, the tone of voice or the small beady eyes in the center of his plump face. Karen studied his features when he glanced over his shoulder. "My name's Clyde. If you need anything just give a holler. Is everyone having a good time so far?"

"Yes," Peter said.

Charlie shoved Peter away. "Get outta my seat. It's my turn to sit next to the window."

"Is not."

"Is too."

For no apparent reason, Byron clapped his hands and shrieked.

"I've had enough of this bickering and noise to last me a lifetime," Thomas said, his voice harsh, losing patience with the children, who said nothing for the next ten minutes.

A familiar ache tugged at Karen's heart. Until now, she'd found it hard to believe Thomas didn't want children, but his tone and the way he'd issued the statement reminded her of her parents' reprisals over the years. In her quest to gain their attention, she'd sometimes gone to extremes and probably deserved some of their stern comments. *If only they'd tempered their criticism with hugs and kisses, she might not have repeatedly tested their love.*

The driver steered the limo into the Wal-Mart parking lot and pulled alongside the curb. He leaned his arm over the seat and looked back at them. "Shop to your hearts' content. Here's a gift card from Floyd for each of you."

"I'm gonna buy lots of toys and candy," Charlie said,

grabbing his card and two others.

"Gimme mine," Peter swung and missed. "You're a butt head."

"You're a boobie." Charlie leaned away and dangled the gift cards from the tips of his fingers.

Thomas snagged all the cards. "Boys, I'm not going into the store unless you promise to keep your voices down."

Three heads bobbed.

"Do you promise?"

"Yup."

"Good." He directed a warm smile at the children. "A man's handshake is the same as giving his word. Anyone who doesn't abide by what he says isn't worth spit."

The boys giggled.

"Do you understand?"

"Yup, if we say we're going to behave, we should mean it," Peter said, a look of awe on his face.

Charlie giggled. "I like what you said about spit."

"Good, then let's shake on it and go have a blast."

The boys and Thomas exchanged solemn handshakes.

Karen undid Byron's seatbelt. The baby leaped onto Thomas' lap. "Love you," he said, giving Thomas a wet kiss.

Thomas climbed out of the back seat with Byron in his arms. Peter grabbed Thomas' free hand.

Charlie hopped out. "How much can I spend?"

Karen ducked her head and asked the chauffeur, "Do you know the value of the gift cards?"

"Sure do. You each get ten buckaroos."

Thirty minutes later, they stood at the checkout, waiting for the cashier to ring up their purchases. Karen had splurged on supplies she might need later today: white shoe polish, double-sided tape, and a small tablet of colored paper. The cashier scanned Byron's stuffed animal and raised a penciled eyebrow. "I know you. You're the lady in that contest."

Peter set his G.I. Joe tank by the scanner. "I told you I'd be good," he told Thomas, who smiled at him approvingly.

Against her protests, Charlie had chosen a toy gun that shot ping-pong balls. When the cashier tried to take the box from him, he tugged at his purchase with both hands. Thomas tapped his shoulder. "You gave me your word."

Reluctantly, Charlie loosened his grip and focused on something behind them. Karen assumed he was checking out the candy display. Any second he'd demand a chocolate bar. He slapped his hand over his mouth. "I can't believe my eyes."

Karen glanced at the magazine display behind her and stared in shock at the perfectly focused picture of her and Thomas in a tight embrace on the cover of a tabloid paper. Thomas grabbed every issue and laid them face down. "We're taking these too."

"Karen, I saw your butt!" Charlie's crisp, clear voice echoed throughout the store.

Chapter Nineteen

Floyd handed George, the freelance reporter, a check and puffed on a thick cigar. "I wish I'd been there to see Karen in that getup. What I'd have given to be the one with my hands on that luscious ass. Thomas has all the fun."

The two men shared a raunchy laugh. The reporter slipped the check in his pocket.

"Keep 'em coming. I want to raise some hell. Those two have been getting along too good. A little negative publicity for them will garner lots of attention for my dealership."

"Bad press always travels fast," George said.

"Which is why I want you to do another job for me."

They discussed the particulars for several minutes. George looked uncertain. "I'm not thrilled with the idea. I could get hurt. That guy's a lot bigger than me."

"Yeah, but you're a hell of a lot smarter," Floyd said to pacify the fool. "If you move quickly, he won't touch you."

"Well . . . I don't know."

Floyd handed George another check. "Call this an incentive bonus." The reporter's eyes grew wide as Winnebago hubcaps. "If you play your cards right, you won't get injured." Floyd pointed a thick finger at the reporter. "I'll triple the money if you manage to get Thomas thrown in jail."

"You must really hate the man." George folded the check in two before tucking it in his shirt pocket.

"I'm just protecting my investment." Floyd gave George what looked like a red plastic jellybean. "All you need to do is snap this open at the right moment and you'll be bleeding like a gutted swine."

Thomas shoved the newspapers into the bottom of a trashcan and strode toward Karen and the children. They climbed into the limo. Charlie folded his arms across his chest and plunked himself at their feet. "I ain't goin' nowhere 'til Peter lets me sit by the window."

"Peter, it's Charlie's turn," Karen said, patiently.

Peter heaved an exaggerated sigh. "All right, cry baby, have your own way."

Karen rubbed the bridge of her nose and squeezed her eyes shut. Thomas could tell the children were wearing her down, too.

"Jerk."

"Butt head."

"Poop head."

With a smug smile, Charlie covered his mouth with his hands and peered at Karen. "My mother sure is gonna be surprised when she sees your bare butt on that magazine picture."

Karen's face turned scarlet. Thomas slammed the door shut and sent bad vibes toward the kids. "Nothing was bare. Karen had on pajamas, similar to the short ones you wear when it's hot outside."

The picture accentuated lots of good points: long legs, a well-shaped behind and firm breasts. Because everyone had been watching him, he hadn't dared examine the newspaper picture for too long, but he'd looked long enough to admire her assets.

"But I saw . . ."

Thomas interrupted Charlie. "What you think you saw and what you actually saw on that picture are two different things."

The child rolled his tongue beneath his top lip and seemed to mull the matter over for a moment. "What were you doin' so close to Karen?"

Caught off guard, Thomas said the only thing that came to mind. "Karen had something in her eye, and I was checking to see if could find it."

"Oh." Charlie lowered his gaze toward his new toy. "Can you get my gun out of the package?" Normally Thomas would have refused, but he figured the gun was just the distraction Charlie needed to get his mind off the magazine picture.

As they neared Salisbury Beach, Massachusetts, Karen was deep in thought trying to think of a way to gain a point advantage. Since Thomas had declared a truce, she hoped she didn't have to worry about his construction company building billboards and hiring bands. Unfortunately, something Thomas had said to the boys earlier that day bothered her: *Anyone who doesn't abide by what he says isn't worth spit.* The less than poetic statement wreaked havoc with her conscience. Since she was behind at the moment, she needed to use every opportunity to her advantage.

She'd crossed her fingers. What she said hadn't counted, which proved she was worth spit. She moaned. Only a woman in advanced stages of dementia would boast of such a thing. Thomas settled his arm over her shoulder and gave her a comforting hug. "I want us to have a good time. Let's forget the past and go on from here."

Thomas didn't realize it, but he'd let her off the hook. By eliminating the past, he'd also canceled out their deal not to compete. "Yes, that's a good idea."

The chauffeur pulled the limo into the crowded parking lot. He climbed out of the car, went around to the back, and removed a picnic basket from the trunk. Thomas, Karen, and the children slid out of the back seat. The driver set the basket next to the car. "Floyd packed a gourmet lunch for everyone. Enjoy folks."

The boys clamored around Thomas. Karen lifted the wicker basket from the pavement. By its weight, she assumed Floyd had packed lots of food.

"Do you boys want to eat at a picnic table or on the beach?" she asked the children.

Peter and Charlie jumped up and down. "The beach, the beach, the beach!"

"The beach," Thomas repeated with a boyish grin.

"Me too," Byron added, giggling softly.

"Then the beach it is," Karen said, returning Thomas' smile and leading the way toward the sand and the pounding surf.

Karen scanned the cloudless sky and turned a bright smile toward Thomas. It was a beautiful day. *And the perfect opportunity for her to whip his butt.* If he could read her mind, he wouldn't be grinning as though he'd struck it rich. *Whip his butt!* She was starting to sound like the kids.

Two reporters hurried toward them. "Are you the people Floyd told us about?"

"Never heard of anyone named Floyd," Thomas said with a nod toward the kids.

"Huh?" Charlie shrugged. "Floyd's the one who paid for Burger King and our toys and our rides."

Peter kicked his brother's shins. "Can't you take a hint?"

Charlie stomped on Peter's foot. Peter stuck out his tongue. "But . . ."

"Boys!" Thomas lifted an eyebrow. Three pairs of eyes riveted on his stern face as he turned to the two reporters, one tall, the other short. "Guys, give us a break."

"We don't get paid unless we come back with good copy."

Karen got an idea. "If you allow us some time to eat, you can follow us around on the rides."

The taller of the two whispered something to the other reporter. "Okay, but don't go trying to give us the brush off."

The reporters stayed a few hundred feet away. Thomas spread out a blanket the chauffeur had given them, and Karen opened the picnic basket. When she'd heard the expression gourmet lunch, she'd pictured cheeses, shrimp, and wine. She was disappointed to see a large container of green Kool-Aid, sandwiches, and potato chips. Charlie plunked himself down beside her. He pulled a sandwich from the baggie and took a bite. "Yum, my favorite, peanut butter."

Thomas whispered, "That stingy son of a bitch."

She poured drink into paper cups and offered one to Thomas. "I agree one hundred percent."

For the first time, Thomas felt as though he and Karen were a team, two people fighting one enemy, Floyd. A warm feeling settled in his chest as the boys ran ahead of them and Byron walked hand in hand with Karen and Thomas.

"Do it again," Byron said, giggling. Raising their arms, Thomas and Karen swung the baby above the ground, then set him back down.

The two reporters tagged alongside with pen, paper, and tape player. The short guy stuck a mike in Thomas' face. "What's it like to wake up every morning with kids that aren't yours?"

"It's not so bad." Thomas enjoyed the boys more than he cared to admit.

"I bet they're driving you to drink."

"It wouldn't be fair for me to blame my bad habits on innocent children."

The tall reporter laughed and motioned toward Karen. "I was hoping you'd give me some dirt on the broad."

Thomas released the baby's hand and stared at the idiot in disbelief. Unaware of the mounting tension between the two men, Karen continued ahead with the boys. The guy must have mistaken Thomas' actions because he slid in closer. "She's a hot looking chick, and I can tell by the picture in 'Gotcha' that you're getting a lot of action. Share the details, and I'll make it worth your while."

Thomas barely controlled his rage.

The reporter sent Thomas a conspiratory grin. "On second thought you watch the kids and give me a turn with the bitch."

Thomas reared back, clenched his right hand, and angled his fist at the bastard's face. The reporter jumped back. For a moment the man's arms swung like the blades of a windmill. He stumbled over a branch, lost his balance, and fell face first against a large granite stone. The reporter crawled onto his knees, blood pouring from his nostrils, he hollered, "Police, help! I'm being murdered."

One minute Karen was walking along enjoying the weather, the next moment Peter was shouting for her to turn around. She saw two armed policemen standing over Thomas as he laid spread eagle on the sand.

A lifeguard was kneeling next to the injured man. "How many fingers am I holding up, sir?"

"Three, you damn moron. The blow was to my nose not to my brain."

"If you had a brain, you wouldn't be talking filth," Thomas sputtered before the policeman snapped handcuffs around his wrists. "Anyway, I didn't touch you. If I had, I'd have blackened your eyes too."

The reporter winced when he touched his nose. "Throw him in jail. He's a danger to society."

Thomas glared at the reporter. A cameraman jumped forward and snapped several pictures.

"Is Thomas going to jail?" Charlie asked.

Peter tugged at the policeman's arm. "Thomas looked like he was going to bonk the reporter, but the man lost his balance and slammed his nose on the big rock."

The officer knelt before the child. "How old are you?"

"Seven."

"Do you know the difference between telling the truth and telling a lie?"

"Yes, anyone who doesn't tell the truth isn't worth spit."

"You're a wise kid." The officer rose and asked the crowd. "Did anyone see what happened here?"

An elderly woman stepped forward. "I saw the whole thing. The big guy never touched the skinny one," she said, swinging her gaze toward the man holding a bloody handkerchief against his face. "You should be ashamed. I heard every word you said. If you were my son, I'd wash your mouth out with lye soap."

Chapter Twenty

"You blasted that guy right on his butt. You sure are strong," Charlie said, looking awestricken. "When I'm big, I wanna be just like you."

Karen came out of the bathroom with Byron in time to hear the conversation. Thomas sat at a picnic table and encouraged Peter and Charlie to join him. "Don't ever use your fists unless it's your last resort."

Peter shuffled his foot against the sandy path. "That man said bad things about Karen."

Thomas nodded. "He sure did, but that didn't give me the right to swing at him." Confusion clouded his features. "I swear I didn't hit him."

Peter patted Thomas' arm. "I know that."

"But you were gonna hit him," Charlie said.

Karen watched the play of emotions over Thomas' face. "I wanted to frighten him. But a man shouldn't raise his fists unless he's prepared to use them."

Peter nodded.

"Maybe," Charlie said. "But sometimes it's easier to bonk someone in the head."

Thomas put an arm around each boy. "Just because it's easier, doesn't make it right."

Byron pulled free. He ran toward Thomas, climbed onto his knee, and planted a kiss on his cheek. Karen was amazed at how strongly the boys had bonded with Thomas. How much she loved him amazed her even more.

Karen's mood was infectious. Everyone laughed and had a great time. Thomas went on the roller coaster with Peter and Charlie, and they squeezed the breath from his lungs. Both boys insisted they loved the ride but refused to go on again. They rode the go-karts, the merry-go-round, and the bumper boats. While Byron took a turn on the pony rides, Peter and Charlie ate cotton candy and fries.

Thomas and Karen stood hand in hand. A strong feeling stirred in his chest, an emotion he didn't dare examine too closely. Although their arrangement was temporary, he'd decided to enjoy today and not worry about the future.

As they strolled along the boardwalk, Karen stopped in front of a booth with a display of antique pictures. "Let's have our pictures taken," she said, tugging at Thomas' hand.

"Haven't we been photographed enough?" he said, noticing the cameraman and the same reporter inching toward them.

For a man who'd looked as though he was bleeding to death two hours earlier, he'd made a good recovery. Upon closer inspection, Thomas saw no swelling on his nose or face.

"It'll be a nice souvenir."

The light in her eyes weakened Thomas' resolve. "Sure, let's go for it."

Moments later, decked out in old-fashioned swimwear, they stood facing the camera. The park photographer scowled at the cameraman behind him.

"Read the sign, buster. I don't allow anyone to take pictures but me."

The reporter handed him several bills. "Your policy doesn't apply to us, now does it?"

"In this case, I'll make an exception." The photographer pocketed the money.

197

"Give me a big smile."

Karen pulled away and winked at the boys. "Now."

The children and Karen turned around and bent from the waist. Cameras flashed. Taped to the back of the boys' swim trunks in white were the words, *FLOYD'S RV'S*. Karen felt a bit guilty but elated she'd come out ahead. She didn't know how many points she'd earned, but the look on Thomas' face when he realized she'd bested him was priceless.

"The limo's not here." Peter eyed the spot in the parking lot where the driver had left them.

"I'm sure he's around somewhere," Karen said, the first inkling of apprehension zipping down her spine.

Except for a groan, Thomas remained silent. Karen knew he was disappointed in her, and in a way she was disappointed in herself. She'd never been a cutthroat businessperson. This contest defied reason. No rules applied and only the shrewdest person would win. To win she needed to change her tactics. She hadn't spent two weeks with three children, two animals, and one maddening man, who confused and amazed her, to go home empty handed.

"Maybe the driver forgot about us," Peter said, sitting on a smooth sun-bleached log. "I sure hope we don't have to stay here all afternoon and all night."

"I bet I know why he's late. He's probably playing with my new gun," Charlie said.

Peter rolled his eyes. "That's the dumbest thing you've said yet."

"Is not."

"Is too."

"Butt head."

"Jerk."

"Poop head."

"That's enough, boys," Karen said, in a tone that brooked

198

no argument. The children lifted startled faces.

"Gee, you're starting to sound like our mother," Peter pointed out, looking none too happy.

She sliced a finger against her throat. "I've had it up to here with your constant bickering. If you don't stop this instant, I'm going to . . . I'll warm your bottoms."

Their pupils widened.

"I liked you better when you was nicer," Charlie said, his lower lip jutting out.

"And I like you better when you're nicer. So there, we're even."

She noticed Thomas' fleeting, smug grin. The boys pouted and avoided looking in her direction. At least they weren't arguing and calling each other names.

"I see it, I see it," Charlie said a short while later, waving his arms excitedly, pointing toward the approaching limo. "He better not have broken my gun."

Peter looked ready to comment, but he speared a cautious glance at Karen and clamped his mouth shut. She'd broken her own rule about how to speak to children, and though she wasn't proud about shouting at the boys, she noticed they'd quieted down.

Once the limo stopped, they scrambled inside. Karen fastened Byron's seatbelt. He fell asleep before they left the parking lot. Charlie hugged his toy gun to his chest. Within minutes Peter's head bobbed against his brother's shoulder. *Peace at last.* Until taking care of the boys, she'd never realized how difficult it was to keep a cool head around children. Although she still didn't approve of all of Abby's parenting techniques, Karen admired her friend's effort. As a single parent, she was doing all right.

Karen had started the trip with lofty ideas. She was going to corral those boys into acting like little gentlemen. With the help of her charts and positive reinforcement, she'd expected them to stop saying bad words and to treat each other with respect. After two weeks, only her expectations had changed. She leaned her head against the seat, closed her eyes, and listened to the whirl of the wheels on the pavement. She was aware of Thomas' leg brushing hers, the heat of him penetrating deep inside.

She opened her eyes and found him looking at her.

"I thought we agreed we weren't going to compete today. You didn't keep your word," he said.

"I never promised. When you suggested we forget about the contest, I said it sounded like a good idea."

"You knew what I meant."

"Apparently, you didn't get the meaning of my words. Which gave me the opportunity to earn some much-needed points."

"I can't trust you."

"That's a fact. Only one of us will drive off with the Winnebago. I intend that person to be me. So from now on, do whatever you can to win because I will too."

"I thought we were friends."

"That's impossible. Until the contest ends, I have to think of you as the enemy." *Ridiculous! He was the man she loved.*

Chapter Twenty-One

An hour later the limo pulled into a parking lot adjacent to the Rocky Oyster Restaurant and Pub. As they climbed out of the vehicle, Karen admired the waves breaking over the sandy beach.

"Can we look for shells?" Peter asked.

Thomas glanced at his watch. "Sure, why not."

They strolled between sunbathers and children digging holes and crafting sandcastles along the water's edge. Peter and Charlie ran ahead of Karen and Thomas, stuffing sea urchins and shiny rocks into their pockets. Byron bent to examine a piece of driftwood encrusted with barnacles.

Half an hour later they were seated at a picnic table on the deck of the Rocky Oyster overlooking the ocean. Thomas sat with Charlie and Peter on a wooden bench opposite Karen and Byron. A blonde waitress clad in shorts and a tank top, arrived with a pitcher of chocolate milk and a bottle of wine. "Floyd called ahead to order your dinners."

"I can just imagine," Thomas said, exchanging knowing looks with Karen.

Thomas turned dazzling blue eyes at Karen. Warmth flooded her senses as their gazes met and held. Karen remembered the feel of his lips and how safe she'd felt in his arms, how she'd craved the intimacy of his embrace, how she'd wanted to listen to his heartbeat as they made love. *Karen, get* back on track. Thomas is the enemy.

The waitress arrived ten minutes later with steaming bowls of fish chowder served with hot rolls, crackers, and a platter of assorted cheeses.

"Enjoy." She set a plate of onion rings in the center of the table. "If you need anything, give a holler."

Karen poured chocolate milk for the boys while Thomas unscrewed the top from the bottle of white Chablis and filled their glasses. "I wonder what Floyd has up his sleeve."

"Maybe he's just being nice."

"Right," he said with a deep chuckle.

Karen loved the timbre of his voice and the way his eyes sparkled with mischief.

Charlie pulled a clam from his chowder. "This looks yucky."

Peter squeezed the clam's belly until it exploded. Charlie's eyes widened. "Yuck!" He whispered something in Peter's ear and the boys giggled.

"Keep your opinions to yourselves," Thomas warned them sternly. "Maybe you should stick to eating onion rings."

Looking disgusted, Peter wiped his hands and shoved the bowl of chowder away from him. "I won't do that again."

"Me either," Charlie said, sticking out his tongue.

Byron blinked comically.

As the children nibbled on the cheese and crackers, Thomas paused a moment and looked at Karen in a way that stole her breath. Gooseflesh pebbled her arms when he reached across the table for her hand, the rough pad of his thumb tracing tiny circles along her palm. For a short moment the children and the other people around them disappeared. They were one, a couple, lovers, and more. If only that were true . . .

She chided herself for being stupid, for craving what she

could never have, but in that moment all seemed possible. All seemed right.

"Look at all the birdies!"

Charlie brought her back to reality, made her realize she couldn't lose focus on the contest. She pulled her hand from Thomas' grasp and sucked in a fortifying breath. Overhead, seagulls dove to catch the bread people threw onto the beach. The gulls' loud squawks resonated in the air as they fought for choice leftovers.

"Those seagulls remind me of you three," Thomas pointed out with a grin.

"How come?" Peter asked, cracker crumbs spraying from his full mouth.

Charlie studied the birds for a moment. "We don't got no feathers."

"No, but you're always bickering with each other."

"I bet the gray one gets my bread," Charlie said, heaving a roll over his head.

"Hey, I was going to eat that," Peter said, shoving his brother.

Thomas uttered an exasperated sigh. The waitress arrived with steamed clams and a basket of fries. "Leave room for the lobsters," she said before sashaying across the deck and disappearing into the kitchen.

Charlie stuck fries in each nostril and growled. Thomas speared him with a warning glance. With a wide grin, the child blew the fries across the table, ducked his head, and crammed a cracker into his mouth.

"Sorry," he mumbled not looking sorry at all.

Byron reached across the table and almost tipped over a glass of water, but Peter caught it. Thomas winked at the older boy. "Good save."

Karen filled a plate with fries and onion rings for Byron.

Until lately she'd never realized how much attention three children required. Thomas grabbed Charlie's hand to prevent him from lobbing the last bun onto the beach.

"To a stranger watching and listening to us, they'd think we're a real family," she said.

"They'd be mistaken."

She hid her disappointment behind her smile.

Thomas dunked a steamed clam in butter and popped it into his mouth. Karen's short, wind-blown hair made her look sexy as hell. The sun cast fiery highlights along the mahogany strands, lighting the embers in Thomas' gut. Fortunately, the racket coming from the boys was enough to douse the potential flames.

The boys were cute, noisy, and had lots of pent-up energy. A lot of the time he enjoyed being around them. But he'd also be glad when they left. They were typical boys. A man who hadn't raised children might believe his offspring would be well behaved and quiet. That man would be an idiot. Thomas had his share of faults, but he was no idiot. Only a moron would plunge into the dark waters of matrimony with a woman intent on having babies.

Yet Karen was what he wanted in a woman. He loved her bubbly personality, and he admired her never-ending patience with the children. She'd be a wonderful mother. In time she'd marry, lie in another man's arms, and make love until dawn. Jealousy flowed unbidden in his veins. The muscles in the back of his neck tightened. He couldn't fathom Karen with anyone but him. An onion ring slammed into his forearm and landed on the deck, breaking his reverie with a jolt.

"Oops," Charlie said, hands over his mouth.

Thomas refilled Karen's glass and admired the graceful

curve of her neck above the collar of her soft cotton blouse.

"I'm surprised we haven't gotten our lobsters yet," Karen said, throwing a quick glance at the clock surrounded by red and yellow buoys on the weathered gray wall.

"There's no hurry," Thomas explained. "It's five o'clock, and it's only an hour drive back to the Winnebago. We need to get there by ten. As long as we leave by seven, we'll have plenty of time to spare."

A gull landed on the deck railing. The boys heaved pieces of breadsticks and cheese. Karen grabbed a roll, tore off a chunk, and aimed a morsel at the gulls on the beach. Flapping their wings, several birds ran for the bread. Karen rose to her feet, pulverized two more buns and aimed at the growing flock. The motion lifted her blouse enough for Thomas to catch a glimpse of her belly button ring. Lust slammed into him with the force of a two by four. He wanted to dip his tongue into the indentation of her navel.

Karen swung, and breadcrumbs rained over the beach. The boys jumped to their feet and scurried onto the sand, shouting like barbarians. Laughing, Karen lifted Byron into her arms and gave him a bun that he tossed at the gulls. She set him down and swung her long legs over the railing. When the waitress arrived with another basket of buns, Thomas grabbed the ammo, charged after the boys, and pelted them with moist bread.

Karen called his name, and he turned. A chunk of bread thumped his forehead. Karen's eyes glowed with mischief before she fired at him again. This time he ducked, and the bread missed him by an inch.

"You'll pay for that." He dashed after her, aimed at her behind, and struck his intended target. *And wished it were his hands making contact.*

Karen and the boys ganged up on Thomas, assaulting him with the leftover rolls.

"When I get hold of you, you'll wish you'd picked on someone else." Feigning outrage, he captured Byron, swung him in the air, tickled his sides, and set him free. Next he grabbed Peter, wrestled him to the ground, and held him down until he pleaded for mercy.

Meanwhile, Charlie filled a bucket he found on the beach with icy water and dumped it over Thomas' head. Taken by surprise, Thomas swore but quickly broke into a laugh. He caught up with the child and lifted him into the air.

"You look like you need a bath," he said, running toward the water with the boy under his arm.

Kicking his feet, Charlie pummeled Thomas' chest. "Help, help," he shouted between giggles.

"It's too late for that." Thomas held him upside down over the breaking surf, dipping Charlie's hair into the salty brine. The boy shouted and splashed until Thomas' shirt clung to his chest. Karen, Byron, and Peter came to the rescue and joined in the fracas. Everyone was damp and covered with sand when they sat down to finish their meal.

The waitress arrived with a tray of hot dogs and fries for the boys. "Your lobsters should be ready in a few minutes."

Thomas saw it was already six. "Tell the cook to hurry, we'd like to leave in another hour."

"I'll be back in a jiffy with your order."

By six-thirty they were still waiting for the lobster. The boys had eaten enough to feed a third world country. Doing his damnedest not to stare at the swell of Karen's pert nipples standing at attention beneath her wet blouse, he focused at the clock. The waitress finally returned at seven with two large red lobsters, setting them down in front of Thomas and Karen.

Karen's face glowed from her day in the sun. Tiny bits of mica clung to her cheeks and nose, glinting in the sunlight. She looked vibrant and happy. Thomas didn't have the heart to tell her they should leave. Even if they left at seven-thirty, they'd still have two and half hours to get back.

He cracked open a claw and dipped the lobster into the melted butter. Leaning forward, he offered it to Karen. Her mouth closed over his fingertips. Jabs of electricity zapped Thomas' hand and made him wish they were alone together, lips and bodies joined. His fantasy halted when Charlie shouted, "It's the Boogie Man!"

Thomas jerked his head around and spotted the familiar bearded man watching them.

"Don't let the kids out of your sight," he said as he jumped to his feet and dashed toward their stalker.

Chapter Twenty-Two

The children scrambled next to Karen and huddled together.

"Will the Boogie Man hurt Thomas?" Charlie asked, his small face twisted with fear.

Although Karen assured the boys Thomas could take care of himself, once he disappeared from sight, she worried for his safety. She watched the slow moving hands of the clock, every second dragging on. Fifteen minutes seemed like an eternity.

When they finally spotted Thomas in the distance, everyone dashed out to meet him.

"I lost him," he said a moment later, running his hand through his hair before glancing at his watch.

Charlie wound his arms around Thomas. "If I'd had my gun, I'd have blasted the Boogie Man."

Thomas cupped his hand over the boy's shoulder. "Next time I may take you along."

Peter crowded in closer. "Me too."

"Definitely."

Byron wrapped his chubby arms around Thomas' knees. Karen picked up the baby. "It's already eight. We'd better head back."

"Are we gonna lose?" Peter asked, jogging next to the adults.

"No way," Thomas said. "As long as that son-of-a-bitch is

waiting in the limo, we should get back to the Winnebago with an hour to spare."

Karen threw a quick glance toward Charlie and was relieved he seemed to have missed Thomas' comment. As they neared the limo, the driver sat up and yawned. "I must have fallen asleep."

They scrambled into the back seat and shut the door. Charlie beamed an impish grin at Thomas. "You had nothin' to worry 'bout. The son-of-the-beach was taking a nap."

They soon found themselves in a traffic jam. As the limo inched forward, Karen glanced nervously at Thomas who was tapping his fingers over the cracked leather seat.

"Once we reach Route 128, we'll make better progress," he said. "We still have plenty of time."

Karen heard the worry in Thomas' tone. A while later Charlie tugged at her arm. "I'm gonna puke."

Sweat beaded Charlie's upper lip and forehead. He was pale, his jaw drooped, his eyes watered. The driver pulled the limo onto the shoulder of the road. Just in time Thomas hopped out with Charlie. With a groan, the child vomited on Thomas' shoes. The driver dashed around back and handed Thomas a roll of paper towels. Thomas ripped off several paper sheets and dabbed at Charlie's face and arms.

Karen watched Clyde release the hood and walk around front. His head disappeared for a moment, and she wondered what he was doing. When he slammed the hood shut a moment later, looking unconcerned, she assumed all was fine.

Thomas slid the soiled paper towels into a plastic bag that had held their purchases. He heaved the bag into the trunk and slammed it shut. Still pale, Charlie fastened his seatbelt. "Sorry, are we gonna lose 'cause of me?"

"No way, sport," Thomas said, glancing at his watch. "We

still have over an hour to get back."

Clyde turned the key, and the engine made a grinding noise. After several attempts, he shrugged. "Looks like the old girl's conked out on me again."

Thomas didn't trust the shifty bastard. He jumped out of the car and ordered, "Pop the hood."

Clyde stuck his head out the window. "What for? I already called for a tow."

"I want to see if I can fix the problem."

"Only certified mechanics work on my vehicle."

Thomas strode to the driver's side, wrenched the door opened, and leaned forward until he met Clyde's gaze. He wrapped his hand around the driver's arm and squeezed.

"Your policy just changed. You now allow only certified mechanics and me to work on your car."

Clyde sneered. "That's a load of crap!"

Thomas tightened his hold. With his free hand, he reached down and released the hood. Swearing under his breath, he inspected the wires between the distributor and the spark plugs. Karen came up beside him. "Can you fix it?"

"Four of the plug wires are cut clear though. That son-of-a-bitch sabotaged our return." Thomas ran to the driver and hauled him out of the vehicle by his collar. "Why'd you do it?"

"I don't know what you're spouting off about."

"Like hell you don't." Voice shaking with rage, Thomas stuck a plug wire inches from Clyde's nose. "Why'd you cut these?"

"It was an accident."

"Like hell!"

"After we left the Cape, I noticed the engine was skipping. When we stopped, I decided to take a look and see if I could spot the problem. My fingernail scraped against the wire and snapped it in two. Those wires were old and brittle."

"That's a crock of bull."

"Honest, why would I damage my own limo?"

Thomas clamped a hand over Clyde's shoulder. "You tell me."

"Stop, that hurts."

Thomas turned fury-filled eyes on Clyde.

"You're going to crush my collarbone." Clyde's face contorted in agony. "Let go, and I'll tell you everything."

Thomas released him, and Clyde collapsed against the car, rubbing his shoulder.

"The other night Floyd and me were tossing back some beers. We were having a few laughs about my draining your water tank when he started feeling down about this contest and the prospect of losing the Winnebago. After a few more drinks, we hatched this plan to offer you an outing with lots of opportunities for everyone to have a good time. No one ever turns down freebees."

A wrecker pulled behind them, and the mechanic walked around the vehicle and stuck his head under the hood. "Who took a cleaver to the plug wires?"

Looking dumbfounded, Clyde shook his head. "Beats me. I took my eyes off the car for a few minutes. The next thing I know it doesn't start. Vandals are running wild all over Massachusetts."

"Can you give us a ride?" Thomas asked the man who'd driven the wrecker.

"No one's going anywhere for a while. I drove in the breakdown lane, or I wouldn't be here now. A tractor-trailer carrying chickens turned over up ahead on 128. There's poultry running amok and bird shit all over the highway."

Clyde slapped his hands together. "The jig is up, caput,

finished, you've lost. You'll never get back before ten."

Thomas leaned close to Clyde. "What's in this for you?"

"Floyd and me are first cousins. Our fathers started the business. I own twenty-five percent of the dealership."

Thomas stood behind the limo talking on his cell phone. Karen assumed he was trying to find a solution to their problem. There was none. Although she believed in setting goals, she also believed in accepting reality. Unlike the speedy hands of her watch, the traffic was barely moving. It was already 8:50. Defeat was only seventy minutes away. She slid into the back seat with the boys.

"Are we gonna lose?" Charlie asked, looking much better.

"Yes," she said.

Peter's face scrunched in disappointment. "My mom says losing doesn't matter as long as you did your best."

The familiar adage didn't console Karen.

A few minutes later, overhead, she heard a *whomp, whomp, whomp,* glanced out the window and spotted a helicopter about to land in a nearby field. Charlie lunged for the door handle. Karen grabbed the back of his shirt.

"I wanna go see the chopper with Thomas."

"No, it's too dangerous to be running around outside."

She watched Thomas crouch down and race toward the pilot. In that instant she knew he'd outsmarted Floyd. In that instant she was certain he'd return to the Winnebago with time to spare.

"I can't wait to ride in the chopper," Peter said, his eyes wide with excitement.

"Me too," Charlie added.

Byron kicked his feet and swung his arms. "Me too, me too."

There was no way Thomas would invite them along. The

last shred of hope disappeared when Thomas hopped aboard, the helicopter lifted off the ground.

Feeling as though a ton of cement had lifted from his shoulders, Floyd hopped down from the Winnebago, lit his cigar, and frowned at the cluster of reporters and cameramen milling around. Hoping to gain more media attention, he'd called the radio and television stations to inform them of Thomas and Karen's unfortunate plight. He filled his lungs, the nicotine and smoke calming his nerves. "The towing company called. Thomas and Karen are stranded about twenty miles from here. There's no way they can get back in time to fulfill their part of our contract. The contest will end at ten sharp."

Mabel, a tall woman reporter aimed a mike at Floyd. "This isn't their fault. Have you considered giving them another chance?"

The brooch hanging over her right tit almost gouged Floyd's eye. Granted he was partially to blame. He'd stepped forward to get a closer look at the same time she made her move. He'd never seen such a big set and wondered whether they were real or implants. They were a cross between large honeydews and small watermelons. He clasped his hands behind his back so he wouldn't be tempted to cop a feel. When he raised an appreciative gaze, the broad's cold eyes greeted him. Floyd wasn't discouraged. He always did like a challenge.

Tight brown curls hugged her head; eyebrows resembling bushy caterpillars hung over mud-colored pupils. A bulbous nose shaped like a summer squash, protruded from her face and hooked over her lips. Kissing the woman would be damn near impossible. Why was he even thinking such absurd thoughts? One more glance at her chest and he had his answer. He could overlook a few imperfections. In the dark only the essentials mattered, and these essentials were the largest he'd ever seen. He turned up the wattage on his smile. "There's nothing I'd love more than to give them another opportunity, but I can't. I hope to run more contests in the future. If I make exceptions for Thomas and Karen, everyone will expect me to give them a break, too. The next thing I know, the next contestants are suing the pants off me because I'm playing favorites."

Floyd heard a helicopter and saw it hovering over the mall like a giant vulture. As it neared, a spotlight arced skyward. Moments later he spotted Karen, the boys, and Thomas waving at the crowd. The reporters ran to greet the contestants. Schooling his features, Floyd stepped toward the Winnebago and propped opened the door. When the Siamese dashed off across the parking lot, he puffed on his cigar and chuckled. A moment later, wanting to be the first to offer his congratulations, he darted toward the helicopter, ready to demonstrate one of his many skills—slinging bullshit.

Chapter Twenty-Three

At exactly 9:40, Thomas and Karen rushed into the Winnebago, followed by Floyd and a woman reporter.

"That was a close call," Floyd said, tapping Thomas' back like a close friend while Bear ran circles around them.

"Fortunately, a member of my brother's graduating class lives on the Cape," Thomas said.

"Imagine that."

Thomas saw the disappointment in his eyes.

"I figure the odds of you two returning on time were slim, but the odds of knowing someone with a pilot's license ready to come to your rescue at a moment's notice must be nil to none."

Thomas smiled at the bastard. "The odds increased greatly this morning when my brother called his friend and asked him to stick around."

"Thank the good Lord for brothers." Floyd waved his arms as though he were at a church revival. "Anyway, I'm pleased as punch you made it back on time." Floyd sent the woman reporter a long, warm glance. "I was telling Mabel how it broke my heart that I couldn't give you two a break."

The reporter clicked on her tape recorder. "Did you and your brother expect trouble?"

"We believe in being cautious."

Joe had warned him not to accept Floyd's offer, but

Thomas had ignored him, hoping to get closer to Karen. He'd been a fool then and an even bigger fool when he'd ordered the pilot to land so that Karen and the boys could accompany him. One clear fact grated on his nerves; he didn't regret going back for Karen, proving he'd completely lost his mind.

"Anyway, you're back now, which is all that matters." Floyd inched closer to Mabel.

They hurried into the Winnebago. Karen slipped into the bedroom, returned a moment later, and started searching the cupboards.

"Luce is missing," she said after looking under the sink, her voice trembling.

One corner of Floyd's mouth quivered upward. "I saw him streak across the parking lot."

"I need to find him," Karen said, running from the motor home.

According to Thomas' watch, it was 9:52. Thomas considered letting Karen look by herself. If she chose to relinquish her chances of winning, that was her problem. But he knew how much that cat meant to Karen, and he couldn't abandon her now any more than he could earlier.

Floyd stayed behind to watch Byron. Thomas dashed out the door with Peter and Charlie. Mabel followed a few feet behind.

"I see Luce," Karen shouted from a distance. "Each time I get close, he runs farther away."

"I'll shoot it." Charlie lifted his gun and sighted down the plastic barrel. A ping-pong ball rolled close to the cat. When Luce leaped forward, Karen grabbed the animal by the scruff of its neck and hugged him to her chest.

The happy look on her face when she hurried toward Thomas was worth all the chances he'd taken to help her.

"It's a good thing I brung my gun along," Charlie said in a crisp voice.

Mabel jotted down a note, then smiled at the boy. "That weapon sure came in handy. Maybe you'll let me borrow it. I've a critter I'd like to send scurrying in the opposite direction."

"What's a critter?" Charlie asked.

She winked at Thomas and Karen.

"It's a short, slick-talking, large-paunch, balding creature."

That night the boys insisted on sleeping with Karen. Charlie set his gun by the side of the bed and climbed under the covers. "If the Boogie Man shows up, I'm gonna shoot him."

Peter slid into bed between Charlie and Byron and wrapped his arms around his younger brothers. "I'll protect you."

Charlie wrapped chubby arms around Peter and kissed his cheek. Karen understood why parents endured all the bickering and the commotion. Beneath the shoving and the name-calling, love grew, bonding the boys together for their lifetime. She kissed them good night and claimed her side of the bed.

"I don't want any feet or elbows in my back."

"Yup."

"Wasn't it nice of Thomas to let us ride in the helicopter?" Peter said a moment later.

"It sure was." Karen had given up hope. She'd closed her eyes and leaned her head against the seat of the limo when the boys had yelled, *"Yippee! Thomas is coming back for us."* She spotted the helicopter landing in the field and a moment later, Thomas running toward them, waving his arms, and shouting for them to hurry. He'd lifted Byron into the crook of his arm. She held onto Peter's and Charlie's hands and together they dashed toward the waiting helicopter.

"Are you gonna win now?" Charlie asked with a yawn.

She sighed. "Unless I think of a way of earning lots of points, I'm going to lose."

"Maybe we'll get lots of points for having our picture taken with Floyd's RVs on our swimsuits," Peter said.

"Not nearly enough points to make a difference."

"Oh."

"This is my problem, not yours."

"We're on your team," Peter reminded her.

"That's definitely a plus. I need a plan that'll gain national attention. There's little chance of that happening."

"My teacher says I'm a really good problem solver. I bet I can come up with a great idea," Peter said.

"Me too," Charlie said, turning on his side.

"Don't give up. Me and Charlie will get you so many points, you'll be sure to win."

"Thanks. Now, let's get some sleep." Her heart swelled with love for the boys.

As she dozed off, she imagined herself sitting in a rocking chair with her child in her arms, inhaling the sweet fragrance of baby powder. She'd lower her face and kiss the downy fuzz on her baby's head.

Before dawn, they were awakened by Charlie's cries. "The Boogie Man is here!"

Charlie jumped over Karen and hid under the blankets, his body trembling with fear. Thomas charged into the room and switched on the lights. "Is everyone all right?"

Karen held Charlie in her arms and tried to calm him. "Shush, you were having a nightmare."

"I saw the Boogie Man. He was looking at me." Charlie peeked over the edge of the blankets at the opened window.

Karen cradled him against her chest. Thomas glanced outside, shut the window, and turned back to the children, his voice laced with alarm. "I'll lock the windows and pull the shade. You boys need to get some sleep. Karen is in here, and I'll be in the living room keeping watch. If we see anyone near the Winnebago, I'll call the police."

Peter cast a timid smile at his brother. "You'll be safe sleeping next to me."

With some persuasion, Charlie stretched out next to Peter and pulled the bedspread over his head. Byron slept through the ordeal, unaware of the commotion.

Once the boys had fallen back to sleep, Karen tiptoed into the living room to speak to Thomas. He was sitting on the couch, a sheet over his bare legs and a cup of coffee in his hand. Before she could question him, he said, "I saw a man taking off in a white pickup right after Charlie shouted. I want to get to the bottom of this. Tomorrow night after the boys are asleep, I'll hide in the Volkswagen in hopes of catching the culprit."

"You need to spend ten hours in the motor home."

"I'll stay in the rest of the day if it means catching the guy."

She admired the strong angle of his jaw. "I don't understand why you came back for us this evening."

He shook his head. "Neither do I."

While Karen and Peter stripped the bed the next morning, she heard the door open and Floyd's voice in the living room.

"Thomas, your picture's on the front page along with a few sentences about my dealership. I doubt there's anyone in Maine or Massachusetts who hasn't heard of Floyd's RVs."

"Wow," Charlie said. "It looks like Thomas is trying to hurt Peter. What do the words say?"

"The caption reads," Floyd said, in a jovial tone, "Bully restrains boy and forces him to plead for mercy."

Charlie kicked a pillowcase across the room. "We was only playing a game."

Floyd continued, "Young man, that's nothing, wait until you see your picture."

A moment later Charlie chuckled. "I look funny up-side-down. It looks like I'm gonna be drowned."

Thomas groaned. "Let me see that."

"Look at the bright side, Thomas. You're winning!"

Floyd's snide laughter grated on Karen's nerves.

"I've called a press conference for this afternoon. I figure I'll milk all the publicity I can before moving on. Tomorrow, you'll head for New Hampshire." He laughed. "I should sign over the papers to the Winnebago right now because there's no way Karen can beat you."

Peter hopped over the bed and hugged Karen. "I've got my thinking cap on. I've already got an idea."

"Do you want to share it with me?"

"I need to think on it awhile longer."

She opened the window to let in some fresh air. "I'm glad you're on my side."

Fearing for their safety, Thomas and Karen watched the boys' every move. If Peter and Charlie went outside, Thomas accompanied them. When Byron took his afternoon nap, Karen locked the bedroom windows. Her stomach clenched when she spotted a white vehicle about a hundred feet away, a late model and not the truck they'd seen on other occasions. She pulled the shade and stayed in the bedroom with the baby, certain if she took her eyes off him, he'd somehow disappear.

"Can we go to Burger King for supper?" Peter and

Charlie asked later that afternoon.

"I'd planned to cook your favorites, potato puffs and fish sticks," Karen told them.

Charlie stuck out his tongue. "Yuck, I hate fish sticks."

"Since when? You ate six when we had them for supper three nights ago."

Charlie's chin rose. "I hate fish sticks—real bad."

Peter rolled his eyes. "Potato puffs are all squishy inside and they stick in my throat."

From across the room, Thomas sent her a look that said the boys were pulling a con job. His mouth curved into a damnable, cocky grin that she'd grown to love.

"Can we, please, please, pleeease go to Burger King?" Charlie asked, clasping his hands and looking pathetic.

"Pretty pleeeeeease . . . tomorrow we'll sweep the floor and dust the furniture like we do for our mom," Peter added. "And we'll . . . even eat fish sticks and potato puffs."

She saw no harm in giving in to their wishes. Every child on occasion deserved to be pampered. "All right . . ."

The cheers drowned out the rest of her sentence.

They walked into Burger King a while later and chose a booth in the middle of the restaurant, where the boys could refill their own drinks and still be closely watched. Karen got a high chair for Byron, and Thomas arrived a moment later with a tray brimming with burgers and fries.

"I'm scared," Charlie shouted.

Thomas rested a calming hand over the child's shoulder. Charlie pulled away. "Don't touch me. You're not my father."

"What's gotten into you?" Thomas asked.

"Dunno." Charlie popped several fries in his mouth.

"Remember, that door swings both ways," Thomas warned him.

"What's that s'pose to mean?"

"If you make another scene, I'll wait with you in the car while your brothers and Karen finish their meals."

Lower lip curling, Charlie didn't utter another word. He polished off the rest of his kid's meal and played with the small toy that came in the package.

Karen had finished her burger when she realized Peter was more quiet than usual. She rested her hand on his forehead.

"Are you feeling all right?"

He jerked back. "How do you expect me to act? You've taken me away from my mother, and I miss her. I want to go home."

Charlie always spoke in a booming voice, but Peter talked in low tones. She was shocked to hear him yelling. Thomas rose from his seat, his expression furious. "I'm not putting up with this nonsense."

Someone behind them gasped. Karen heard whispers. The manager rushed toward them. "What's the problem?"

"There's nothing wrong here that a swat across the behind won't cure." Thomas scooped Charlie in one arm, and grabbing Peter's hand, motioned for Karen to follow with Byron.

Charlie wailed and beat his fists against Thomas' chest. The manager followed them out the door. "What's wrong?"

"I want my mama!" Charlie's fists rubbed dry eyes.

"My brother is wicked tired. He'll be fine once he gets some sleep," Peter said, winking.

The manager knelt on one knee and looked closely at Peter. "You'd tell me if anything wasn't right?"

The boy nodded. "Sure, can you do me a favor?"

Concerned filled the manager's eyes. "Anything."

Peter retrieved a napkin from his pocket. "Take care of this for me. I forgot to throw it away."

Although Karen thought Peter's request strange, she let

the matter slide, thankful their ordeal was finally over. The boys fussed about getting into the car and created such a disturbance the strangers in the next vehicle stared at Karen as though she were a criminal. After more threats from Thomas, the boys hopped into the back seat.

Finally they pulled out of the Burger King parking lot. Squad cars with flashing lights screeched to a halt around them. Armed officers stormed the car and opened the doors. One policeman grabbed Karen's arm and pulled her out of the vehicle. Another policeman yanked the front seat forward. "Are you boys all right?"

"Yup."

"Me too."

"We are now," Peter said.

"You should be commended." The officer smiled at Peter while helping the children out of the car. "Handing the manager the note was quick thinking on your part."

Peter pointed at his head. "Me and my thinking cap came up with the idea."

"When we get to the station, I'll get all three of you an honorary badge."

"Yippee," Charlie shouted before Peter kicked his shin. "But I'm still scared."

The officer squeezed Charlie's shoulder.

"He's not frightened of us," Karen said, totally confused at the disgusted look on the officer's face.

The policeman holstered his gun. "There's been a mistake, all right, and we're going to fix it."

When Karen glanced over her shoulder, she saw Thomas with handcuffs around his wrists. Customers inside the restaurant pressed their faces against the plate glass windows. Other people clustered in groups, whispering and sending her dirty looks.

"What's going to happen to the children?" Hot tears stung Karen's eyes as she stared at the officer's unyielding back. Another officer clamped handcuffs over Karen's wrists. "The proper authorities will see they're returned to their parents."

"But his mother can't care for them because . . ."

Before she could explain, he cupped his hand over her head and pushed her into the back seat of the cruiser.

"Lady, look this way."

She turned toward the voice and spotted a smirking cameraman, the same guy who'd tried to pick a fight with Thomas. The last shred of her patience vanished. She considered giving the jerk the one-finger salute. Unfortunately, her wrists were locked in handcuffs behind her so instead she made a face and stuck out her tongue. The cameraman snapped her picture, capturing the moment for posterity. The door to the police cruiser slammed shut. The sound of sirens blasted her eardrums.

"But I haven't done anything wrong," she said to the policeman sitting in the front seat of the patrol car.

The officer glanced over his shoulder and regarded her with cold eyes.

"Honey, save your breath and tell it to the judge."

Chapter Twenty-Four

Through the glass panel in the next room, Karen saw the three boys sitting on the bench. Sucking his thumb, his head bobbing against Peter's arm, Byron had fallen asleep. Charlie swung his short legs and closely examined the fake police badge hanging from his T-shirt. Peter's head hung low as he dashed a hand over his tear-streaked face.

"Don't be too hard on the boys," the policewoman said. "The Captain chewed out the oldest and explained the seriousness of faking a kidnapping. I think Peter's already learned his lesson. Anyway, they did it for you."

Peter had confessed to masterminding the plot to gain media attention and earn points for Karen, who'd assured the police she had no knowledge of their prank. Fortunately, they believed her, or she might be cooling her fanny behind bars.

Charlie had fussed inside Burger King to draw attention. When the manager followed them outside to the parking lot, Peter handed him a napkin with the words: *We've been kidnapped.*

Later that night after the boys had fallen asleep, Thomas explained he'd be spending the night in the car, waiting for their stalker to pay a visit. Karen shivered. To ease her fears, he wrapped his arm over her shoulder and felt immediate longing for the woman who'd never be his. "I'll sneak outside after midnight. Earlier today I took the bulb out of the dome light in the Volkswagen so no one will see me opening the door."

Karen leaned into him. He pulled her closer and filled his lungs with her scent. His heart swelled with emotions; a possessive feeling took hold. Though he knew better, in his mind, she was already his. A crock of bull, he assured himself because he was a sensible man, someone who knew what he wanted and what he didn't want. In this case, that meant babies. He'd pass on that so-called joyful experience. *Even if he had a change of heart, it was too late.*

"Keep the door locked and put my phone next to the bed. If you hear a commotion outside, call the police."

She raised frightened eyes. "Keep the phone with you. If you spot the stalker, call for help."

"I'm not giving the bastard a chance to escape. If he comes near the motor home, I'll jump him and make sure he stays put until the police arrive."

"I'll worry about you."

"The guy's puny and a head shorter than I am." Thomas figured he could easily restrain the man.

She stretched on tiptoes and kissed his cheek, her firm breasts beneath her cotton blouse, brushing his chest. His pulse skipped a beat. "That's not much of a kiss for a man ready for battle." Instead of having a comical ring as he'd intended, his tone was deep and sensual.

A seductive smile lifted the corners of her mouth. She wrapped her arms around his neck and angled her lips against his. Her tongue slid into his mouth. A while later with a hard-on that wouldn't quit, Thomas crept from the Winnebago, erotic images dancing in his head.

A tired-looking Thomas and the smell of fresh perked

coffee greeted Karen the next morning. Thomas frowned. "I'll try again tonight. He's bound to show up sooner or later."

"Maybe I should take a turn waiting in the car."

"Not on your life. It's too dangerous." He poured coffee into a cup and handed it to her. "Anyway, it's important you stay with the children."

Later that morning while Thomas slept and the children sat in front of the television watching cartoons, Karen called her mother, who answered on the second ring and uttered an almost unperceivable gasp.

"Mother, what's wrong?"

Silence preceded a long-suffering moan. "I've been to a doctor for my migraines. Ever since I saw the picture of you in the paper, clad in a scrap of nylon, hanging onto that man like a dog in heat, my head has been splitting."

Karen's heart twisted with a familiar ache.

"If that wasn't bad enough, there's another photo of you with turkeys on your posterior, posing for the camera, your behind in the air. Where's your pride?" Her mother continued in a hysterical tone, "Just when your father convinces me it can't get any worse, I see you on the news being carted off to jail in handcuffs like a common criminal."

"That was a mistake," Karen explained, her erratic pulse drumming in her ears.

"Some mistake! I'll never again be able to face my colleagues or our relatives."

"Once the contest is over, the gossip will die down."

"That can't happen soon enough to suit me. Meanwhile, the pain in my head won't quit."

Hot tears rimmed Karen's eyes. "Mother, I wish I could help you."

"My health is in your hands. Quit the contest this minute,

and show the world you're better than the image you've portrayed."

Karen wanted to explain she was doing this for her parents and that she planned to give them the Winnebago as a surprise, anniversary present. Suddenly Karen realized that wasn't the only reason.

For once, she was standing up to her mother. In a confident tone that rivaled how she felt, Karen said, "I'm sorry you feel that way . . ." She tightened her trembling fingers around the phone. "But I won't quit."

The line went dead.

Late that night Thomas crept toward the Volkswagen. He inched the door open and settled his long legs under the steering wheel. As if his limbs remembered last night's ordeal, his muscles cramped in protest. He stretched his right calf onto the passenger side, leaned his head back, and waited. Sometime later, yawning, he tapped his fingers against the dashboard and tried to stay alert. He'd slept a little during the day, but not enough to feel rested.

Since he didn't want to draw attention to himself, he couldn't listen to the radio. He tried counting backwards from one hundred, and nodded off, jerking awake a moment later when his head dropped to one side. He ran a hand over his eyes and tapped his cheeks with his fingers, hoping to stay vigilant. But as time slowly passed, his eyes closed, and he drifted off to sleep.

He came to with a start and realized he'd been sleeping for almost an hour. The clouds covered the moon and cast the parking lot in darkness. As Thomas squinted toward the Winnebago, he imagined shadowed figures creeping toward the motor home. He rubbed a kink from his neck. A light flicked on inside the kitchen. He spotted Charlie entering the bathroom and leaving a moment later. The light went out. In the distance he heard a door shut and the soft patter of feet approaching the vehicle. But when the noise stopped, he wondered whether he'd imagined it. He tipped his head and heard a soft shuffle, like someone crawling on their knees.

Propelled into action, he yanked open the door and threw himself over the perpetrator. A sharp object jabbed his ribs. Charlie's high-pitched voice rang out. "I come to help you, and I brung my gun."

Thomas stood and pulled the child to his feet before shoving him, his weapon, and a paper bag into the back seat of the car. He considered taking the boy back to the Winnebago, but dismissed the idea. "You need to be quiet."

"Yup."

"How did you know I was out here?"

"I heard you and Karen talking."

"If I leave the car for any reason, lock this door."

"How come?"

"Just do as I say."

"Yup." The kid's voice drilled into Thomas' eardrums.

Thomas glanced over his shoulder. "You should whisper."

"Okay. I loaded all my ping-pong balls into my gun." The volume of his voice intensified with each word.

"Quiet," Thomas said, placing his finger over his mouth and realized his actions were futile in the pitch darkness. "No matter what, don't leave this car unless I say so."

"Yup."

If their stalker was within two miles, he'd heard Charlie's voice and had hightailed it in the opposite direction.

"This is fun," Charlie said, standing and leaning over the

front seat, snapping bubble gum in Thomas' ear. "Would you like a snack?"

"What do you have?"

"I brung some peanut butter crackers and cans of Pepsi."

Thomas' throat was parched. He took the can from Charlie and started to pull the tab.

"Be careful," Charlie warned too late.

Cold drink sprayed over Thomas and the front seat.

"Oops, I might a shook up that can 'cause I like lots of bubbles."

Thomas swore under his breath and was ready to abandon his mission when he spotted the lights of a vehicle about three hundred feet away. The lights went out. He ran a sticky hand over his face and waited. Behind him, Charlie tapped his shoulder, "Is that the Boogie Man?"

"Be very quiet, and we'll know soon enough."

Charlie inhaled a shaky breath. "I wanna go back inside with Peter and Byron."

Thomas couldn't allow the boy to leave the vehicle, or all their efforts would be in vain. "If this isn't our man, I'll tuck you back in bed in a little while."

"Yup." The one syllable quivered with fear.

In the distance a dome light flicked on. Thomas wasn't certain, but he thought the driver had a beard and a long coat.

"It's the Boogie Man," Charlie said, jumping into the front seat. "I'm scared."

"You're a brave kid," Thomas said, hoping to calm the child. "I need your help."

"Yup," he replied, his tone ringing with doubt.

"I'm going to open the door and stay down low, just like you did when you came over here."

"Don't go. I'm scared."

Thomas patted his shoulder. "I've left the window opened

an inch. Once I leave the car, you lock the door. When I shout, 'Now, Charlie,' you pull this switch that'll turn on the high beams. Toot the horn. Karen will come and get you."

"Don't leave me."

"I don't blame you for being frightened, but it's too dangerous for you to come with me. I need you to do as I say."

As Thomas opened the door and knelt beside the car, Charlie scooted to the driver's seat.

"If anyone other than me approaches this car, you toot that horn with all your might."

"Yup, and I'll shoot him with my gun."

"Don't open the window or the door." Thomas hated abandoning the child, but he had no choice. He crept toward the motor home, throwing an occasional glance over his shoulder at the Volkswagen.

He spotted a wavering flashlight beam approaching and heard raspy breathing. For the first time he realized he'd put Karen and the boys in grave danger. The man could be armed with a knife or a gun. Thomas would never forgive himself if . . .

Focusing on the man gaining ground, he hid behind the Winnebago and flattened himself against the vinyl siding. Muscles tightened as he pounced on the stalker.

"Now, Charlie," he shouted.

The horn tooted, lights came on. As Thomas yanked the culprit to his feet, a volley of ping-pong balls rained over them.

Chapter Twenty-Five

Karen dashed outside with Peter. She recognized Barney, Floyd's employee, a scraggly beard hanging under his chin.

Charlie scurried to Karen's side. "We don't gotta be scared no more."

Barney lowered his head. "I never meant to frighten anyone. I was just doing my job."

Thomas peered threateningly at Barney. "What job is that?"

"I keep tabs on how many hours a day you spend inside the Winnebago."

"You must be exhausted," Thomas said sarcastically.

"As a matter of fact, this is one of the most tiring jobs I've ever done. I sure would like to sit for a spell."

Karen hugged Peter and Charlie to her side. "Make yourself comfortable. Can I get you something to drink?"

Disbelief streaked across Thomas' face. "Don't treat Barney like a guest. He's terrorized us for over a week."

She smiled at the man she loved. "It was all a misunderstanding."

Thomas looked at her as though she'd lost her mind. Karen released her hold on the boys and rested reassuring fingers over Thomas' hand. "Barney didn't mean any harm."

Floyd aimed a foxy grin at Karen. "In all my years I've

never seen such a comeback. Getting those boys to fake a kidnapping was a stroke of genius."

Karen's pupils widened. "But I didn't . . ."

"Don't play innocent with me. Remember who you're talking to. I know a conniving woman when I see one."

Karen swung her gaze toward Thomas. Was that shock or guilt he saw in her brown eyes? Thomas remembered being shoved into a cruiser and how he'd felt sorry for Karen when he'd caught a glimpse of her, looking startled and ready to cry. Had he gone through the humiliation of being frisked for weapons so she'd earn points for the contest? Surely, Karen wouldn't stoop so low.

Floyd plucked an unlit cigar from the corner of his mouth and turned a bright smile at Thomas. "It looks like you're dead in the water. This gal pulled the wool over both our eyes."

"Is Karen winning?" Peter asked, smiling.

Floyd clapped a hand over the granite countertop. "She sure is. You boys did a great job."

Charlie's face split into a wide grin. "I pretended to be scared in Burger King."

Floyd winked. "Your performance deserves a trophy."

Charlie high-fived Peter's hand.

Thomas had explained to the boys about the severity of their actions. They'd hung their heads in shame and assured him they understood. Seeing their smiles grated on his nerves. He waited for Karen to reprimand them.

"I put on my thinking cap," Peter said proudly.

Floyd cupped his fingers over Peter's shoulder. "Your thinking cap would come in handy at my dealership."

"I thought I stood little chance of beating Thomas," Karen finally said, not addressing the issue about the boys. Her priorities were clear to Thomas.

"The fake kidnapping's been played across the country along with some overseas stations. You're winning by a landslide."

"Oh," she said, a trace of victory in her tone. As if in afterthought, she frowned at the boys. "Wipe those grins off your faces. What you guys did was very wrong."

To Thomas, her comment didn't ring true.

Floyd turned to the boys. "These kids deserve a reward for a job well done. Here's twenty bucks for each of you."

Cheers rang out, and greedy hands circled the bills. Thomas waited for Karen to tell Floyd where he could put his money. When she didn't instantly react, he swore and stormed out of the Winnebago, disappointment squeezing his gut.

Hearing Floyd's news had knocked Karen off balance. She was winning by a landslide. So why wasn't she doing back flips?

"You can't keep the money," she told the boys once she'd regained her equilibrium.

"Why not?" Peter asked, guilt flickering in his eyes.

"I think you know why."

Peter's gaze avoided hers.

"Yeah, how come?" Charlie asked, his tone challenging.

"You shouldn't be rewarded for doing wrong."

"It's the boys' money," Floyd pointed out. "It's not fair for them to go away empty-handed. If it's wrong for them to profit from their actions, then it must be wrong for you, too."

His comment sliced through her. "I didn't know what the children had in mind."

"The outcome is still the same. You're punishing them while you reap the benefits. Where's the justice in that? Anyway, do what you have to do. Meanwhile, I've scheduled a press conference for four o'clock. Make sure you're bright

234

eyed and bushy tailed, ready to smile for the camera."

Karen felt responsible for the boys' prank. If she hadn't asked for their help, they wouldn't have pulled their hoax. "Boys," she said in a gentle tone, confusion welling inside. "Give Floyd back the money."

Peter did as he was told.

Charlie scrunched up his face. "Gee, that's not fair."

Floyd returned later that afternoon, feeling like a new man. With Thomas out of the picture, his only adversary was Karen, not a worthy opponent for the likes of him. Karen's main weakness was her conscience, not a condition that afflicted him. He grinned and hurried into the Winnebago, spotting Thomas sitting on the couch with his dog. Floyd looked around. "I expected to find your bags packed and ready to go."

Thomas made a crude comment.

Floyd threw back his head and laughed. "Now that would be a trick and half."

Karen came out of the bedroom with the boys, dressed in neat clothes, their hair slicked back. The discord between the couple was palpable. Pleasure blossomed in Floyd's chest.

"I'll wait outside," Thomas said a moment later, not sparing Karen a glance.

Floyd's shriveled heart swelled joyfully. With a little luck, Thomas would leave, then Karen would follow suit. The Winnebago would be his. Of course, he'd take them to small claims court to pay for the damages. He'd end up with the motor home along with thousands of dollars in free advertising. Whoever coined the expression *life sucks* had never walked in his shoes.

Guilt gnawed at Karen's conscience, marring the thought

of a potential victory. How could she smile at the reporters when she'd benefited from the children's wrongdoing?

"So how's it feel to be trailing?" a reporter asked Thomas.

He beamed a cocky grin. "I'm not worried."

Reporters directed their microphones at him. "Are you surprised Karen outwitted you?"

He shrugged. "Nothing surprises me any more."

"Have you strategized your next move?"

Thomas struck a calm pose. "I have a few tricks up my sleeve."

Charlie went to stand next to Thomas and smiled up at the reporters.

"What do you have to say for yourself, young man? It's because of your actions that Thomas is losing."

Charlie's lower lip curled. "I don't wanna have Thomas lose."

Thomas rested his hand over the boy's shoulder and faced the reporters. "Karen and I are playing this game, and I won't have you guys making the children feel bad about who's winning or losing. The contest isn't over yet." He flicked a quick glance at Karen, making it clear he wasn't quitting, then turned his attention back to the child. "And if I do lose the Winnebago to Karen, it won't be because of anything you've done. Don't worry about the contest. It isn't your problem."

Charlie cast a watery smile at Thomas. "I wanna see both you and Karen win."

Thomas grinned at the gathering crowd. "No matter the outcome, Karen walks away a winner. According to the tabloids, what woman in her right mind wouldn't want to spend four glorious weeks with a hunk like me."

Laughter broke out.

"What's a hunk?" Charlie asked.

"It's what you and your brothers are going to be when you grow up."

That said, he sidled next to Karen and planted a kiss on her unsuspecting mouth. Cameras flashed. She jerked away and shoved him hard. Thomas made a show of losing his balance, his thousand-watt-smile aimed at the crowd. "This little lady could knock any man off his feet."

The crowd roared.

A while later inside the Winnebago, Floyd pulled a cigar from his shirt pocket. "Thomas, you're a natural born actor. You never broke a sweat in front of the reporters. But you can't fool me. How's it feel to be treading water with your feet in cement flippers?"

"Cement flippers will either drown me or make me stronger. I'm not giving up."

Floyd smiled through his disappointment. Thomas' cell phone rang so he excused himself and moved several feet away. "When? Will she be all right?"

Floyd saw the anguish on Thomas' face.

"The hell with the contest," Thomas said a moment later, his voice catching. "I'll be there as soon as I can." He flipped his phone shut. "My sister's been rushed to the hospital with a ruptured appendix. I need to be there when she wakes up from surgery. I'm taking the Volkswagen." As if in afterthought, he glanced at Floyd with bleak eyes. "I'll make arrangements to have the car returned tomorrow."

Floyd estimated it would take at least three hours to reach Maine, longer in heavy traffic.

"According to Barney, you've spent only nine hours today inside the motor home. There's no way you can return by eleven. If you leave now . . ."

Without a word Thomas strode past him. He stopped in

front of Karen and the boys. "Promise me you won't give up. I don't mind losing to you, but I don't want to lose to Floyd."

He rushed out the door, jumped into the vehicle, and drove away. Although Floyd felt some compassion for Thomas, he was thrilled only Karen remained. He sighed and sneaked a peek at her hooters. "It's a damn shame Thomas won't be able to finish the contest," he said, not meaning a word.

Teary eyed, she sniffed several times. "Can't you make an exception and allow Thomas to return in the morning? He could make up the time tomorrow."

She was a weak, softhearted broad. Floyd frowned and spoke in his practiced, sympathetic voice. "According to my lawyer, I can't bend the rules."

"Is Thomas' sister really sick?" Peter asked.

"Yes."

"Thomas looked sad when he left," Charlie said.

"He's very worried." Karen brushed a strand of hair from the child's forehead.

Peter moved close to Karen and reached for her hand. "I got an idea. Why don't we go to the hospital, too?"

"Yeah, why not?" Charlie asked.

Karen bit the inside of her mouth. "I've only driven the Winnebago once, and that was a horrible experience."

"You did drive very slow," Peter pointed out.

"And you almost hit a truck," Charlie added.

Peter laughed at the memory. "The back wheels were on the sidewalk. Thomas was shouting for people to take cover."

"Thomas never asked me to drive again," Karen said with a sigh.

The woman had nice boobs but no guts, Floyd thought to himself. She didn't stand a chance against the proprietor of the most publicized RV dealership in New England.

Chapter Twenty-Six

After Floyd left, Karen closed her eyes and pictured her parents' faces when she handed them the keys to the Winnebago. Would she be disappointed again? Her parents had never intended to have children. She'd been their little mistake, the one blemish on their otherwise perfect life. Growing up, Karen had felt like an outsider. Even as an adult, she craved their attention, the need to belong. This might be her last chance to tighten their bond. *She needed to win the Winnebago.*

As a teenager, she'd gone to extremes so they'd notice her. Getting good ranks had never raised an eyebrow, so she'd resorted to more desperate tactics. The tattoo of a tiny yellow butterfly on the small of her back had incited a riot in their household. But she'd succeeded in getting a rise from her parents. The day Karen pranced through the living room, her navel adorned with a jeweled belly button ring, her mother had taken to her bed for the entire weekend.

She couldn't risk losing the motor home to Thomas. Even if she did go after him, there was no guarantee he'd leave his sister's bedside to finish the contest. Although Peter and Charlie peeked at her with questioning glances, she pretended not to notice until Charlie jumped to his feet and settled himself next to her.

"So, are we gonna go?"

"No," she said and watched Peter frown.

"But it's not fair." Charlie bounced on the cushion.

"This is a contest. I don't have to be fair."

Charlie's lower lip curled. "I don't care 'bout the contest. I wanna go get Thomas."

"It's not going to happen," she said in a firm tone, hoping he'd drop the subject.

"You're just saying that 'cause you're 'fraid a drivin'."

"That's not the only reason."

"Cluck, cluck," Charlie said, tucking his hands in his armpits, and flapping his arms like wings. Peter jumped to his feet and started clucking too. Byron followed suit. Soon all three boys were strutting in front of her, clucking and giggling. She smiled. "I admit it. I'm a chicken. Are you satisfied?"

Peter stopped dancing and slipped his hand in hers. "If you change your mind about driving, we'll be your co-pilots."

"You don't understand," she said, not sure she understood. "I need to win this contest."

"Floyd said Thomas could never catch up."

"We can't believe anything Floyd says."

"Thomas didn't leave us behind when he got the chance. If he hadn't come back in the helicopter, we'd have already lost."

"I know that." Guilt gnawed away at her.

"We should give Thomas a chance." Charlie's sharp tone drilled into her overloaded brain.

"My mom says one good turn deserves another," Peter added.

She steeled herself against their arguments and her own misgivings. She needed to look out for herself, or no one else would, a fact instilled during her less than perfect childhood.

Thomas huddled in the hospital waiting room with Joe, his nerves taut, and his hands clammy. He rested his elbows on his knees, and laced his fingers together. "What's taking so long?"

Tension creased Joe's features as he thumbed through a National Geographic Magazine and stared blankly out the window. "I'll ask the nurse to check again."

Thomas glanced at his watch. It was almost 10:30. "It's only been twenty minutes since she spoke to us."

"It sure seems longer than that." Joe stood up and started pacing across the room. Six steps one way and six steps back until Thomas lost count. "Sit down. You're making me dizzy." Thomas wondered whether his other brother knew about Suzie's operation. "Did you get hold of Paul?"

"Yes, he wanted to take the next plane out, but I persuaded him to stay put. I promised I'd call him the instant we heard from the doctor." Joe dropped into the chair opposite Thomas and broke into a smile. "Suzie sure kept life interesting. Remember the time she climbed the oak out back and refused to come down?"

Thomas had been at his wits' end. But he could smile about it now. "She was afraid I'd warm her behind with dad's belt."

"She knew you wouldn't hit her. You were just a big bag of wind, always threatening us and never following through."

Thomas ran a finger over the day's growth of beard. "A bag of wind, is that how you kids saw me?"

"When you started hollering at us, we'd tune you out."

"I'd see the blank looks on your faces and shout louder."

"All that matters is that you kept us together."

Thomas heard soft rubber soles coming their way and tried to prepare himself for the news, good or bad. Without a word, a nurse continued past the waiting room. Thomas glanced at his watch. Only two minutes had passed. A doctor in scrubs entered the waiting room. "You the O'Leary brothers?"

A stone settled in Thomas' stomach. For what seemed like an eternity, he waited for the doctor to speak. Fearing the worst, he tried to read something into the man's sober expression. Earlier today Thomas' biggest concern had been how he'd regain the lead in a senseless contest. His priorities had since changed. He no longer gave a damn about Floyd or the Winnebago.

The doctor leaned against the door casing. "It was a close call, but your sister should be fine."

Joe blew out a long breath. A weight lifted from Thomas' shoulders.

"She'll be in recovery for another forty-five minutes. We're keeping her in intensive care overnight. You'll be allowed to visit for five minutes every hour. But your sister needs her rest. Once you've seen her, go home and get some sleep."

Joe staked claim to a chair by the window. Determined to remain until dawn, Thomas stood and shook the doctor's hand. "Thank you."

After the doctor left, Thomas strolled across the room and looked through the rain-splattered window down at the wet parking lot. Hazy halos around the streetlights reflected in the puddles, giving the night an eerie glow. He heard footsteps behind him, felt a hand on his shoulder.

"Thomas."

At the sound of Karen's voice, his heartbeat quickened. He turned. Dark rings circled her eyes. Fatigue lined her face. He saw Joe watching them with interest.

"Where are the children?" Thomas asked, surprised how calm he sounded. Knowing Karen had come for him meant a lot.

"Barney's watching them."

"Why are you here?" he asked, still not believing his eyes.

She shook her head as though unsure. "You have only fifteen minutes left before you lose the contest. If you hurry, you can still make it."

Though tempting, he considered the offer for only a moment. "I'm not going anywhere until I've seen my sister."

Joe interrupted. "The doctor said Suzie would be fine."

Thomas sent him a mind-your-own-business look.

"You could come back after midnight," his brother continued, avoiding Thomas' gaze. "There's no sense you losing out on the contest. You've put too much effort into it already."

Ignoring him, Thomas circled his fingers around Karen's elbow and felt a sharp sense of awareness. "I appreciate you giving me this chance, but I'm going to have to turn you down."

Karen wagged her finger under his nose. "You can't turn me down. I've spent the longest four and half hours of my life, maneuvering the Winnebago over the pitch dark roads with boys clucking every time I eased my foot off the gas!"

With Karen trailing by several yards, Thomas dashed into the Winnebago and was greeted by Charlie and Peter. Barney was stretched out on the couch, cell phone in one hand, tablet and pen in the other.

"Bet you're surprised to see us," Peter said.

Bear and Charlie ran to Thomas' side. The dog pushed its muzzle against Thomas' hand, wanting to be scratched. Thomas rubbed his fingers through the dog's thick coat.

"Karen drove us here," Charlie said. "Guess what? We almost knocked over a light pole."

Peter rolled his eyes. "And it wasn't our fault the dumb

State of Maine didn't make the bridge tall enough for our satellite dish to go under."

"I see." Thomas reached in the cupboard for a dog treat. Bear scarfed up the bone, then stretched out on the floor under the table.

Barney jotted numbers on a piece of paper. "I hope you appreciate what Karen went through to save your behind."

"Behind means butt." Charlie sent Karen an impish grin.

Karen frowned. "It's late. I want you and Peter to get ready for bed."

Peter looked over at Thomas. "Will you be here tomorrow morning when we wake up?"

"That'll depend on Suzie's condition."

The boys hurried toward the bedroom with the dog and cat at their heels, giggling and shutting the door. Barney limped across the room and opened the refrigerator. He helped himself to a slice of blueberry pie and a glass of milk, sat at the table and dug in with gusto. He must have caught Thomas' look of dismay because he smiled timidly.

"Karen said for me to make myself at home. I'm hoping Karen wins, not just because of this pie, which is the best I've ever tasted, but because she's a woman with a big heart." Karen's smile widened. Barney forked a large bite into his mouth. He chewed a moment. "Spending nights in my car has put my back out of whack. In the morning I've had trouble standing straight."

Thomas scowled. "Spying on people is a rough occupation."

Barney missed the sarcasm. "It certainly is. In this weather, the dampness settles into my bones."

"What a shame," Thomas said.

Karen slid a piece of pie into a plate. "That's why I insisted Barney spend the night in here. You can sleep on the couch,

Barney will take the bed over the table."

Barney flashed blueberry stained teeth at Thomas. "Me and you are going to be bunkmates."

Thomas pulled Karen aside. "You can't trust Barney. Who knows what he's going to tell Floyd."

Her forehead furrowed. "I don't know what I'd have done if Barney hadn't volunteered to come along. We were stuck in a traffic jam and he knew of a shortcut. If it weren't for him, I wouldn't have arrived in time."

"How long is he staying?"

"Just for tonight."

Karen was one special lady, always looking for the good in people, always willing to give a person a second chance. "I owe you," he said, taking her hand and smiling.

"I'd say we're even."

"Did the boys mention something about you knocking over a light?"

Her cheeks turned pink. "The utility pole is crooked but still standing."

"And the satellite dish?"

"It didn't fare quite as well."

The next morning, Floyd's face flushed crimson. "From a distance I spotted a small ding on the motor home. Because it's cloudy, I thought it was a shadow, but look at this mess."

Karen inspected the rear fender and the twisted bumper. "It didn't look that bad last night."

A strangled sound emerged between Floyd's lips. His eyes looked ready to explode from their sockets. "By the time you win, this piece of machinery won't be worth jack shit. Tell you what I'm willing to do. I'll give you two thousand bucks if you pack up and leave this morning."

While he sputtered, she stole a quick glance at the satellite dish above them, cocked at a strange angle. Last night as she'd inched the Winnebago under a bridge, she heard metal scraping, which became a loud thump once they cleared the stone structure. She pulled into the breakdown lane, dashed around back, and aimed the flashlight beam at the satellite dish hanging over the back by one thin wire. She heaved the apparatus onto the top of roof where it remained perched. Fortunately Floyd hadn't noticed it yet.

"You could do a lot with that kind of money."

"Thomas can't catch up. I'd be a fool to take your offer."

"Stranger things have happened," he said, grinning slyly.

Chapter Twenty-Seven

Thomas slid into the chair beside his sister's hospital bed and laced his fingers through hers. To his left a bleep on the green screen monitored her heartbeat. Clear fluids dripped from a bag into a long plastic tube through a needle into Suzie's arm. He studied the slow rise and fall of her chest, listened to the soft sigh she uttered as she stretched and was alarmed to see her grimace in pain. He hurt right along with her and if it were possible, would have gladly traded places. He traced the pad of his thumb over her knuckles.

After a moment her eyelids fluttered open. Looking confused, she licked her parched lips and glanced around the room. She attempted a weak smile. "I hurt all over."

"The nurses said you'd be sore for a while." She nodded, and her eyes drifted shut. He didn't want to lose the connection.

"Can I get you something, anything?"

"Water," she whispered.

He picked up the glass and placed the straw into her mouth.

With effort she sucked in a few drops. "I'm glad you came." The few words drained her, and soon she fell back to sleep.

"I'm not leaving," Thomas told Joe a moment later.

"Suzie's going to be fine."

"I want to be near in case she needs me."

Joe clamped a firm hand over Thomas' shoulder. "If there's any change in her condition, I'll call you."

"No amount of money can take the place of my family."

"You raised us to never give up. I think there's more brewing than you want to admit. I think you're afraid to be around Karen." Joe slipped a dollar bill in the soda machine and punched in his selection.

"You're out of your mind."

"I saw the way you and Karen looked at each other. What's going on between you two?"

"Nothing." *Everything.*

"Hah."

"We'll never be more than friends. She wants children and I don't."

Joe issued an exasperated groan. "Don't give me that crap again about how you've already raised a family." He shook his head. "We were teenagers. I know we gave you a hard time, but we hated you bossing us around."

Joe's tone had risen dramatically, and Thomas noticed a man in a dark suit listening to their conversation. He took his brother by the elbow and moved several feet away in hopes of talking privately. "I didn't want to be in charge."

"You sure acted like you enjoyed shouting orders."

"For a while I was on a power trip," he said.

Joe's freckled face split into a grin. "Through it all, we stuck together, and we turned out all right. Anyway, a newborn wouldn't give you all that flack."

"Babies grow up to be teenagers." Thomas' tone should have ended the subject.

Joe didn't take the hint. "You're a stubborn jackass. Given the chance you could still end up with a baby in your arms."

"You know that's not possible." Certain he'd never want

children, Thomas had taken care of the matter. Now he suspected he'd made a whopper of a mistake.

"Check with your doctor. Men have vasectomies reversed all the time. Suzie's emergency surgery proves you should live life to the fullest because you never know if there's a tomorrow."

Thomas could no longer ignore the truth; he loved Karen and desperately wanted to spend the rest of his life with her. Unfortunately, he couldn't ask her to give up her dreams of having her own babies. *But maybe there was a chance . . .*

When Thomas turned, he saw the man in the dark suit, a few feet behind him, jotting notes in a small tablet. The man jerked his head up and made eye contact then took off at a gallop.

"How's your sister?" Peter asked later that morning, biting into a donut.

"The nurses have gotten her up already. She's being transferred to another room," Thomas replied, finally believing his sister would recover.

"Does that mean you're finishing the contest with us?" Peter swallowed the last of his glazed donut.

"I'll let you know in a little while. First I need to speak to Karen."

Karen glanced at him with a questioning look. "Why don't you boys finish up and go play in the bedroom."

"Can we use your phone to call our mother?" Peter asked.

Thomas threw his phone at Peter who caught it. "Thanks."

"I'm gonna tell mama all 'bout hitting the pole last night. I'm also gonna tell mama I miss her." Charlie licked jelly from his lips and led the way down the hall. Soon the sounds of the children's voices echoed from the bedroom.

Karen refilled their cups with coffee and sat down at the table across from Thomas. "What's up?"

"During the night, I had lots of time to reevaluate my priorities. I'm sick and tired of doing Floyd's bidding, of looking like a fool in the newspapers. I've been portrayed as a hotheaded jerk, a child abuser, and a kidnapper."

She traced the rim of her coffee cup with her index finger. "The contest has been a lot rougher than I'd expected, but we only have a little more than a week left."

He leaned back in the chair and stretched his right leg under the table. "With the press following our every move, it could be one hell of a long nine days." He leaned forward and circled his chin with tan fingers.

She could smell his spicy aftershave. Her senses prickled with desire. "What are you saying?"

"I don't want to compete any more. I want us to join forces, sell the Winnebago, then split the money."

She jerked back in her chair. "You must think I'm stupid. I racked up lots of points when the kidnapping story hit the overseas news."

"Other stories might be covered by the media here and abroad. Who's to say I won't catch up? From the start, I've been a strong competitor."

He had a point. Floyd's offer of two thousand dollars hadn't tempted her, but half the price of the motor home did. "I'm not saying I'm even considering it, but I doubt we could team up even if we wanted. We signed a contract with Floyd."

"According to my attorney, the paperwork we signed never stipulated we couldn't work together. The contract states the person responsible for obtaining the most publicity for Floyd's RVs wins. Nothing in the contract says we need to compete for thirty days, only that we have to remain inside the Winnebago for ten hours daily for a month."

"I've watched enough reality shows on television to know I shouldn't trust you. What if you're trying to trick me?"

"You have my word. There can only be one winner, and you'll be that person. If you agree to what I've suggested, I won't compete. You'll claim the prize, and it'll be up to you whether you follow through and share the money with me. You can't lose. Otherwise I'm going to do my best to beat the pants off you."

A rush of heat washed over her at his choice of words. His mouth lifted in a cocky grin, letting her know he was aware of his phrasing. Was he merely flirting or keeping her off balance? He leaned closer. She saw the sincerity in his eyes. She wanted to believe him, but could she? Thomas' voice mellowed, its deep timbre weakening her resolve, making her believe every word.

"Are you willing to throw away a sure thing in exchange for a long shot?"

Floyd's face twisted in rage. Just who did Thomas and Karen think they were? The uppity bastards planned to team up.

"No one screws with me and gets away with it."

Thomas spoke in a shitty, calm voice that aggravated Floyd even more. "You've already gained world-wide attention for your dealership. You're in a win-win situation."

"You're reneging on our agreement," he said, pointing a finger of blame at Thomas. "Karen, I'm shocked you'd stoop so low. You've always held a special place in my heart. I'm begging you to reconsider. If my business goes down the tubes, my employees will lose their jobs."

Her eyebrows arched. "I've put my parents through enough."

Floyd could have spit out bolts of lightning. "Mark my word, you'll regret this."

251

Instead of quaking in her shoes, she swung around and climbed into the Winnebago followed by Thomas. They'd pay for crossing him. His day that had started out in the toilet could only improve. The Winnebago shot out from its parking space. From the corner of his eye, he caught a glimpse of something hurling toward him. He ducked and felt the breeze from the satellite dish as it flew past his head and landed at his feet.

Thomas eyed the boys in the rearview mirror. "I've made reservations at Moose Lodge on Moosehead Lake. We've already spent over eight hours inside the Winnebago, and since it's a long drive, we'll easily make our ten-hour quota."

Karen threw a glance over her shoulder. "But first we're going to visit your mother."

"Yippees," rang out in triplicate.

"Mama's gotta surprise for us." Charlie kicked his feet and bounced on the seat cushion.

"I asked her what it was, but she said we'd have to wait until we saw her," Peter added. "Are we almost there?"

Byron clapped his hands and chanted, "Poop head, poop head, poop head."

Charlie cupped his hands over his mouth and giggled. "I'm gonna tell mama I saw big boobies on TV."

The boys were trying to yank Karen's chain. By her startled expression, Thomas knew they'd succeeded.

"Remember your mother's going to ask whether you've been good," Thomas reminded them.

Peter wrapped a protective arm around his younger brothers. "It doesn't matter 'cause mom loves us no matter what we do."

When Karen pointed to a green apartment building, Thomas maneuvered the motor home along the curb. Hand in hand they walked into the complex. Thomas felt a sizzle clear to his toes. Karen fired up his libido with a simple glance or a warm smile.

With Karen and Thomas at their heels, the boys charged into the living room where Abby sat with her leg propped up on a recliner. Thomas grabbed hold of Byron's collar, or he'd have jumped onto his mother's lap.

Tears flooding her eyes, Abby turned toward her sons and ran anxious fingers over their faces, leaning forward to plant kisses on their cheeks. "I've missed you boys so much."

"We missed you, too," Peter said.

"I missed you more," Charlie added.

"Did not."

"Did too."

As if afraid she'd disappear, Byron wrapped his fingers tightly around his mother's wrist. While the boys leaned into Abby, Karen made the introductions.

"I can't thank you two enough for taking such good care of my sons," Abby said, smiling at the children.

"They're good kids." Thomas sounded as though he'd enjoyed having them around.

Abby's usually disheveled hair was neat, Karen noticed. There were no stains on her blouse, and she'd taken the time to apply a little lipstick and makeup.

"You look rested," Karen told her friend.

"I wish I could say the same for you," Abby said with a knowing smile before turning back to her sons. "What have you been up to?"

"All sorts of stuff," Charlie said.

"Karen almost got the Winnebago stuck under a bridge," Peter said.

"And the roof scraped real loud," Charlie added. "But I wasn't scared."

"I've missed you guys so much. I want to hear about all your adventures."

Peter swung his arms animatedly. "We went to the beach. Thomas got mad at a reporter."

Charlie dragged his hands from his nostrils to his chest. "Blood came from the man's nose, down all over his shirt."

Peter elbowed Charlie aside and moved closer to his mother. "I thought Thomas was going to jail. But he didn't, and then we went on rides and had a good time until we had our pictures taken with our butts in the air and turkeys on our swim trunks."

Abby's eyes danced with merriment. "Wow."

Peter continued. "Then we went on a real helicopter ride."

"The blades went whomp, whomp, whomp over my head. We had to run like this," Charlie said, dashing bent at the waist across the room and back again. "It was lots of fun."

"We got arrested, too," Peter said.

Charlie's eyes widened. "Karen and Thomas had real handcuffs on their wrists, and we got rides in real police cars, and I got to press the siren."

Laughing, Abby wiped tears of joy from her face. "I'm sure glad to hear you guys had a good time."

"We had a television dish and instead of cartoons, we watched people with no clothes on," Charlie added, cupping his hands inches from his chest and glanced over his shoulder at Karen, who threw him a warning look. "I can't say the bad word, but they were real big."

Abby ruffled his hair and kissed his forehead. Charlie traced his fingers over Abby's cast. "Is your boo boo getting better?"

"I'll be in a cast for at least another month."

"Does that mean we can't live at home for a long, long time?" Peter asked, sniffing.

"Yesterday the doctor put a walking cast on my leg."

Both Peter and Charlie locked eyes with their mother. Abby swung her arms victoriously. "It means I can start taking care of you again."

Chapter Twenty-Eight

When Karen heard they were spending the night in Greenville, Maine, she'd expected a rustic cabin, not a large two-story structure with wrap-around porch, surrounded by wildflowers. Behind the log structure, grassy fields dotted with white pine and hemlock bordered a lake. A moment later Thomas gave the clerk their names and signed the register. While he was talking to the woman behind the desk, an elderly man wearing dark trousers, a white shirt, and a bow tie crossed the wide pine floor. "Welcome to Moose Lodge, Miss." Wisps of white hair stuck out from the sides of an otherwise bald head. Bushy eyebrows hung over warm gray eyes. "Follow me, Miss," he said, taking her suitcase.

Karen considered waiting for Thomas but since he'd been very quiet on the ride, she decided to go on ahead. They rode the elevator to the second floor and continued down a well-lit corridor. The old man opened a thick oak door and stepped aside for her to enter, setting her bag near the chair. He pointed down the hall. "If you get hungry, there's a pantry with a fully stocked refrigerator. 'Deer Crossing' is one of our most popular rooms because of the feather mattress in the four-poster bed and the hot tub in the private bath, guaranteed to warm your body, heart, and soul."

Had Thomas known the boys were about to bail out, he

wouldn't have ordered the bouquet of flowers for Karen's room or the lodge's finest bottle of champagne. While the children slept in the bedroom, he'd wanted to sit under a starlit sky with Karen on their balcony, holding hands and kissing. He'd looked forward to spending this evening together away from the Winnebago without worrying about the situation getting out of hand. Unfortunately, life never went as planned.

He stared out his window at the fog-enshrouded sky, rain pelting the pane of glass. Thunder rumbled in the distance. No children, no stars, nothing to do but spend a night in a bedroom next to Karen's, the adjoining door the only barrier. *Two measly inches of wood.* His room, *The Loon's Nest*, would be more appropriately named the Loony Bin. By dawn he'd go mad. He wanted Karen with an intensity that frightened him. For one night, he'd wanted to make believe Karen was his, to pretend they were alone, and to steal a few kisses as they sat on in the wicker lounge overlooking the sparkling water. Unfortunately, there were no children to run interference.

His throat grew parched, and he ran his tongue between his lips. He needed to keep his distance. After dinner he'd walk Karen to her door, plead exhaustion, then run for his life.

Karen inhaled a reinforcing deep breath and knocked on the adjoining door. For a moment her heart stilled. Thomas swung open the door and looked down at her as if something was terribly wrong. She wanted to throw herself in his arms, to hold him and never let him go. Instead she stepped back and watched him amble across the room and look out the glass doors to the balcony.

"You seem upset," she said, waiting for an explanation.

"I'm fine. Just tired."

"I know it's more than that."

Frowning, he turned to face her. "It's supposed to rain all night and tomorrow morning, too."

She nodded. "Why are you changing the subject?"

His Adam's apple bobbed up and down. "The dining room is open until eight. Did you want to go now or later?" he asked, focusing a moment on the rain-swept landscape.

"It doesn't matter."

He wore dark trousers and a white shirt unbuttoned at the neck. Thomas stood less than ten feet away in her bedroom. All Karen could think about was unbuttoning his shirt to his waist and running her fingers over his chest. His heated gaze swept over her, almost scorching the thin material of her dress before lingering on her mouth. "You look very pretty." He stepped a little closer.

Her breath lodged in her throat. "Thanks. And I loved your flowers and the champagne. Well, I don't know if I like the champagne because I haven't tasted it yet, but I'm sure it'll be good." She was rambling but couldn't seem to stop.

"Perhaps we can share a toast later."

"That might not be a good idea," he replied.

Asking what he meant wasn't necessary. She felt the undercurrent drawing them closer.

"Do you like the room?" he asked, taking another step.

"Yes, it's fine." She moved toward him. Her lungs constricted, making breathing almost impossible. As if in slow motion, she watched him circle his arms around her waist. She felt warm and safe. His touch set off a riot of emotions. *I love you*, she thought, wanting to share her feelings with him. Without thinking, she added, "The bed has a feather mattress." His blue eyes darkened several shades. She slid her tongue over her lower lip. "I've never slept on a feather mattress."

258

"If we don't leave this instant, you won't be sleeping on this one either."

"Oh." The sound came out in a choked whisper.

"Ever since we dropped the boys off, I've been consumed with thoughts of making love to you. I know we shouldn't. It's not fair to you . . ."

A shiver skittered down her spine. He dropped a feather light kiss on her forehead, the side of her face and lingered on her mouth a moment, gently nibbling on her lower lip. "Tell me to leave, and I will." His gaze traveled over her face like a warm caress.

All she had to do was say no. She didn't even have to say the word, just turn and start toward the door. Although Thomas wasn't offering her happily ever after, she wanted to be with him more than she'd thought possible. In that instant, she made her decision. If she couldn't have him forever, then at least he'd be hers tonight. She traced the side of his face with her index finger and looked into his eyes.

"I want you to make love to me," she said, "and come morning, I'll have no regrets."

He crushed her against him and captured her mouth in a kiss that wrenched a moan from her throat and dashed away any lingering doubts. As his tongue mated with hers, she ran her fingers through his hair, drawing him closer, filling her lungs with his masculine scent. She felt his erection straining against his trousers. Knowing she was responsible for his condition sent a shiver of awareness through her body. With infinite gentleness, he unzipped her dress and slid it over her shoulders. The green silk puddled on the floor.

"I've dreamed about seeing you like this." His appreciative gaze swept over her partially clad body before he claimed her mouth and cupped his hand over her right breast. Her nipple puckered against the lacy fabric. He unfastened the clasp on the front of the bra. It too joined the clothes at their feet.

Her fingers trembled when she started to unbutton his shirt, but he brushed her fingers aside and accomplished the task in record time. He threw his shirt across the room, stepped out of his shoes and trousers, and stood in his boxers. As he held her tight and rained kisses over her face and neck, she reached down and ran her fingers over the tented material of his boxer shorts, tracing the length of him. Just for one night, she'd pretend he was hers. Then she'd let him go. For a moment, she questioned her sanity.

Her last rational thoughts shattered when he hooked his thumbs into the waistband of her skimpy panties and slid them down. He scooped her up in his arms and laid her down on the bed, stretching out alongside her. She enjoyed exploring every inch of his hard body. Outside thunder boomed and lightning sliced across the sky as they sank deeper into the feather mattress.

He settled himself over her, and she wrapped her fingers around his erection that swelled on contact. His groan was all the encouragement she needed. He kissed a path to her breast and continued down to her stomach, dipping his tongue into her navel, flicking her belly button ring. He raised his head and spoke in a deep tone. "You're a wicked woman, tormenting me with this small piece of jewelry."

In the growing darkness she saw a sensuous glint in his eyes. He leaned over her and opened a small foil wrapper he'd put on the nightstand. Feeling bold, Karen took the condom from him and unrolled it over his length. She saw the surprise and pleasure on his face. He entered her with one smooth thrust. As they moved to the frantic beat of their hearts, Karen's love for him overwhelmed her.

Waves of pleasure undulated through her body. Shouting

her name, he climaxed, sending her over the edge. Bursting with emotions, she whispered, "I love you, Thomas."

A while later after Thomas' heart rate slowed, he lay next to Karen pondering what she'd said. *I love you, Thomas.* His heart clenched with a certainty he'd done wrong. Karen deserved better than what he was offering. Yet she was a grown woman, old enough to know her own mind, and he hadn't forced himself on her. He still felt troubled. As sure as he'd draw another breath, there'd be a next time. He was not able to stop himself, nor did he want to. Like an addict craving his next fix, he looked forward to the days ahead.

They cuddled together for some time, until Thomas' stomach gave a hungry groan. He glanced at the bedside clock. "I'm starving, and we've missed dinner," he said, sliding a finger over Karen's belly.

She sprinkled light kisses along the base of his neck. "We can get something from the refrigerator down the hall."

Thomas felt complete. He'd found what had been missing in his life. Unfortunately, their time together would soon be over. He instantly shifted his focus because tonight was theirs. He wouldn't allow his concerns to interfere with perfection. Tonight had been perfect, the kind of experience he'd never forget, the kind of experience that had filled his senses and his heart. In a moment of weakness, he heard himself say, "I love you, Karen."

She pulled away a little and looked into his eyes. "I've dreamed of hearing you say those words."

Tell her now. Tell her you can't have children. His lungs constricted. He couldn't bring himself to speak. He wanted to hold onto her for as long as possible.

Looking serious, she ran a finger along his jaw. "What happens to us after the contest ends?"

You'll leave when I tell you the truth. "I figured we'd go out for a few months and get to know each other better."

She glanced down before raising an anxious gaze. "Is there any point in that? You know I want babies."

"Yes," he replied, kissing the top of her head so she wouldn't see the guilt on his face. This was the perfect opportunity to broach the subject.

"You don't want any children," she said, her tone anguished.

"I didn't think I did . . ."

Her eyes lit with hope.

He felt like a heel.

"But now you do."

"Maybe, but . . ."

He was ready to blurt out his ugly secret, but she kissed him senseless.

"Before taking care of the boys, I thought I wanted at least four children, but I've come to my senses," she said with a laugh. "I never realized how much work there was in caring for three small boys."

What if he couldn't give Karen the baby she so desperately wanted? He needed to tell her now, let her know all the facts and decide for herself what she wanted to do.

"I'd be content to have one baby," she finished on a sigh. "I want a boy with blue eyes like yours."

"A little girl would be nice." He imagined himself holding their tiny daughter in his arms. He saw Karen's face in miniature, a perfect bowed mouth, ten fingers and ten toes. His heart clenched at the realization he'd sabotaged his future. What if his vasectomy was irreversible? Then he'd lose Karen for sure, and his dreams would shatter. Gusts of wind rattled the windows. Lightning cut across the sky. The lights flickered, once, twice, then went out.

"We've lost the power. I guess that means you won't be able to cook for me," Thomas said with a growl, hoping to change the subject.

"Just like a man, always thinking about your stomach?"

"A man needs sustenance. If we had electricity, I'd slap your fanny and order you to the pantry for my meal."

He planted a kiss on the tip of her nose.

"I read in the newspaper you packed a gross of condoms."

"So . . . ?" he asked, missing the point.

Her soft laughter tickled the hairs on his chest. "We don't have time to eat."

Chapter Twenty-Nine

Floyd dashed inside Barney's room at the Bangor Motel.

"How did you manage to lose a thirty-nine foot motor home?"

"Sorry, Boss."

Floyd heaved an exasperated sigh. "They're bound to show up. Every newspaperman in Maine is on the lookout for those two lovebirds. I've let the word slip that Karen and Thomas are joining forces." Floyd grinned when he thought of the portable tape player in his briefcase, and the doctored tape guaranteed to knock Karen on her ass. When she ran off, Thomas would follow.

The phone rang. Floyd picked up the receiver. "I've found them," came George's voice.

"Where are they?"

"Do I get the usual bonus?"

Greedy bastard. "Sure, sure, get on with it."

"They're holed up inside Moose Lodge in Greenville."

Floyd's grin widened. "They didn't spend the night in the Winnebago?"

"According to the old man, the couple's been there since six o'clock yesterday."

"I'm on my way."

Sunlight slanted through the lace curtains in the window

when Thomas woke up. He glanced down at Karen curled up next to him, his arm looped over her waist, her breasts pressed against his chest. After the power returned, they'd used the hot tub, drank more champagne, and tumbled into bed, lightheaded and ready to make love again.

For the first time since his parents' death, he felt whole. For years he'd walked around with an empty feeling. Now that he'd found what had been missing in life, he couldn't simply walk away. He needed Karen as much as he needed fresh air. He loved her, but would she stay by him when he told her that he was sterile? Maybe they could work out something. Maybe not.

Peter, Charlie, and Byron had opened his eyes. Though they were capable of stretching any man's patience to its limits, he'd enjoyed playing with them and felt certain he was now better prepared to raise children. He'd changed his mind about having a family of his own.

Would it already be too late?

After feeding Luce and taking the dog for a walk, Thomas returned later that morning with bagels, cream cheese, fruit, assorted pastries, and juice. He'd expected to see Karen sitting up in bed. Instead she called out from the shower. "I'll be out in a sec."

He set the food down on the bed, strolled into the bathroom, and caught a glimpse of her naked body through the rippled glass door. Mesmerized he watched her tip her head and rinse shampoo from her hair. He stripped and stepped into the shower, enjoyed the way her eyes widened when he took the soap from her hand. She stood on tiptoes and kissed him. "I was hoping you'd join me."

He leaned into her and soaping his hand, massaged her breasts. His erection sprang to life. He worked his way over her flat stomach and down her legs, stopping a moment to brush his fingers through the triangle of soft hair at the apex of her legs. As she leaned her head against him, he kissed a path along her neck. Curving his hands over her shoulders, he licked the water droplets from her eyelashes.

"You're beautiful, and I love you," he murmured, seeing the glow in her eyes, feeling like a coward for not telling her the truth, knowing he couldn't put it off much longer.

He put on a condom, cupped her behind, and supported her back against the shower wall. Lifting her over him, he angled his body and slipped inside. All concerns fled when she wrapped her legs around his waist and rode him hard and fast. They climaxed together, and Thomas knew he'd never again be the same.

They clung together until their heartbeats slowed, and they caught their breath. Thomas opened the door to the shower and grabbing a towel, patted Karen dry. He started with her breasts, belly, and legs, then did her shoulders, and started to work his way down when he spotted the yellow butterfly on the small of her back. "You're full of surprises," he said, thinking he'd seen everything there was to see last night.

"Do you like it?"

"I'll never look at another butterfly without getting turned on."

"Wondered whether you two would miss your curfew," Floyd said, shaking his head and pointing to his watch. "Looks like I had nothing to worry about."

"What do you want?" Thomas asked harshly, his tolerance for the man nil.

Karen squeezed Thomas' hand. He flashed her a don't-you-worry grin. Floyd tugged at the briefcase in his hand.

"I've got some news to share, and I didn't want to do it over the phone."

Thomas unlocked the door to the motor home and followed Karen inside. Floyd and Barney joined them. When Thomas flashed a quick glance at Barney, the man ducked his head and studied the laces on his shoes.

"Would anyone like some coffee?" Karen asked, always polite, always kind.

Before Thomas could object, Floyd settled his bulky frame on the couch. "Don't mind if I do."

"None for me," Barney said, looking uncomfortable.

Karen filled the cups and sat opposite Thomas at the table. "So what's this good news you have for us?" she asked.

"In a way it's good, in another way it might be bad." Floyd lifted the cup to his lips and drank.

Thomas frowned. "Get on with it."

"Your patience is shot to hell. You must've had a long night," Floyd said with a snide laugh. "Thomas, you lucky bastard, you're now in the lead."

At first, Thomas didn't grasp what he was saying. It sank in when Karen gasped and covered her mouth with her hands. "That's not possible. I was way ahead."

Floyd crossed one ankle over the other. Thomas sandwiched Karen's right hand between his. "It doesn't matter who wins. We're selling the Winnebago and splitting the money."

Floyd's eyes glazed over. He flashed Thomas a look of victory. Thomas wasn't worried, but he could tell that Karen was.

"Give my points to Karen."

Floyd snickered. "You can walk away now and let her win, but you can't give her your points. Not that I believe for a minute you'd actually do that."

"Karen," Thomas said, tightening his grip on her fingers, urging his strength to flow into her. "You've nothing to be concerned about. Either way, we're splitting the pot."

Floyd cleared his throat. "Mighty touching, but I like Karen too much to allow this charade to continue." Several feet away Barney looked out the window as if afraid of making eye contact. Floyd removed a small tape player from his briefcase. "My conscience has kept me awake at night, and I regret making the deal with you, Thomas, which is why I'm coming clean."

"What deal?" Thomas shook his head.

Floyd pushed the play button. The tape recorder hummed and static crackled for several seconds. Thomas didn't know why he was nervous. He'd done nothing wrong.

"*Thomas,*" came Floyd's voice, "*I can't afford to lose the Winnebago to either of you.*"

"*That's a crying shame.*" Thomas remembered his sarcastic reply. The bastard had proposed a deal. What did Floyd have to gain by playing this tape back now?

"*I'm a sensible man. I know when I'm beat. Losing is bad enough, but I couldn't take losing to a woman.*"

"*I've no intention of losing to a woman.*" Thomas heard his cocky laughter. Her hand stiffened under his touch.

"*But you can't be sure she won't win.*"

"*Give me a break. If all else fails, I'll charm her off her feet. She won't know what hit her.*" The hairs on the back of Thomas' neck lifted uncomfortably. He sounded like a jerk. The conversation had taken place during the first week, when he'd been curled up on the couch like a pretzel, unable to sleep.

"This isn't as bad as it sounds," Thomas said to Karen, confusion clouding her eyes.

More static then Floyd's voice. "*I have a sure fire way for both of us to come out of this on top."*

"What do you have in mind?"

"Wrap that little gal around your finger, sweet talk her sense-less, persuade her not to compete." Thomas heard the sound of Floyd's fist hitting his palm. *"Whammo, when she least expects it, the axe falls. She loses, and me and you split the money from the sale of the Winnebago."*

The conversation had ended with Thomas telling Floyd what he could do with his great idea. Feeling confident, Thomas winked at Karen. Looking startled, she didn't return his smile. A moment later he was shocked to hear himself say, *"You got yourself a deal."*

Chapter Thirty

Karen knew Thomas would never betray her. Feeling sure of herself, she beamed Floyd a confident smile. "You're wasting your time. I don't know how you did it, but I don't believe what I've just heard on that tape."

Floyd looked at her as though she were a moron. "You're so far gone, you can't see the truth right in front of your nose."

Thomas kissed her forehead and turned cold eyes at Floyd. "Leave before I throw you out."

Floyd reached in his briefcase and heaved a handful of tabloid newspapers on the counter. "The public wants to know everything about you. The press is happy to dig deep."

When Floyd left, Karen sat at the table and thumbed through the newspapers. When she reached the last one, she spotted a picture of Thomas and her on the front page. The headline read:

No pitter-patter of little feet for these Lovebirds.

The article went on to explain that Thomas was unable to have children due to a vasectomy he'd had in his mid twenties. Thomas groaned, his stricken expression confirming her worst fears. "I was going to tell you."

She couldn't believe her ears. "When?"

"I wanted to tell you yesterday, but . . ."

"First you needed to finish wrapping me around your little finger," she said because she was angry he hadn't trusted her enough to tell her the truth. "I've been such a fool." Though confused, one fact was crystal clear; she needed to escape.

"I'm leaving!" She jumped to her feet, grabbed her suitcase, and threw in some of her clothes. Thomas cupped his hand over her shoulder.

"Don't go, stay and we'll talk." The lines around his mouth deepened. "Honest, I was going to tell you today."

"I may be gullible, but . . ." *I'm not stupid.* She couldn't finish the sentence because it didn't ring true. From the start Thomas had said he didn't want children, yet she'd fallen in love with him and had allowed him to manipulate her.

Thomas' shoulders drooped. She raised her chin proudly and locked gazes with the man she loved. "I'll drive the Volkswagen home and make arrangements to get it back to you." She scooped her cat off the top of the refrigerator and carried her suitcase out the door. "I'll send someone to pick up the rest of my things later."

Thomas followed her outside, wrapped his fingers around her arm. "Don't leave."

"The contest isn't worth the cost," she said. "Come with me and tell Floyd to shove it."

She saw the indecision in his eyes and realized she'd asked him to choose between her and the grand prize. If he loved her enough, they'd join hands and walk away together. They'd discuss their problems and maybe reach an understanding.

He shook his head. "I can't let Floyd win. Stay and give me a chance to explain."

She was willing to accept Thomas under any terms, but he

needed to prove he loved her with the same intensity. "I'm sorry, but I can't."

Hugging Luce to her chest, she watched Thomas unhitch the Volkswagen and thought how much her life had changed in the last few hours. She threw her suitcase into the car and slipped inside with her cat.

"What about us?" Thomas asked before she shut the door.

"We never stood a chance."

She wanted desperately to wipe the anguish from his face, yearned just one more time to run her hands over his chest and feel his heart beat beneath her fingertips. She started the engine. As she drove away, she watched Thomas in her rear-view mirror until he disappeared from sight.

Tires spinning over the gravel road, she tightened her grip on the steering wheel and fought the impulse to return. As she distanced herself from the Winnebago, the hollow feeling inside worsened. She'd always reacted quickly and then later questioned her reasoning. Maybe she should have stayed and listened to Thomas' explanation. Maybe she was grasping at thin air for something that didn't exist.

Right or wrong, she'd made her move. Now it was up to Thomas. Did she mean more to him than a Winnebago worth a quarter of a million dollars?

Several days later Karen sat at Abby's kitchen table, certain her life was falling apart. "I'm on a roll. First I lose the contest, and now my car is on the fritz." *And she'd lost her heart.*

Abby slid a plate of chocolate chip cookies toward her. "Did the mechanic say when your car would be repaired?"

"It's supposed to take a few days."

Abby sprinkled sugar in her cup. "Has he called?"

"Who?"

"You know who."

272

"No, and he won't. He made his choice, and that's that."

"I don't blame Thomas for finishing the contest and seeing to it that sleazebag Floyd doesn't win." Abby pointed a finger of blame at Karen. "You're too emotional, and I'm not surprised you jumped up and quit. I'd have stuck it out. Instead of running off, you should have given Thomas a chance to explain."

"There was nothing to explain. He lied to me about wanting children," Karen said, doing her best not to cry.

"Maybe he does want them."

"If Thomas loved me, he'd have come after me."

"Consider this. If you loved him, you'd have stayed around long enough to have a serious discussion."

Karen had never thought of it that way. "For once I wanted someone to love me more than anything else in the world."

Abby anchored her elbows on the table and propped her chin on her meshed fingers. "Your parents did a number on you. When are you going to stop vying for their attention? If you haven't won them over after all these years, isn't it time you accept them for who they are, and go on with your life?"

Karen heaved a sigh.

Abby put her hand over Karen's. "For your own peace of mind, you need to talk to Thomas and find out where the two of you stand. Only he can answer your questions."

Before Karen could digest this information, Charlie shouted, "Come quick, Thomas is on TV!"

Heart drumming, Karen raced into the room in time to see the camera span the interior of Floyd's showroom. Balloons fell from an overhead net. Gobbling roared from speakers. A fat, cigar-smoking turkey strutted across a makeshift stage, handing lollipops to the children and sales brochures to the adults. He cocked his feathered head, and leaning close to the mike, flapped his wings. "Remember at Floyd's we talk turkey."

The camera lens settled on Thomas. Karen focused on his deep blue eyes. The stubble on his face added to his rugged appearance and drew her attention to his mouth, lips she longed to kiss. Did he think about her? Did he lie in his bed at night and remember their lovemaking? Did he long to hold her as much as she craved his arms around her?

A reporter aimed the microphone at Thomas. "Do you intend to keep the motor home or sell it?"

Thomas flashed a victory grin at Floyd. "I've decided to donate it to a good cause."

The next morning Karen opened the door to retrieve her newspaper and found a manila envelope on her stoop. She picked it up along with the newspaper and was about to shut the door when she saw the Winnebago parked at the curb. Her heart lodged in her throat. Hoping to see Thomas emerge from the motor home, she ran down the steps and tried to yank the door open but found it locked.

Barefoot and clad in a cotton nightgown, she peeked in the window but saw no one. A passerby whistled. Blushing, she hurried back into her apartment, tore open the manila envelope, and collapsed in a nearby chair. The keys and the paperwork for the motor home landed on her lap along with a folded note from Thomas. Her pulse drummed as she read the few short sentences.

Dear Karen,
I've registered the Winnebago in your name. Do with it whatever you want.
I've missed you.

                                          Thomas

Confusion welled inside. She could now give the motor home to her parents. But did she want to? Abby was right. Karen needed to accept her parents as they were. They cared for her, but something was missing in their relationship, and probably always would be missing.

She glanced down at Thomas' handwriting and traced his signature with her index finger. *I've missed you.* She read that last sentence several times, clinging to the hope that maybe he cared for her. Dare she hope he even loved her? There was only one way to find out.

She'd go see him. Then they'd talk and find out where they stood. Jumping off the chair, she rushed into the bedroom, dressed quickly, grabbed the keys to the Winnebago, and hurried out the door. Once she was sitting in the driver's seat, her nerves tightened. The last time she'd driven the motor home, she'd almost wedged it under a bridge. Crossing her fingers, she turned the key in the ignition, started the engine, and slowly pulled away from the curb.

The Winnebago crawled along Lisbon Street, hogging both narrow lanes. Karen swore silently at a delivery truck sticking out beyond its parking space. She squeezed past the truck, going so slow the mileage didn't register on the speedometer. Behind her drivers tooted horns and shouted obscenities.

Karen was thankful when she turned onto Main Street. Several cars honked and whizzed past her. Stopping at a red light, she loosened her death grip on the steering wheel. Too soon the light turned green, ending her reprieve. Lifting her foot off the brake she turned onto Bates Street and edged the motor home over railroad tracks. Ahead she saw the sign, O'Leary Construction Company.

Hands clammy, heart drumming, she inched the Winnebago down the gravel incline toward a loading dock.

Behind her in a pickup, a large built man with arms like tree trunks waved and shouted, "Move it or lose it, lady."

She meant to ease up a little on the brake and give the gas pedal a tap. But her foot slipped, and the Winnebago lunged forward. Wood cracked and splintered. As if in slow motion, she watched the metal roof over the loading dock topple onto the motor home.

Thomas heard the racket and ran outside. He saw the front of the Winnebago buried under a pile of debris. Thinking Karen was hurt, he pushed aside several boards and forced opened the dented door. He rushed to her side and ran anxious hands over her face and arms. "Are you all right? Is anything broken?"

She grimaced, and he was certain she was in pain. He grabbed his cell phone. "Don't move! I'm calling an ambulance."

"I'm all right," she said, resting her hand over his. "I wish I could say the same for the Winnebago."

"The hell with the Winnebago."

She rose to her feet, and he took both her hands, entwined his fingers through hers.

"I should have told you about my vasectomy before we made love. But I had intended to tell you later that day. I never got the chance because Floyd showed up."

"I shouldn't have run off the way I did," she said, tears rimming her eyes.

"Do you still love me?" he asked, a band of fear tightening around his chest.

"Yes," she whispered, giving him hope.

"The doctor says there's a good chance my vasectomy can be reversed, but I can't be sure. If you marry me, I may not be able to father your children."

One corner of her mouth tipped upward. "Is that a proposal?"

He nodded because he couldn't speak past the lump in his throat.

"YES! I'll marry you."

He wrapped his arms around her. "I love you," he whispered, claiming her mouth in a kiss that left him yearning for much more—a family, a wife, and growing old together. "Are you sure you want to team up with me for the rest of your life?"

Her kiss was all the reassurance he needed.

Epilogue

Eighteen months later

Karen cradled her son to her bosom and watched him suckle on her breast. She glanced up at the television screen in time to see a short, fat turkey waving his wings at the crowd.

"Thomas, hurry, come in here."

Wrapped in a towel, droplets of water cascading down his chest, he ran into the living room and dropped a kiss on their infant's forehead before claiming her mouth. Losing herself for a moment, Karen forgot why she'd called him into the room until gobbling echoed from the television speakers. They looked up, smiled.

"At Floyd's we talk turkey. For a measly one hundred and twenty-five bucks, you can buy a chance to win the grand prize."

"Maybe I should buy a chance," Karen said.

"No way, I can't go through that again."

The camera focused on a new Winnebago.

"That motor home looks better than ours did when you were done with it," Thomas said with a grin she loved.

After extensive repairs, they'd sold the Winnebago for a third of its retail value. They used some of the money for their honeymoon and banked the rest for their son's education. A knock on the door interrupted her thoughts. Thomas dashed into the bathroom to get dressed.

"Come in," Karen said, and watched her parents enter, their arms laden with gifts for their grandchild.

"There's the sweet angel," her mother said, her voice choked with feeling. Since the baby's birth, her parents had showed signs of being wonderful grandparents.

The turkey leaned in close to the mike. "Folks, this is a once in a lifetime opportunity. If I draw your number, you walk away with everything."

A moment later Thomas came up behind Karen and rested his fingers over her shoulder. Karen handed the baby to her mother. They exchanged a warm look, giving hope to their strained relationship.

Gobbling roared from the speakers as the turkey raised his wings. "Winner takes all!" he shouted to the cheering crowd.

Her heart overflowing with love, Karen brushed her mouth against her husband's cheek. Thanks to the contest, they'd won a slightly dented Winnebago, they'd found each other, and they had a son they loved with all their heart. *Both she and Thomas were winners. They'd walked away with everything.*

About the Author

Diane Amos lives with her husband, Dave, in a small town north of Portland, Maine. They have four grown children, a finicky Siamese named Sabrina and an energetic miniature Dachshund named Molly. Diane is an established Maine artist. Her paintings are in private collections across the United States. She is a Golden Heart finalist and winner of the Maggie Award for Excellence. *Winner Takes All* is Diane's third novel. For more information about Diane and her books, check out her Website at www.dianeamos.com.

CB 1/06

✗ NE 1/06

MG 4/06

8/05

ML